fatal journeys

lucy taylor

fatal journeys

lucy taylor

Overlook Connection Press

2014

For Danel Olson

introduction

by jack ketchum

Lucy Taylor's no stranger to travel.

By her own accounting she's *"been on safari in Zimbabwe, jogged with a troop of baboons in Zaire, ridden a camel in Coober Pedy, Australia, hang-glided in Queenstown, New Zealand, gotten married on a beach in Fiji, scuba dived in St. Lucia, lost her passport, plane ticket and wallet in San Miguel Allende, Mexico, pony trekked in Iceland, and confessed her sins to a priest in Paris."*

Me, I'd like to hear about all of this. Particularly that last one.

But that's just me.

She's possessed of an adventurist spirit.

Elsewhere she's said that *"the safest I've ever felt in my life is when I'm in a foreign country where no one knows me, and I know no one, and no one on the planet, to the best of my knowledge, knows exactly where I am."*

I understand that and maybe you do too. When I was thirty I went to Europe for the first time and lost myself for four months in Greece. I've never been happier.

But there are places you really shouldn't go.

Places that are dangerous to the heart, mind and body.

And these are the journeys she's taking you on here. Some very far away geographically. Some much closer to home.

You travel to New Guinea, where women are still dragged from their beds and burned as witches. To Iceland, where a wandering spirit exacts sorrowful, endless vengeance. To the back roads of Mississippi on the Fourth of July in search of a child-killer.

9

You encounter deadly shape-shifters in an African desert, your husband's ghost in Japan, soul-eaters on the icy slopes of Alaska. Your own drowned sister on your mother's wedding day in the luxurious Bahamas.

You travel to Thailand to kill your best friend.

Commit multiple murder and urge a child you love toward her longed-for North Pole.

So many dangerous places to go.

Themed anthologies are common these days, some good, some not so good. And they've been around for a long time. Martin H. Greenberg was undisputedly the king of them. He compiled an astonishing 1,289 books before his death in 2011, a great many of them themed. Things really took off back in the late 90's with the success of the HOT BLOOD series of erotic horror tales, edited by Jeff Gelb and Michael Garrett. In which both Lucy and I cut a lot of our respective teeth.

But themed *collections* by one author are another matter. Offhand, except for this one—and unless you count Sherlock Holmes and other single-detective, single-author mystery collections—I can't think of one. So this is a pretty unique book.

Obviously the theme here is travel, locomotion, motion—and style-wise the stories themselves mirror that theme. These stories sail and drive you through them, diverse as they may be. THE BUTSUDAN has a quiet, measured pace, suitable for a story set in Japan, while HOW REAL MEN DIE jostles you through the streets and bars of Thailand with hard-boiled bravado. But both are under total control.

And that means *they* control *you.*

Lucy Taylor's never been one for trivial subject matter even when she's having the most fun with you, even when donning her cape and crown as "Queen of Erotic Horror."

(Sorry, Lucy. I just had to bring that up.)

But it seems to me that her sense of *gravitas* has grown over the years.

Oh, she's still telling a rousing good story, full of unexpected twists and turns, grabbing you with her characters. But inside the overall theme of journeying there are other—some of them very important—themes. About love and loss, friendship, the perils of childhood, redemption, freedom. She doesn't toss them in your face. But she doesn't toss them away, either.

So in that sense you're in for a very rich journey here indeed.

Dangerous, though, and dark.

So pack your luggage well.

Bon voyage.

— Jack Ketchum, 5/4/13

Summerland

On that cloudless, blindingly bright morning, when everything in her life was about to change, twenty-two-year-old Sonya Olendski motored out from the dock to a reef about a mile offshore, dropped the anchor, and stretched out in the dinghy, feeling peacefully indolent as she gazed out at the flat, unbroken horizon, basking in silence and solitude.

Peace at last! At least temporarily, she had escaped the swarm of Olendskis and Olendski family friends who were descending on the Paradise Island beach house for her mother's wedding the next day, none of whom—with the exception of her older brother Julian—she gave a jot about.

She'd left the three-story, eggshell-colored mansion known as Summerland, just as breakfast was being poured, Bloody Marys and Yellow Birds all around, half-potted relatives blundering about the kitchen, spilling things, laughing obnoxiously loud. Cousins Troy and Martin behind the boathouse, snorting controlled substances, Aunt Tanya bouncing around in a string bikini with her new, surgically enhanced rear end jutting out like a pair of flesh-colored balloons. And Mother, desperately vivacious, her face Botoxed to the impeccably bland smoothness of a Noh mask, issuing orders to the Bahamian staff, while her fiancé, one Harbinger Rampling of Traverse City, Michigan, sprawled on the veranda, reeking of Ricardo Gold and New Money. And Julian, her poor, long-suffering brother tasked with overseeing the construction of the wedding arch under which the two bling-laden lovers would speak their vows (as if Julian knew any more about construction than she did, they'd be lucky if the thing didn't collapse before the couple got to the part about in sickness and in health.)

What did I even come here for? She thought disconsolately, but the question was ingenuous, she knew. She was here for a respite from her job in New York as a buyer for Saks Fifth Avenue, to sip rum drinks on the veranda overlooking the blue diamond Caribbean, and to spend time with her brother, of course, dear Julian. How long had it been? A year already? He'd given up on the MBA from Berkeley and was working in Australia now, setting up tours from Adelaide to Alice and beyond for well-heeled Americans, passing his time Down Under with some little sheila he'd shacked up with in Sydney. He hadn't brought her with him, which didn't surprise Sonya in the least. Julian was a solitary creature, a great catch if the right girl could snare him, but slippery as an eel and apt to give a nasty shock if he were cornered.

The tropical sun beat down on her, delicious and stinging as a keen little switch. The cradle-rock of the dinghy lulled her. She felt like a turkey basting. Rousing herself, she leaned over the side and splashed water onto her face, looking down as she did so to where the reef sloped away, the water darkening from pale, translucent turquoise to a rich royal blue hemmed in with gorgeous corals. A school of orange and white clown fish darted above the clustered antlers of some staghorn coral. It was as she was watching the fish weave in and out among the skinny branches of the coral that she saw the dead girl.

Dear God!

And recognized her.

In that first, stunned instant, her mind tried to deny what she was seeing, to reinterpret the pinched, discolored face and undulating auburn hair as a lushly colored sea fan waving languidly beside some kind of grotesquely speckled flounder whose yellow and brown scales and gills created a weird facsimile to a human face.

Her *own* face. The same face as her twin sister Vonnie, who'd disappeared from Paradise Island three years ago and was presumed dead.

Even as she thought about her sister, Sonya was reaching for her mask and snorkel, preparing to dive down, perhaps even try to drag the pitiful thing up into the light of day. But what then? Surely a drowned body would be too heavy for her to shove into the dinghy and, even if she were capable of such a feat, the idea of sharing the small boat with that dead, repulsive thing that so resembled *her* made her stomach lurch.

14

Masked now, she hung over the side again and plunged her face in. She saw the clown fish and the coral, but the body of the girl was…where? Then, *there* she was, the spectral hair and bloated fingers fluttering up beseechingly, *Come down here with me, Sonya. Now!*

With a jolt so fierce it made her gasp, a buried memory surfaced like a reanimating corpse:

Vonnie hiding in the tangle of ferns outside the boathouse that last summer, waiting for her, whispering urgently: *Sonya, come here! I had the strangest dream last night, I have to tell you. Come here! Now!*

Black panic seized her. She gave a strangled shriek, tore off the mask, gunned the motor and roared back to the dock.

It was, she later reflected, the worst decision of her life.

《《——》》

Summerland, the name given by her father to the four million dollar 'cottage' he'd purchased on Paradise Island, Bahamas, in the late 80's, was a rambling palm-shaded estate flanked by tennis courts and a sapphire-tiled pool surrounded by meticulously tended gardens of hibiscus, wild banana trees, bamboo, and birds of paradise. The lush foliage did much to mute the clamor, but as Sonya hurried toward the house, up the gated path past the gazebo, the din of merriment echoed through the tropic air like strange, off-kilter birdcalls.

A trio of young women in wide-brimmed pastel hats and micro swimsuits lounged on chaises by the pool, the fervor of their conversation noticeably quieting as Sonya dashed past. On the stairs to the tennis courts, she barely missed a collision with Aunt Willis, who tittered, "Your mother's been looking all over for you, dear!"

Sonya made some vague sound of acknowledgment and rushed on. She was hoping to see Julian or, if not Julian, then Uncle Frank, who had a steady head about him when he was sober, but she was intercepted near the gazebo by her mother. The adrenalin was still roaring in her veins. She hadn't taken time to arrange a coherent version of what had happened and blurted, "I saw a body out on the reef! It looked like Vonnie!"

15

"Keep your voice down. People will *hear*," hissed her mother. Roberta Olendski wore a sheer white tee over a black bikini top, a sarong patterned with scarlet hibiscus blossoms, and a sneer of perfectly visible disgust under a shabby layer of maternal solicitude. Gripping Sonya's arm, she led her away from the house into a series of cloistered nooks adorned with ceramic gnomes and stone benches. Julian and a pair of workmen were laboring on the wedding arch somewhere amid the greenery. She could hear the beat of hammers and male voices, abrupt, incurious.

Her mother stood very close and pronounced each word as though Sonya were a foreigner of limited English. "Now repeat what you just told me. Calmly. What exactly did you see?"

"I took the dingy out over the reef. There's a woman's body in about twenty feet of water."

Roberta's brightly lipsticked mouth drooped the way it always did when Sonya shamed her—the rejection from Bryn Mahr some years ago, the suitors from good families that she'd snubbed, the 'C' in social studies in second grade.

"You say it looked like Vonnie?"

"It *was* Vonnie. I'm almost sure!"

"You saw her clearly?"

"Yes."

"What was she wearing?"

That stopped her as though her mind had run full tilt into a wall. She'd been so focused on the face…*her face.*

"I—I'm not sure. I don't remember. She might have been naked, I don't know. For God's sake, what does it matter? It looked like Vonnie, and she was dead. Do you need to know more?"

"And what do you want me to do about it? Organize a search? Call the police, the rescue divers? I won't do it. I won't play into your childish games."

"But what if it *was* Vonnie?" Her voice was like shattered glass now, cracked and jagged. She tried to contain it, was conscious that the hammers pounding in the background had stopped, the men silent now, attentive, the Bahamian staff undoubtedly entertained by the quarrel they were overhearing as much as Julian must be appalled.

"How could it be your sister? That's absurd. No one's seen or heard from her in three years." Sonya opened her mouth, but Roberta raised a hand for silence "Oh, don't rehash the same old theories. She didn't run away. She had no reason to leave Summerland. That local girl, the one whose body washed up right before Vonnie disappeared, that wasn't a coincidence. Whoever killed her murdered Vonnie, too. You know how your sister carried on. She crossed paths with the man who killed that local girl."

"The girl's name was Havana Brockton, Mother. And the police never arrested anyone. They've never closed the case."

"They never will close it, either," said Roberta savagely, "but that doesn't change the fact that your sister's *dead*. God only knows what happened to her—I don't want to know, I'm not sure I could live with it. But I do know this, that even if Vonnie was alive, she didn't find out about my wedding, secretly fly into the Bahamas and somehow manage to drown herself in a place where you'd be sure to find her, all within the past twenty-four hours. Even for a person of Vonnie's dramatic abilities, that would be asking a lot."

"Fine. If you don't believe me—" She turned and started back along the footpath toward the house. Her mother's voice, alarmed now, clawed after her.

"Wait! What are you going to do?"

"I'll call the police myself."

"You won't!" Roberta's nails bit into her shoulder, spinning her around. Sonya could see tendrils of peach-colored lipstick filling in the little vertical lines along her mother's upper lip, ugly souvenirs from a one-time smoking habit. "You're doing this to spite me, aren't you? To spoil my day and grab the spotlight for yourself! Like the Christmas we were all in Aspen and you decided to nick your wrists and create a fine hullabaloo. Oh, you are so full of envy, consumed with it, aren't you? I wish you'd stayed in New York City. I wish you'd go back there if you're intent on ruining the most wonderful day of my life!"

"This isn't about you, Mother! It has nothing to do with you!"

From the corner of her eye, she saw a space open in the greenery and Julian glided through. A slender, agile-looking man in his late twenties with startling, sky blue eyes, he wore white chinos and a blue short-sleeved shirt unbuttoned to reveal a wedge of deeply tanned skin. "What's going on? No one's going to ruin anything." He put one hand on his mother's shoulder, the other on Sonya's. "What is it, Sonya? Too little sleep? And what's your story, Mom? Pre-wedding jitters?"

Thank God for Julian, Sonya thought. Always the centered one, reasonable, clear-headed, making himself useful when everyone else was either running around like headless chickens or soused out of their minds. His calm, even baritone was comforting. Sonya felt herself soothed. She told him what she'd seen.

As she spoke, he cocked his head and listened with the thoughtful earnestness of a priest or a very good bartender, his face betraying no emotion beyond a single furrow between his brows, deep enough to slot a coin in. "Wow, Sis. A body? Okay, I suppose it's possible. Not that you saw Vonnie, of course, but someone. That could be. Was the body caught in something, entangled somehow? In fishing lines maybe or seaweed?"

Confused, Sonya shook her head.

"Because if it was really a drowned person, they'd bob to the surface, right? That's why they call them floaters. So if a dead body's just hanging out down there, it would have to be weighted or snagged on something, otherwise the gases—."

Their mother waved her hands as if flailing at attacking gulls. "I'm not listening to this! It's too morbid and disgusting."

Behind her, the voice of Sonya and Julian's stepfather-to-be, Harbinger Rampling boomed "Disgusting? Only thing disgusting is I haven't kissed my gorgeous bride in ten or fifteen minutes!"

He loomed up behind Roberta, a muscular silver-haired man with gorilla forearms and an over-sized bald dome like a gourd. He put his arms around Roberta and bent to nuzzle her neck.

"What's this you're arguing about? Something fishy on the reef?" He chuckled at his wit and looked at Sonya. "A body, did I hear you say?"

"Don't listen to her," said Roberta. "Her imagination's too vivid for her own good. She saw her own reflection in the water and scared herself."

Her dismissive tone and obvious desire that the matter be

immediately dropped was all it took to spur Harb into manly action. Within minutes, he'd recruited Uncle Frank to assist him in a search while, despite Sonya's protests, Roberta dispatched Julian back to the construction of the arch. The three of them, Frank, Harb and Sonya, then motored out to the reef in Harb's thirty-eight foot cruiser, The Midnight Oil, where Frank snorkeled on the surface and Harb made steady inroads into a cooler full of Kalik Gold. Sonya, meanwhile, gnawed her nails, feeling more unsure of herself by the moment and parched as well, since Harb had neglected to stock up on an exotic beverage like water.

By noon, they'd moved the Midnight Oil a half-dozen times, following the edge of the reef. Sonya had begun drinking beer, trying to get her courage up to enter the water. She knew she should help Uncle Frank—this mission was at her behest, after all—but the mere idea of going underwater made her lightheaded with fear. She could barely bring herself to gaze over the side. As though what was down there, whatever she'd *thought* was down there, was some sort of evil omen aimed at her. She could not forget the way the dead girl's fingers had seemed to coax: *Come join me, for we both know the truth, you're looking at yourself.*

Or the memory—vivid now after being so long suppressed—of Vonnie calling to her from behind the boathouse, telling her about the peculiar, frightening dream.

Harb interrupted her reflection. "There's a lot of coral down here. You think this is where it was?" He clearly wanted her agreement, but Sonya wasn't sure. Had they gone out far enough? Too far? If only Julian had come along. He was methodical and tireless and, best of all, he had the lungs of a seal.

Uncle Frank, meanwhile, was finding only the detritus of passing boats—empty rum bottles and a man's white deck shoe, a plastic cooler tilted on its side which he reported housed a moray eel that came thrusting out, teeth aglitter like a set of steak knives. It was after this, Frank's up close and person encounter with the eel, that the two men declared the expedition at an end.

Uncle Frank must have seen her look of confusion and defeat. He draped a sun-fried forearm across her shoulder and said, "Whatever you think you saw, it's gone now, hon. Forget it. This is a happy time—your mom's wedding day tomorrow!" He handed her a Kalik Gold and raised one of his own. "To Olendskis now and to Olendskis of the future!"

Sonya accepted the icy can, holding it against her throbbing forehead as the yacht motored toward land, the sunlight glancing off the waves like quartz crystals, stinging her eyes. *Vonnie,* she thought. *I saw you. I know I saw you.*

«« —»»

Back on land, the party had moved outside, people bogeying to a reggae band by the pool, fruity drinks and snacks of grouper fingers, johnnycakes and guava duff being served by red-jacketed waiters.

Sonya couldn't bear the thought of chitchat with a horde of tipsy, inquisitive relatives. She grabbed another beer from the cooler and headed up the beach, disconsolate, too embarrassed to face Julian, wondering if she was going crazy.

Beyond the grounds of the P. I. Hilton and the thatched bungalows of the Sivananda Yoga Ashram, she cut across a field of coconut palms, past a group of fleshy, dark-skinned gussy-maes in bright, ankle-length dresses, toting baskets full of handmade necklaces and trinkets carved from coconut shells. The women called out to her, offering their wares—straw handbags and turtles made of tiny cowries, polished conchs shell with knobby spires and gleaming pink interiors.

"Morning Missy!"

"I guh see you on duh beach today?"

"That be Miss Vonnie from Summerland," she heard one say and whirled around, mouth open, mute, shocked to be mistaken for her sister. Didn't these women remember Vonnie's disappearance, covered at the time in local news? How could they not *know*?

Then again, how could *she* not know whether or not her sister was dead? If Vonnie were still alive, wouldn't she *feel* it? For Vonnie had been her other half, as near to her as her own skin, as familiar as her heartbeat.

As young girls, they'd been inseparable, and although Sonya

20

was shy and bookish and Vonnie a Tom-boy who'd rather hike alone into the forest around their Michigan home than go to dances or muddle over books, they loved each other with the singular devotion of two people who, when looking into each other's eyes, perceived their own reflections.

Holidays then were spent at Houghton Lake, in a lofty A-frame set deep in the thick woods, a house mysterious and foreboding as a witch's fairy tale cottage, constructed of spun sugar and candy canes and secrets.

Vonnie and Sonya shared the loft at the top of the A-frame, where they could hear the wind rattle and stomp about the roof and imagined that gremlins were using the shake shingled slopes to go tobogganing. They pretended they were in a secret attic, hiding from ogres, or stowed away in the belly of a sailing ship, having barely escaped capture by pirates. They searched the Atlas for exotic-sounding names—Goreme and Peshwar and Cap d'Antibes—and speculated how it would be to live in these exotic places, the new names they'd take, the people they'd pretend to be, the daring exploits they'd undertake together.

Life was all about pretending, Sonya had thought. The only difference was that most people didn't seem to know that they were doing it.

On cold nights, with autumn settling in, they'd snuggle in bed and whisper together about a world that seemed so wondrous and strange or, sneaking outside in the dark, they'd marvel at the silent, star-bright sky, an awe-inspiring spectacle that their parents and even older brother Julian, so shy and so reserved, seemed oddly unaware of.

One such night, out of the blue, Vonnie had said, "As soon as I'm old enough, I'm going to run away and hide someplace far away. And when I do, Mom and Dad will never find me! Do you know why?"

Sonya shook her head. She didn't like to hear Vonnie talk this way, didn't understand why she would want to leave. Things weren't that bad in the Olendski household. Dad yelled sometimes and Mom drank a lot and Julian seemed a cipher at times, barely a ghost in his own home, but she knew from school and from TV that other families were unhappy too, and some much worse than theirs.

Vonnie said, "Mom and Dad will look for me at first, to keep up appearances, but they won't look for very long. You know why? Because the truth is they'll be relieved."

"That's silly," Sonya said. "They love you, Vonnie. Mom and Dad would look for you like crazy. Why wouldn't they?"

"Because I see them as they really are, and they can't stand that," Vonnie said. A tiny fleck of iridescent blue, a chip of topaz, marred the brown of her left eye, the only obvious, discernible difference between her face and Sonya's. "It makes them uncomfortable. That's why when I run away, I know they'll let me go."

"You don't mean that," said Sonya airily, parroting her mother.

Her sister looked at her with disappointment and regret. "I do too mean it! It's not good for me here and not good for you, either. Can't you feel it?" In response to Sonya's blank expression, she went on,"It's like when you're just on the verge of coming down with the flu, not sick yet, but your body tingles in a weird, yechy kind of way and the inside of your skin prickles and you know you've picked up a nasty bug. Sure enough, the next day you wake up ill. That's what it feels like to me living here. All the time!"

"Is this another of your visions?" Sonya scoffed. She knew her sister 'saw' or 'felt' things sometimes and it scared her. Like the time Vonnie had told her to be extra nice to their math tutor Mrs. Elms, because this was the last time they would see her, and two nights later Mrs. Elms was killed when a drunk driver slammed into her Camry. Or the time that Mr. Beaumont from next door, who was sad because his wife had left him, invited them to see his new puppy, and Vonnie refused to go and told Sonya she mustn't go either. How angry Sonya had been with her sister! And years later, seeing the police cars come, and hearing about Mr. Beaumont's 'special room', where two other little girls from the neighborhood said dreadful things had happened.

"I don't have visions," said Vonnie, "I just get glimpses, like peeking through a curtain. You could do it too, if you'd let yourself. You've got the same gift I do, Sonya, maybe more, but you've got a wall up around the part of you that sees."

What if Vonnie had been right, thought Sonya, and this morning, looking through the clear water, she had actually been given a glimpse beyond the curtain? What if Vonnie had actually drowned three years ago, and she was only now able to 'see' it?

The idea that her sister was truly dead rocked her like a punch. All these years, she had been the only one who held out hope. The rest of the family agreed with Roberta, that Vonnie had been killed by the same man who murdered Havana Brockton, undoubtedly a local man, for everyone know that Bahamian men boozed and brawled and beat their women. In hushed tones, they would add that Vonnie must have gotten involved in something tawdry and awful, for she'd made no secret of her sexual indulgences, had flaunted them, in fact. She'd been with men and women both that last summer on P.I., acted like a hooch-addled sailor on leave, fucking everything that surfed or limbo-danced or slammed Bacardi, the lean ebony dock boys with their bright white smiles and singsong dialects, the drunken, muscled frat boys on summer break, the pasty marrieds looking to be rescued from monogamy and boredom, she'd done them all and laughed about her exploits, she was a whore, a slut, a strumpet, she'd even hinted that…but Sonya wouldn't, couldn't, go there.

She climbed a low ridge, hardly more than a bump of sand and grass, and stared out at the water, trying to triangulate in her mind exactly where she'd dropped the dinghy's anchor. What she'd seen this morning hadn't looked like any vision, but a dead body in all its swollen, mottled horror. If a killer was about, maybe even the same person who'd murdered the Brockton girl and her sister, wasn't it her responsibility to do something?

Go the police?

Sonya decided she didn't want to risk looking even more foolish. The officers of the Royal Bahamian Police Force were no fans of the Olendskis—there'd been too many lawsuits and scandals over the years, disputes over Summerland's property boundaries, a drunken spat Mother got into at the casino of the Atlantis that made the front page of the Nassau Guardian, Daddy's swept-under-the-rug fling with a local politician's wife and whispers of a bastard child— then Vonnie's disappearance. The police would laugh at her.

She finished her beer and chucked the can, wishing for another. *Lovely, I'm turning into a lush like Mother.*

The path she was following curved round again, leading her back toward the beach and an ancient stretch of grey seawall, erected she supposed at the same time as an old fort that had once stood here and decades earlier been torn down. The stones were chipped and cracked like bad teeth, their sides festooned with barnacles and encrusted with kelp.

Along the dilapidated seawall, she saw a man stretched out on his side, the bottoms of his bare, dirty feet turned toward her.

Oh drat, she thought, for this spot was special to her, one of the few places she could generally be alone. Then she did a double-take and realized, to her relief and chagrin, that the man was Julian. Rather than call out, though, she stood looking at him with fondness and a pleasant dash of jitters, the way she would always stop a foot or so away from a high balcony, craving the view but fearful of getting too close, afraid the secret urge to leap might prove overwhelming. The truth was she relished watching her brother when he didn't know she was doing it. Tracing the clean hard lines of his body gave her pleasure. They were angular and cleanly geometric, bronze and sleek and sculpted, like the metal of a copper-colored Lamborghini their father had once owned. The only part of him that moved were a few wisps of hair tossed by the breeze and the lazy rise and dip of his ribcage.

She said softly, "Hey Julie Boy," and the way he turned and sat up, languidly, like a lazing cat, made her realize his surprise was only feigned, that he'd been pretending not to know that she was watching. That Julian, in one way or another, was always pretending. Julian, so beautiful and yet so shy, he'd spent his life pretending he didn't realize others were always watching him, admiring, envying, coveting.

"Hey Sister Girl, I wondered if you'd come along. I know this is your hideaway. How was the boat ride?"

"Aside from the fact that Uncle Frank almost capsized the dinghy going into the water and Harb tried to feel me up? It was fucking dandy."

He looked stricken. "I'm so sorry."

She felt a surge of anger. "I wanted you to come with us. They'd have taken it seriously if you'd been there."

"I know, but Mother latched onto me, looked fit to be tied. You know how crazy she can get when she feels things slipping out of her control."

"Things like you, me, Harb?"

"World peace and nuclear disarmament. Not to mention the impending nuptials."

"Speaking of which, what are you doing here? Why aren't you working on the arch?"

"We finished it, so I took off. Too much drama. You know Mom's friend Lexy Dalton, the one who married the Hong Kong real estate exec? She got caught going down on one of the waiters behind the boathouse."

"You're joking!"

"Ha, I'm the one who caught her! I was looking for a place to smoke a blunt and what do I hear but sounds of high-velocity suction? A regular little Hoover, our Lexy."

The image made Sonya smile. "Good for her."

"And Aunt Willis has taken to her bed with stomach cramps, says the conch fritters were off, so Mother called a doctor over in Nassau to come see to her. Mother's howling pissed at you, you know. Thinks the whole episode this morning was you getting back at her for marrying Harb."

"Oh, I'm mad jealous, for sure" said Sonya, rolling her eyes.

Julian swung his feet over the wall on the land side and stepped into his sandals, which waited like obedient dogs alongside the wall. He performed a magnificent stretch, like someone waking from profound sleep or a shape shifter climbing back into his skin. Then abruptly, "Do you think Harb is marrying Mother for her money?"

"Of course he is! Rampling, Elliot, and Chung Construction's going bankrupt, everyone knows that. Mother's his recovery plan. Why else would he marry her?"

"Well, she drinks as much as he does. And she appears to like to fuck."

"Which makes a good match in some circles, I suppose." They were silent a moment, the air whispering back and forth between them like children carrying secrets. Sonya sat down next to her brother. Like him, she sat facing the land but looked back once, quickly, at the water nibbling and lapping at the decaying wall. She was surprised how gentle the waves looked. Bathtub wavelets made by rubber duckies, small and inconsequential, barely there. Looking at them you'd never guess the same water had wrought this much damage to the stones.

Julian sighed like a man laying down a burden. "Sister Girl, can I ask you something? Don't get angry. But did you really see a body that looked like Vonnie? You didn't just imagine it?"

"Of course I didn't! You're as bad as Mother if you think that"

"I know, but—look, I see things all the time when I'm out snorkeling. Then I dive down for a closer look and surprise! The shark I thought I saw turns out be kelp moving with the current or what looked like a skeleton reaching up from the sand to grab me turns into a half-buried anchor. I get spooked a lot. The light plays tricks. My mind plays tricks. And if you and Uncle Frank and Harb couldn't find anything…?"

"I don't think we were ever in the right place. Uncle Frank and Harb were both three sheets to the wind. And Uncle Frank splashing around like a hooked pelican, it's a wonder he didn't draw sharks."

"Well, whatever you saw, it wasn't Vonnie. You know that, right?"

"But it seemed so real, Julian. If you had seen her yourself— look, let's get the dinghy and go out again. Just for a bit, while we've still got lots of daylight. If we don't find anything, I'll let it go. I promise."

"You're letting your imagination get the better of you."

"You know, it's funny. That's the same thing I told Vonnie right before she disappeared, when she told me about this awful dream she'd had."

"Really? What was it about?"

"It was about you, Julian."

"Go on."

She gave a dismissive little wave, the kind favored by Roberta. "I'd forgotten all about it until this morning when I saw the body, but—it's silly, Julian, really, Vonnie's imagination, I'm sure. Forget I brought it up."

She expected him to argue with her, was surprised when he only stretched again and yawned profoundly.

"Let's walk, Sister Girl." He held out his hand to her.

"Now? In this heat?"

"Hey, we Olendskis are like tropical plants. We thrive in a hot-house environment."

She hesitated another moment, then took his hand.

They stepped down off the wall and started back into the grove of palms, headed inland. There were stones here too, chunks of sea-wall visible amid the foliage. Sonya realized that the water must have overturned them during a storm and pushed them along, pounding them into the moist soil like fists smashing teeth.

Julian stopped suddenly, laughing softly as he pulled her to him. He slipped a thumb under the sides of her bikini top and peeled it down. Her back arched like a drawn bow and she pressed her hips against his and they sank together, heavy as the stones around them, into the soft earth, Julian's mouth and hands frantic as he kept murmuring, "Sister Girl, my Sister Girl," and Sonya clutched his hair and sighed, "My wicked little boy" and laughed with a delight that was mocking and skittish at the same time and threw herself into him like he was crystalline pure water and she near dead of thirst.

Later, naked, slick with sweat, she gasped, "Oh God I've missed you, Julian! I didn't think we'd ever do that again," and he snorted a laugh. "You're wrong, Sister Girl. We'll do this 'til we're old and dotty, while we're married to other people and procreating their kids, every chance we get, we'll still be fucking each other like minks. And you know why? Cause a husband or wife is always replaceable, they're strangers, bottom line, not family, not the honest to God blood and bone of family." He seized her hand. His palm felt hot and damp. She could see his heartbeat in a blue vein at his temple. "We won't stop wanting each other, Sister Girl. Not ever. How could we? We're in each other's blood."

She hugged him hard. "We're all we've got, aren't we?"

"I'd say so."

She slipped into her shorts and fastened her bikini top. "Will you come out with me for just a quick look, Julian? Please?"

He shrugged and stared up at the sky, where a single cloud, like a lost sheep, roamed the blue. She saw his Adam's apple bob as he swallowed. "Why don't you let it drop? We could make Happy Hour at the Hilton."

She punched his shoulder. "You just *had* Happy Hour, you goose."

"Okay, you're right, but I'm parched now. You wore me out. Let's go drinking."

A sly smile, a more appealing version of Roberta's, crimped the corners of her mouth. "What if I told you Vonnie said she only *thought* at first she'd dreamed about you? That later on, she realized it wasn't a dream at all, that it was *real*?"

He canted an eyebrow. "I don't follow."

"Remember the hammock at the edge of the beach where Vonnie used to like to sleep?"

Julian looked surprised, then vexed. "I don't remember one hammock from another. But if you're getting ready to say Vonnie claimed something happened between her and me, it didn't. Not in a hammock. Not anywhere."

She balled a fist and whacked him on the shoulder. "Shut up, you filthy-minded brat! That's not what I was going to say at all! The hammock isn't there anymore, it blew down, but three years ago it was. Daddy used to tell her not to sleep there. He said it wasn't safe, that anybody could be passing by and see a girl alone and take advantage—anyway she told me that she woke up and saw you, coming down the path in the moonlight, and you were carrying a girl in your arms. She said she looked drugged or unconscious. You carried the girl out to the beach and then *into* the water, but then she lost sight of you and she fell back to sleep. When she woke up again, she thought it was all a dream. But then, a few days later, the body of the Brockton girl washed up and…it was right after that that Vonnie disappeared."

She stopped abruptly, expecting Julian to retort with sarcasm or anger, but instead he spoke matter-of-factly, like someone discussing the choices on a menu. "So that's it? You mean, Vonnie thought I killed that girl, that I took her out and drowned her."

"She didn't know what to think. She was afraid to say anything, afraid you knew she'd seen you. And she would never have gone to the police, Julian, not Vonnie and not me, either, but—that's why I never really thought that she was dead. Because she always said she'd run away, she'd told me she had friends—men who skippered boats and would let her crew for them, no questions asked—I always wondered if she ran because of what she thought she'd seen."

She was silent then, waiting for an explosion or rebuke. Instead Julian only shook his head and exhaled forcefully, like one recovering from an unexpected blow. "Oh, God, Sister Girl, you mean to tell me you've been carrying that around all this time, what Vonnie told you? Jeez, why didn't you just come to me? Why didn't *she*? What happened that night, I could have cleared it all up."

"You could?"

He made a show of bugging his eyes and gawking at her. "Well, *what*, you think I killed a woman? Jesus, Mary, and Joseph, Sister Girl, I don't even step on ants, I don't eat veal, for Christ's sake, and you think I'm out there killing women."

"Not women, Julian, just the one."

"Oh, well, only one, that hardly counts then, does it?" He raised an index finger, made his voice deep and stentorian. "Objection, Your Honor, my client's not a killer. It's just that it was on his bucket list, commit a murder, just to see what it would feel like. No danger here to society, Your Honor, none at all." He was laughing now, so good-naturedly that she joined in, too, not sure what they were laughing at, only knowing that it felt right and good, laughing with her beautiful brother in the sunlight.

"What happened then?" she said, wiping away her tears with the back of her hand. "You mean the man Vonnie saw was someone else? It wasn't you?"

"No, it was me, and the young woman in my arms was dead, all right, dead *drunk*, that is. I was at the pool bar at the Hilton as usual and this girl—her name was Michelle, she was from Canada—we clicked, you know, incendiary chemistry right off the bat, and I invited her to come back with me to Summerland. We could've gone to her room, of course, but she was sharing a suite with a couple of other girls and anyway I wanted to impress her, let her think she had a shot at marrying into fantastic wealth before I gave her the heave ho. What better way to plant the hook than to show off Summerland?" He had the grace to offer an embarrassed shrug before continuing. "We got as far as the gazebo, but we never made it to my room. We'd been slamming Yellow Birds and Goombay Smashes all night, and then I'd bought a pint of rum to nip from as we walked. Right by the tennis courts, she got violently sick, then dropped like she'd been clubbed. I couldn't wake her up, I wasn't sure if she was even breathing. I did the only thing I could think of. I picked her up and carried her straight out into the water, dunked her down like a Holy Roller doing a baptism. She woke up and projectile puked all over me, and it was coming out the other end as well, so I piled her into Daddy's golf cart and whisked her right back to the hotel. Rounded up her roommates who came down to tend to her. So you see, the only thing that died that night was my fantasy of a beautiful romance."

"So the Brockton girl—"

"—was not my date, I promise you, just some poor thing got herself drowned, maybe even murdered, but not by me."

She was almost shaking with relief, a reaction that perturbed and shamed her. Until today, she hadn't thought about Vonnie's story since that awful summer and didn't realize how desperately she'd needed Julian to refute it, to explain what Vonnie actually saw.

Now she hugged him fiercely, rocking them both to and fro. "Oh, God, I *knew* there had to be an explanation! If only I hadn't doubted you, if only I'd just gone to you and asked."

"Really?" Julian said. He looked forlorn. "You doubted me, Sister Girl?"

"Only a tiny part of me," she said, holding up her thumb and index finger a quarter inch apart. "Just the smallest part."

«« — »»

For a man whose energy was usually boundless, Julian seemed exhausted, sapped. On the walk back to the dock, he seemed utterly spent, so much so that Sonya wondered if he even had the strength to go out snorkeling. Once out over the reef, though, he gamely donned his mask, snorkel, and fins and followed Sonya's hesitant and sometimes contradictory directions without complaint. He seemed drained, but at the same time solicitous and tender, stroking her cheek once when she'd lamented her poor navigational skills, telling her not to worry, he didn't mind.

The water, which that morning had been smooth and flat as a glassine envelope, was choppy now, small swells rippling along the surface. They moved the dinghy from one spot to another, finally stopping at a place where the drop-off into the deep water was fringed with branching coral. Sonya cut the motor. At once they were engulfed by silence.

She leaned over, peering into the water. "Julian, I think this is where it was!" She turned to him. "I know you're wiped out. Will you go down one more time and have a look?"

"No problem, Sister Girl."

He slid over the dinghy's side and kicked down. For a few seconds, she could see him gliding along the edge of the reef, surfacing now and then to blow water out of his snorkel and inhale, working his way toward the place where the water darkened. Then he must have begun to descend, because she lost sight of him. Time crawled by and she glanced around nervously, expecting him to surface.

When he didn't, she felt a rush of irritation and alarm. In the boat, he'd seemed so listless and exhausted.

Come on, Julian. What the hell are you doing?

Another twenty seconds. Something was wrong. Without hesitation, Sonya grabbed her mask and snorkel and jumped over the side.

She kicked down, looking frantically around, and spotted Julian almost immediately. He was hovering above a staghorn forest that descended into a steep ravine, where the sunlight dwindled and the water turned blue-black. He was seemingly mesmerized, staring at something in the deeper water. Sonya put more heft into her strokes, kicked harder.

As she swam to him, he turned around. His blue eyes, magnified behind the mask, looked distant, vacant, the eyes of no one that she knew. For an instant, she had that same prickly sensation she'd had earlier, that he'd known all along she was there, that he was only pretending to be distracted, and she felt a bite of fear.

But then he held his hand out to her and beckoned, a familiar, calming gesture he'd made to her a hundred times. Reflexively, instinctively, she took his hand.

«« — »»

On the other side of the world, in a small Croatian village that Sonya and her sister had once discovered together in the pages of an Atlas, the young woman who called herself Evelyn Marquis awoke with a gasp. She tasted sea water, her heart was thundering, and her throat blazed. For a horrific instant, she thought her lungs were filling up with water, and she turned to the man asleep next to her, thinking to wake him, wanting him to hold her as she died.

But then the terrible sensations passed. Her breath came easily. Her heart calmed.

Evelyn Marquis turned onto her side and dropped back into dark, dreamless sleep.

Soul Eaters

"The great peril of human existence consists of
the fact that our diet consists entirely of souls."
—Inuit saying

Heading south on a week-long cruise to Vancouver, the Sea Mist sailed out of Whittier, Alaska, a little after six p.m. and plunged into mushroomy fog. Most of the six hundred plus passengers were snugly inside, eating dinner, gambling in the casino, or enjoying one of several nightclub acts. Only a handful, untroubled by the cold, remained on deck. Had the fog not swathed the ship like a chilly grave cloth, one of them might have seen the body tip over the starboard side around seven-fifteen. But the fog was a co-conspirator with the killer, and so the body plummeted, mute and unobserved, into the high, choppy seas.

《《——》》

At eight o'clock that evening, Hugo Santiago was beginning his rounds on Deck Five in a dour mood. Earlier, he'd ventured out on deck, but the knife-blade wind drove him back inside, feeling as trapped and frozen as an ice cube in a tray.

So dispirited was Hugo that he barely bothered to acknowledge Inz, the lusty Bolivian maid with whom he'd enjoyed a romantic, if short-lived, romp the previous cruise season.

"Ah, you forget Inz already," she teased, bending forward to rearrange the soaps in her cart while providing Hugo with a view of bountiful cleavage. She wore the standard maid's uniform, blue with white piping, but always managed to forget a button or two on the blouse and further jazzed up the ensemble by adding pink socks short enough to reveal the tattoo of hot lips on her ankle.

33

Hugo gave her plush rump a firm pinch as he passed, wondering if she might be persuaded to help him muss up the sheets in an unoccupied cabin or even get down on her knees in the linen closet, but she yelped and slapped him so hard across the back of the head that he actually stumbled forward.

"Dammit, Inz!" he said, rubbing his scalp. "Why're you acting like this?"

She snorted and looked at him like he was dried puke she had to scrub off a carpet. "Better question is what you doing *here*, Hugo? What happen to all your too-good-for-Inz plans? I thinking you and your rich sugar mama jet off to Buenos Aires, live happily after ever, no? Hot smoking Imelda who does tango on your cock, tight like sixteen-years-old virgin, you say! Why you freezing your skinny ass off on board fucking ship? What happen? Hot lover she ditch you, no?"

This last smirked with a kind of snide exuberance that made Hugo want to choke her.

"I got tired of her," he snapped and continued on down the corridor, reflecting as he did so that if he didn't laugh at his current situation, he'd have to weep.

Here he was back in Alaska when, above all, Hugo hated the cold.

Born in the steamy swelter of the Yucatan, he yearned for the heat of his homeland, for sultry breezes and turquoise seas—above all, for the heat and solace between Imelda Thomasina de Hidalgo's remarkably well-toned and energetic thighs.

He wondered idly what she would say if he called to beg her forgiveness. If he could only come up with a reasonable explanation that was flattering to her ego—anything but the truth—as to why he'd departed her bed in the middle of the night and run like a gangbanger fleeing a police raid.

As he pondered this, he gave the door to cabin 518 a perfunctory rap, got no response, and used his passkey. He entered a spacious suite divided into a sitting area with flat screen TV, computer and bar, and a luxuriously furnished bedroom. He hesitated, sniffed the air. An intriguing scent permeated the cabin: the subtle but compelling odor of sex, musky and hormonal, like the pale vestige of some lingering depravity. So enticing that his nostrils flared and his penis threatened to declare up periscope.

His mood began to lift as well. Since he knew from the manifest that the cabin's occupant was a single woman, he looked for evidence of recent hijinks, but the russet bedspread looked untouched and the few items of clothing in evidence were folded neatly, hardly an indication of passion-fueled haste. He felt let down. Vicarious thrills from the escapades, infidelities, and generally scandalous behavior of some passengers were one of the perks of a cruise ship job. Participation in these shenanigans, although technically forbidden, was, of course, an even bigger incentive to sail the seas. And if, like Imelda, the woman happened to be rich and single…?

With a mental note to try to meet Cabin 518 as soon as possible, he went into the bathroom, where he left fresh towels, replaced the pastel soaps, shampoos, and body lotion and folded the bottom square of toilet paper into a triangle. He took time to check his appearance in the mirror. He was a slender, wiry man, only five six, but with almond eyes, high Aztec cheekbones and a sensuous, full-lipped mouth that, for most women, offset the lack of height. He noted with some satisfaction that he still looked smart and crisp, even though his black bow tie was a tad askew and his red jacket (one of three) with his name and the cruise ship logo embroidered on the right lapel would soon be due for a laundering.

Back in the bedroom, he plumped the pillows and smoothed the coverlet before placing a foil-wrapped Godiva chocolate and a copy of the next day's activities between two tasseled duvets.

Before leaving, he checked the closet to get an idea of 518's taste in clothes—obscenely expensive designer stuff plus furs that could have populated a small zoo if their owners were still alive. Imelda, who dressed like Spanish royalty but disdained fur, would have turned up her Castillian nose.

He assumed the woman's jewelry would be locked in the room safe but—*ay, Dios mio!*—she'd left a stunning pair of ruby ear rings and a matching bracelet on the night stand by the bed.

So, in addition to smelling like a wet dream, she was also a trusting soul, thought Hugo, ever more intrigued. He picked up the bracelet, trying to determine if it was real or one of those bagatelles you could buy for a few hundred bucks at The Real Deal on Deck Nine.

Real, he judged.

And almost jumped out of his highly polished shoes when a blast of freezing wind gusted into the cabin, as the woman whose jewelry he was fondling shoved back the sliding door and stepped inside off the balcony.

She was petite and winter pale with shoulder-length black hair threaded with silver. Early to mid-50's, Hugo guessed. She wore black ski pants and a long-sleeved sweater under a fleece-lined parka soaked with spray—no hat, no gloves, no neck warmer— what was she thinking? He realized he was still holding the bracelet and placed it back on the night stand, making a brushing motion with his hand in a lame attempt to pretend that he was dusting.

"Why are you in here?" the woman asked. She spoke with a pronounced but indeterminate accent that reminded him of Helga, the Bulgarian social director.

"Just doing the turn down," Hugo said, hoping desperately she hadn't seen him scrutinizing her jewelry like a cat burglar tallying up the take.

The wind was rioting around the room like a vandal, but she took her merry time closing the slider. When she finally latched it shut, she brushed bits of ice from her hair and said, "I haven't seen a schedule. Can you tell me at what time the ship will reach the Torngasak?"

"I'm sorry, *what*?"

"Oh, I forget. Torngasak is the Inuit name. You call it the Hurtigruten Glacier after some nineteenth century Norwegian sea captain."

"Ah, the Hurtigruten. Day after tomorrow. Mid-day probably."

"Will we get close?"

"Very close. The fjord where the Hurtigruten terminates is narrow, so the maneuver's tricky. The captain has to exercise some care. If you're interested, you might want to sign up for the glacier walk."

Her face brightened.

"A bit strenuous, but well worth it," he added enthusiastically, thinking he'd as soon swim naked with killer whales as go tromping around on a creaky slab of unstable ice that might fracture under his feet at any moment.

She was staring at him so intently that for a second he wondered if he'd actually spoken the thought out loud. The silence stretched between them like an invisible cord and—no mistaking it—the tang of rut wafted from her pores like heat throbbing from a stove.

He shifted his feet. The floor seemed to slip away underneath him.

"I'll be going then. Is there anything else you need, Ms.—" At the start of every voyage, he'd trained himself to memorize the names of his cabins' occupants off the manifest, "—Kent."

The woman's wide-set eyes, dark brown with hints of amber, appeared to size him up. A conclusion was evidently reached, and she gave a knowing smile. "Forget formalities. Call me Naqi. And I'll be needing a pair of binoculars."

Hugo didn't want to point out that what he'd had in mind was more along the lines of extra towels or truffles on the pillow instead of mints.

"You'll find excellent binoculars in the gift shop on Deck Four."

She removed her dripping parka and slung it across a chair. "I need binoculars, not information about where to buy them. And by the way—"

He began nodding with what he hoped was appropriate contrition.

"—why were you holding my bracelet when I came in? Do you plan to steal it?"

Hugo's face flamed as though he'd been locked inside a freezer, but he rallied, reminding himself of what Imelda used to tell him—before he gave her reason to believe otherwise—that he was more than a mere steward, he was a gentleman as well. Invoking his former lover's lofty cadence, he said, "I confess to you, Ms. Kent—Naqi—that I am a man with a weakness for beauty which sometimes gets me into trouble. But I take nothing that isn't freely offered. I am a man who—"

She closed the space between them like a shadow sliding over a bare wall, pressing herself to him as though they were old lovers, her touch so wickedly assured that he lost both balance and composure and stumbled back onto the pristine expanse of heretofore unrumpled bed.

"I know what kind of man you are," she said, peeling off her sweater before she cupped his face to kiss, tracing the curve of his cheekbones, the sweep of his lips, with her thumbs.

While he removed his clothes, she opened up the closet and began yanking down furs, tossing them onto the bed. Onto these— the luscious sable and ermine and mink—they sprawled naked and tussled and rolled on the thick, sumptuous bedding of pelts.

Her skin was still damp with spray. On her mouth was the tang of the ocean. When he tongued between her thighs, the scent of sex he'd first detected upon entering the cabin unfurled in his brain like fever.

She slid back and straddled him, matching her rhythm to the pitch and sway of the ship, bending forward so he could tongue and suck her nipples.

Then suddenly, alarmingly, Inz's hiss in his head—*Hot lover, she ditch you, no?*—followed by a jolt of anger and the knife thrust slam of his heart.

He rolled the woman over and got on top, riding a rush of violent need, his blood full of razors and heat. Tired of tameness and the bitter swill of self-hate for the things he'd fucked up.

Pounding his pain into her.

When he hooked her legs over his shoulders for a deeper thrust, he felt her own powerful contractions tugging him deeper still, and there was a disorienting instant of naked lust meeting primal terror when he feared he might not be able to withdraw. Arched beneath him, she saw the dash of panic in his eyes and pulled him down to her even as she released her inner grip, the moment so fleeting and unexpected that, as Hugo continued to ram himself inside her, he could only think he had imagined he had briefly been held captive.

Later, she wrapped the furs around them like a soft dark cave where they could nuzzle and caress, whispering sweet, foreign words to him before she fell asleep. He lay there, aware of the passing time and turn-downs still to do, of the ship picking up speed as it plowed south into deeper water. Finally, carefully, he extricated himself from her embrace and began to gather up his clothes.

She woke up while he was struggling to get his legs into his trousers as the ship swayed, her flat gaze detached and—to Hugo—disturbingly neutral. Imelda, he reflected, liked to watch him dress, too, but appeared far more appreciative.

"Come back tomorrow night with the binoculars," she said. "By then I'm sure I'll have thought of something else I need."

Despite his best intentions, he could feel resentment bunch his forehead. *What, she couldn't be bothered to buy the damned binoculars herself? Or she took pleasure in tasking underlings with petty favors?*

He was getting ready to say something to that effect when he saw what looked like a trail of blood drops flying at his head and couldn't suppress a grin as he snatched the ruby bracelet from the air.

《《—》》

The binoculars required some finessing—nimble fingers and a deep-pocketed jacket put to good use while the gift shop manager was texting—but worth the risk. Naqi rewarded him with another bout of enthusiastic debauchery, insisting that he stay the night, huddled with her in their nest of furs.

He slept like a stone until, sometime in the wee hours, she shook him awake. "Get up! A glacier is about to calve."

Half zombified with sleep, he grabbed a robe and stumbled outside. The ship was gliding through a fjord, past spectral cliffs of blue-white ice that gleamed pearlescent in the moonlight. Naqi stood silhouetted in the shimmering light, the muscles of her naked back clenched as she gripped the rail. He opened his mouth to complain about the cold, but she shushed him. The seconds ticked.

There came a vast and vibratory rumble, as though a furious sea beast, aroused and rampant, had thrashed to life under the water. Explosive cracks, like a barrage of artillery fire, rent the night, as a colossal shelf of ice crumbled into the water, flinging up a mammoth geyser of spray.

"It's happening!" cried Naqi, exultant, triumphant as though in this purely natural phenomenon she found some sort of personal redemption.

Hugo gaped at her. He'd seen camera-laden passengers shiver outside in freezing cold for hours at a time, staring at a slab of ice in hopes a chunk would rupture off into the sea—a fool's mission, he'd always considered it. But now, seeing the ecstatic look on Naqi's face, he felt a tiny jolt of doubt and wondered if there was more to what he'd just witnessed than was immediately apparent. "How did you know that was going to happen?"

She shrugged as though such abilities were commonplace. "The glacier tells me. When I'm this close, I can feel it creak and vibrate. Before it calves, the ice groans and shudders like a woman giving birth."

Hugo could feel the cold knifing through the bottoms of his bare feet up into his ankles and knees. The prospect of bundling with Naqi in that warm mountain of furs suddenly seemed irresistible. He took her hand. "C'mon, you've seen it. Let's go back to bed."

She shook him off and stood riveted, staring at the cliffs of ice. He saw that she was trembling, too, blue moonlight sliding over the goose bumps on her skin. When she spoke, her voice was hushed and reverent. "The Inuits say that once there was a tribe called the Claw People, who fed off human souls. They caused much death and suffering. The people cried for help to Aguta, the god who gathers up the dead, and he froze the Claw people in the ice."

She spoke with such gravity that Hugo wondered if she half believed what she was saying. He looked into the blue-black water that was now subsiding back into deceptive stillness and, though he saw no sign of lurking evil, no souls being consumed, her words still touched some atavistic fear within him, of things unseen and unimaginable set loose to feed upon the world, and a shiver skimmed his ribs like the legs of a spider. He looked at the looming wall of ice that the ship was passing and thought: *Hell isn't fire and brimstone like the predicadores rant about. Hell is cold and sleet and knife-edged wind, an eternity in ice.*

Hell is here.

40

《《—》》

By dawn, the first brash streaks of violet light revealed otters frolicking among the ice floes and a bald eagle soaring over forested slopes. A moose with candelabra antlers lumbered along the shoreline, then dipped back inside the veil of greenery, its lumbering movements seamless as a sigh.

Bundled in furs, Hugo and Naqi watched as the ship traveled past dense, foreboding forests where no light penetrated and huddled trees scraped brittle-looking branches against a frozen sky.

Naqi slid her hand through his. "It's so beautiful, but you don't want to be here. I can tell your heart is somewhere else."

He shrugged. "Too cold, that's all."

"It's more than that." She took his face in her hands, kissed his forehead, eyelids. He brushed her hair back, saw diamonds glinting in her earlobes like tiny stars.

"Tell me where you would go," she said, "if you could live anywhere at all."

He knew at once. "Buenos Aires."

"You've lived there?"

"For a few months, yes. It's a beautiful old city, the people are kind, the air like flowers—" He smiled at a memory that flashed by like an unexpected kiss. "They have enormous tango halls where passionate women wrap their legs around the men and look like they're making love right on the dance floor." He laughed softly. "I never became good at tango, but it was enjoyable to try."

"You were in love with someone in Buenos Aires. Perhaps someone you left behind?"

He studied the passing forest. A fox ran along the shoreline, something bloody hanging from its jaws. "I work on a cruise ship. I'm always leaving people behind."

"A lonely life," said Naqi. "I understand that. My life is lonely, too."

"It doesn't have to be."

They were silent for a moment, watching the fox rip its prey. Hugo lifted Naqi's hand to his mouth and licked the palm, breathing in the carnal perfume of her skin, feeling himself stiffen. She leaned toward him as though she were about to bestow a kiss and whispered, "I wonder, have you ever seen anyone jump overboard?"

The question, so unexpected, rattled him profoundly.

"Why would you ask me such a thing?"

"I suppose because sometimes I imagine doing it myself. When the sea is tranquil like this, it seems to beckon me. Like a lover holding out his arms for me to jump."

"Don't talk crazy" Hugo said. "You wouldn't last five minutes in that water."

She studied him. "I'm going on the glacier walk this afternoon. I want you to come with me."

He'd been maneuvering himself to press against her, but now he tensed and pulled away, snapping in exasperation, "Do you think I'm here on holiday? I'm not a wealthy man. I can't just take off work to keep you company! I can't—"

She sighed and tapped a finger to his lips. Slipping one of the diamond studs out of her earlobe, she placed it in his palm and curled his fingers round it.

Light danced in her eyes like a candle flame, and she whispered, "Find a way."

«« — »»

He was coming out of Naqi's cabin, straightening his tie, when Inz zipped around the corner toting a pile of towels, and almost knocked him flat.

"Watch where you're going!" he said and Inz gave him a sneer. "You spending all night with that old woman, don't you?"

"Don't be stupid. I just brought her tea."

Inz's lip curled. "You bringing her your cock is what you do."

"Bitch. What's wrong with you?"

"Tonio told me you weren't in your bunk last night."

"What, my bunkmate waits up for me now?"

"If you fucking a passenger, Hugo, you are—how they call it?—history, you know that."

"Hell, if that's what I was doing—which I'm not—the cruise line should pay me double."

42

"Ha!" scorned Inz. "You *wish*." She wrinkled her nose like she was smelling something nasty. "How you even getting it up for grandmama, eh, Hugo? At least Brazilian bitch has flair and spice. But this old cow…!"

Jealous bitch, go fold your fucking towels, thought Hugo, but he held his tongue. Instead he slid his arms around Inz's waist and pulled her close. "Why do say these things, my Inz? Why do you make me angry? Don't you know when all is said and done that you're the one I want?"

He tried to kiss her, but she made a disgruntled moue and turned her head.

On impulse, Hugo dug inside his pocket and took out the diamond stud. "Look here. I wasn't going to give it to you yet, but since you doubt me…" When he dropped the earring into her hand, her eyes widened and glazed over.

"I need to ask a favor, though."

«《——》》

Hugo worked the first half of his shift distractedly. Around noon, when he felt the ship slow down and turn slightly to starboard, he put away his cleaning cart and went outside. Already most of the passengers were gathered on the Sea Mist's upper decks, taking photos of the massive Hurtigruten glacier that Naqi called the Torngasak. Now, even with a thick cloud cover and snow starting to fall, the Hurtigruten gleamed as if lit from within, its pressure ridges and crevasses outlined in a luminous shade of turquoise so bright it burned the eyes. The water around the glacier's terminus was dense with brash ice, small ice fragments that, over time, had accumulated from its numerous calvings. He looked around for Naqi, didn't see her, and took the elevator down to Deck Five to let her know that he'd arranged for someone to complete his shift. If she asked why he wasn't wearing the diamond, he'd tell her that ear rings violated the dress code for male staff.

A pair of French-Canadian girls who occupied the cabin next to Naqi's waylaid him as he was coming up the hall. Flirty and boozy and reeking of gin, they peppered him with questions about the zipline excursion in Ketchiken, an activity that involved strapping on a harness attached to a cable and bee-lining through the treetops of the Alaskan rain forest at breakneck speed.

"A once in a lifetime experience! You've got to try it!" Hugo was enthusing, when suddenly he saw Naqi crack the door to her suite and slip the Do Not Disturb sign into the key slot. She then closed the door quickly without seeing him.

The Canadians kept asking questions (and Hugo, glibly, invented answers as they popped into his head—"of course no one has ever fallen from a zipline, the equipment was designed by NASA engineers"), but as soon as he could extricate himself from their tipsy exuberance, he went to Naqi's door and unlocked it with his passkey.

She wasn't in the suite or the bathroom or in the little alcove with the mini-bar, which only left the balcony. With her name on his lips, he went outside, automatically pulling the slider shut to retain the heat in the room.

His mind, expecting one thing, stuttered to a stop when what he saw was quite another.

The balcony was empty.

Incredulity was followed by cold, gut-loosening dread. This couldn't be. She was playing a game. She was in the cabin, but somehow he'd missed seeing her. He went back inside, checked the sitting room and bedroom again, then the closets, the bathroom, the shower. Had she slipped outside while he was distracted by the Canadians? Impossible, he'd been looking right at her door.

Back to the balcony.

"Naqi!"

The wind jabbed at him like a blade twisted by a sadist.

Bits and pieces of their earlier conversation stormed through the gathering turmoil in his mind: *I understand loneliness…Have you ever seen anyone jump?* Who the hell asked a question like that?

He leaned over the railing, into the black and glittering chop, and knew with sickening certainty that she was down there, probably already dead.

He leaned out, yelling her name, but the ship was moving so fast, it seemed to fly across the waves. Panic clawed at his belly. Vertigo made his eyes seem to spin in their sockets.

She'd done it. She'd jumped.

Por Dios!

Behind him, he heard a throaty cough, like a laugh or sneeze being stifled.

He whirled and saw her perched on the adjacent balcony, the binoculars around her neck. Her lips were pressed tight with suppressed mirth, as though she'd caught him doing something foolish but felt it would be unkind to laugh. But then she began to giggle, while he gaped at her with nothing less than horror.

To get from the balcony where Hugo stood to the one she was now on, she'd had to traverse five feet of yawning space with nothing but the Gulf of Alaska below. The railings themselves were not flat but cylindrical, always damp with spray. Standing on one would be like trying to walk across a greased broom handle stretched between two swaying chairs.

"Stay there!" he ordered, even as she climbed atop the railing and leaped, clearing the gap between the two balconies and landing nimbly, her knees absorbing the shock of the fall.

"I'm sorry. Did I scare you?" she said, looking not repentant in the slightest.

"Are you crazy? What the hell are you doing?"

"That balcony is wider. I can get a better angle for viewing the Torngasak."

He waved his hands, a man fed up. "You're *loca*! What the hell is there to see? Nothing! Just ice and rocks and more ice!"

She looked at him as though he'd claimed the frescoes in the Sistine Chapel were just so much graffiti-tagging.

"For years," she said, "I've studied glaciers. They fascinate me, and the Torngasak is a favorite. I've cruised past it, but I've also hiked its valleys and moraines, I've drunk from its melt-pits and shivered out a storm in one of its ice caves. Never any sign of thaw. But now the ice is melting. The glacier's heart is bleeding out and everything will change."

And Hugo, squinting at the towering glacial cliffs, suddenly felt a bone-deep chill, as though the glacier really were a living thing, now in its death throes, and he preparing to trudge across its dying bones.

"Go dress for the outdoors," said Naqi. "The Zodiacs are loading."

《《—》》

Instead of going straight to his bunk in the dormitory to change clothes, Hugo gave in to the impulse that had been tugging at him ever since he told Naqi about Buenos Aires.

Taking out his cell phone, checking to see he still had service, was like picking a sore, the blind craving of an alcoholic reaching for a bottle, a gesture so automatic and reflexive that it went unchallenged by his conscious mind until he was scrolling through the address book to punch in Imelda's number. He almost hung up, but some inner momentum, borne of feelings he couldn't really acknowledge or explain, powered him on. Numbly, he tolerated the hollow bleating of the phone until someone picked up on the other end.

Silence like a nuclear winter reverberated through the phone.

"Imelda? Estas alli?"

"*You.*" A pause while she seemed to collect herself. "Well, this is unexpected."

He found himself speechless. He'd forgotten how sublime her voice was, how soothing and mellow, the voice of a fairy godmother laced with an erotic subtext.

"Imelda," he said. "I'm so happy you answered. Are you alone?"

"I'm always alone now, Hugo. Where are you? What are you doing?"

"I'm on the Sea Mist, headed to Vancouver."

"Still at sea? I'm surprised. I thought you'd have built that house in Merida you always talked about, that you'd be living the good life by now."

The good life costs more than it used to, he felt like saying, and money draws people to you for all the wrong reasons, like flies buzzing over carrion, but given what had occurred between them, it was a sentiment he could ill afford to voice. "All these months, I've wanted to call you. I want us to meet somewhere, in Vancouver or maybe I could fly down to B.A. I need to see you. I need to explain why I left."

"I'm sure you'd come up with something quite original."

Was she chuckling or holding back a sob? It was hard to tell.

46

He talked on, the words erupting out of him, wheedling and desperate.

"I'm so sorry, Imelda. The way I left was crazy, cowardly! I had this idea I wasn't worthy of you, that I would be a burden to you, an embarrassment, that I'd never fit into your world. I was a fool, I don't know what I was thinking."

"Stop!" She spat the word like an invective. "Tell me, Hugo. How did you squander the money? Was it drink? Gambling? *Putanas*? Maybe just bad real estate or too many greedy relations with their hands out."

"I don't know what you mean."

"Don't insult me. My sons admitted what they did. The older one is a chronic alcoholic like his father was, maudlin and sentimental. He drinks and listens to samba music and confesses his sins like a child. Now he and his brother regret their meddling bitterly, because I've disowned them both."

"Imelda, it isn't what you think. I had no choice. Your sons threatened to kill me. They said they'd burn down my family's house in Merida. They threatened to—"

Her laughter crackled through the phone like broken glass.

"How much did they pay you, Hugo? How much did it cost them to make sure you wouldn't be filching too much of their inheritance?"

"It wasn't about the money. I was happy with you. I felt—"

"Felt *what*, Hugo?" she said, the words so slathered with contempt they dripped like honeyed offal.

"I was in love with you, Imelda. I still am. I want to come back."

As he spoke, he caught a glimpse of black hair billowing. Naqi emerged from a stairwell beside a glass-enclosed poster that touted the charms of that evening's singing sensation. It was the first time he'd seen her outside her cabin. His heartbeat quickened, and he found himself turning away to conceal the cell phone.

Imelda was saying something he hadn't heard.

"I'm sorry, what—?"

"Find some other wealthy fool," she said and the phone went dead.

«《——》»

Four orange inflatables holding twenty passengers each were launched from the back of the Sea Mist, accompanied by two guides. The hike would be short and only mildly taxing, suitable for people with more stamina for gorging themselves at the buffet than trekking across a glacier. Now, with snow flurries beginning to make visibility iffy, its duration would be curtailed even more, a development unlamented by Hugo.

The Zodiacs put in at an area of bare, vegetation-free bedrock left behind as the glacier had retreated. Naqi and Hugo followed up the rear as the guide led them up a path paralleling the ice. To one side rose a dark forest of fir and Sitka spruce, to the other loomed a wall of massive seracs, jagged pinnacles of glacial ice resembling frozen giants wearing pyramidal hats. There was a sound that Hugo couldn't place, a constant crackling like soda water fizzing.

Naqi, as though reading the question in his eyes, said, "Haven't you ever heard bergy sizzle before?" When he looked blank, she added, "It's the sound of air bubbles being released as the glacier melts."

She took his hand as they huffed uphill, pausing frequently for the guides to explain some aspect of glaciology, which Hugo almost entirely tuned out. The snow was falling harder now, dusting the bedrock and accumulating in the branches of the spruce and fir whose roots found tenacious purchase in the thin, rocky soil. Beyond the sediment deposits, the frozen river flowed, eons of glacial ice, cracked and grooved and fissured.

The group gathered on an outcropping of rock while the guide described how seracs formed by the intersection of crevasses. Hugo found himself contemplating an ice ridge, white as bone, that rose like a bent and twisted spine, a bridge to the end of the world. Naqi's hand slipped out of his. When he reached for her, she was gone.

Behind him, Hugo saw only snow, and beyond that, a glimpse of blue-white cornices dissolving into the pixilated frenzy of whirling flakes. He yelled Naqi's name, and a fat woman in a pink Lands' End parka turned her hooded face to shush him, plump finger to pursed lips.

He muttered something rude and turned away in time to glimpse a grey-white blur, low to the ground, that dashed between two outcroppings of rock. He blinked, unsure what he had seen.

Behind him, the group was moving on, the guide's commanding voice fading so quickly into silence that Hugo had the impression a crevasse had yawned under their feet and swallowed up the lot of them. Thinking that Naqi might have returned to the Zodiacs, he turned and started to retrace his steps.

Within a few hundred yards, the trail was blocked by a fallen Sitka spruce, toppled by the glacier's advance into the adjacent forest. He hadn't seen the spruce before and paused to reorient himself, bedeviled by the wind and snow and the skin-crawly sensation that black eyes within the blue-tinged shadows observed him and sensed his fear.

Whichever way he turned, impossibly fleet shadows meteored across the periphery of his vision.

Skirting the fallen tree, he quickened his pace, heedless now of whether he was still on the trail or veering toward a crevasse or treacherous snow bridge. He began a sliding, stumbling run. Wolfen bodies razored into view, their lean forms resembling frantic scissor strokes opening up dark rents on a sheet of white paper. With synchronized precision, they flanked and circled him.

They were wolf-like, but unlike any wolves Hugo had ever seen on nature shows or pacing behind bars in zoos. Long, ribby torsos extending from humped, muscular shoulders, snouts low to the ground like truffle-rooting swine, eyes fierce little nuggets of tar shot through with red. Their grey pelts mirrored the glacial ice, tinged with glimmers of blue, so that, viewed from behind the whirling snow, they seemed to shiver, ghost-like, incandescent.

Naqi's command came from behind him. "Don't move, don't make a sound." Silent as shadow, she inched out from a vertical furrow at the base of a serac. Hugo, moments before the animals appeared, had looked right at her hiding place and seen nothing.

Crouching, she circled slowly and dropped to her knees. Her hands shook as she removed her left glove and put out her hand, fingers splayed. She swung her head from side to side, long hair dragging the ice as she emitted sounds that Hugo could only associate with loss and bitter mourning.

At first Hugo hoped the group from the ship—who surely must have noticed their absence by now—would hear her frightful keening, but the wind was gusting vigorously and wailed along in a high, vicious soprano, the noise as white and undifferentiated as the flakes boiling around them.

The attack came too fast for him to see—a flash of fur and fangs and two white snail-like objects that skittered across the snow, trailing slimes of scarlet.

Another of the shaggy, grey-white animals approached, its piggish snout agape with teeth that would do credit to a butcher's arsenal, snuffled at the bloody morsels and gulped them down.

"Come," Naqi hissed. Grabbing his arm, she started crawling backward, their pace torturously slow, Hugo expecting any second for the pack to fall upon them and tear their throats out. When they were finally far enough away, she yanked him to his feet and steered him cautiously around a series of snow-filled crevasses and onto a flat stretch of bedrock that gave way eventually to forest.

When they heard the guide yelling for them, Hugo called back and they were quickly taken to the Zodiacs and ferried back to the ship. Naqi kept her wounded hand wrapped in a scarf and tucked inside her parka. Back on board ship, she refused all Hugo's entreaties to go to the infirmary. In the elevator, she stared straight ahead with empty eyes and gritted teeth. When he tried to comfort her, she shook him off.

"You're bleeding! Let me help you!"

She turned away, but not before he saw the cold resolve in those black eyes flicker like a candle dimmed and pain twisted her features.

"Leave me alone," she said. "Don't come to my cabin again."

And left him standing, stunned and furious, when the elevator door opened.

«« — »»

A stiff drink, he thought. Make that a half dozen shots of Tecate to get the circulation going in his frozen body and tamp down his rage. How dare the bitch dismiss him like a servant! He bolted for the closest lounge, the Yukon Territory on Deck Three. Along the way, he passed the Photo Op Shop, where shots of passengers taken when they first boarded the Sea Mist were posted on bulletin boards for purchase, arranged by deck and cabin number. He hurried past, then suddenly, remembering something Inz had said, he halted and went back.

Inz had been wrong to describe the woman in 518 as old. 'Old', in Hugo's estimation, hovered somewhere between sixty and eighty. Maisie Kent from Bristol, England, looked mummified, an ancient crone with cropped white curls, pearly teeth, and a jaw-dropping diamond the size of a pea on her withered finger. She bore as much resemblance to Naqi as the Bering Sea to a duck pond.

《《—》》

Hugo threw aside the Do Not Disturb sign and stormed into the suite. Cold assailed him. The balcony door was open, and, a fierce wind blustered through. Blood speckled the carpet, and a warm, coppery reek tainted the air.

He strode to the balcony, automatically slamming the slider shut behind him. This time the fact that the balcony was empty didn't alarm him. He shouted Naqi's name like an oath.

At once, she came out onto the balcony that belonged to the adjacent suite, looking at him as he must have stared at her, with horror and dismay. Blood still flowed from the stumps of her amputated fingers, but not nearly enough to account for the amount staining her pants and parka. Her clothes were slick with it, her hair stippled red.

Hugo shouted above the wind. "Who the hell *are* you? What happened to the woman in 518?"

Behind her, gold curtains caught by the wind, swirled out the open door. Something wrong there, Hugo registered, but was unwilling to take his eyes off Naqi. He had not forgotten she was perfectly capable of jumping between the balconies. He found himself taking a step backward.

"You say you've never seen anyone fall overboard," said Naqi, taking a step closer. "I myself have seen it several times. Usually, it

51

all happens in a flash, the person who's about to fall doesn't fully understand what's happening or what it is they're seeing. But that old woman surprised me. She looked into my eyes and saw me as I really am. She saw into my *soul*. No one has ever done that before. It took courage. I made sure she was already dead before I threw her overboard."

"Jesus, why would you kill her?"

"Why do you think? I'm not officially on board the ship. I needed her cabin."

She moved forward again, closing the distance between them and blocking his view of the curtains, which flapped wildly behind her. At the same time, Hugo felt the vibration of the Sea Mist's engines and knew the ship was about to leave its current position and sail up the fiord. Naqi felt it, too. For the first time, her eyes left Hugo and she looked at the shore.

"There!" she said. At the glacier's terminus, where bare bedrock gave way to forested banks, Hugo saw blurred movement, grey shapes milling and massing behind the swirling snow.

A nauseating cold stabbed his belly. He stepped away from the railing, at the same time that Naqi mirrored his movement on her own balcony.

With her good hand, she pointed toward the shore. "My kind have been imprisoned in the ice for eons. Whether it was Aguta who caused it or something else, who knows? The few who escaped have been wandering ever since, waiting to be reunited with their tribe."

Hugo barely listened. He was looking at the slider, sickened to see he'd closed it on his way outside. He would move toward it casually, he thought—calmly, like nothing was happening—he'd go inside and lock it, and call security to report the murder of a passenger.

"The old ones have accepted my offering," Naqi said. "Now I can rejoin my kind."

Hugo inched closer to the slider. "Your fingers…you offered them your fingers?"

She gave a funny smile. Behind her, the wind whooshed beneath the drapes, billowing them inward, revealing gobbets of meat and bone protruding from a pink sock that was ripped and blood-soaked.

"Inz!" he cried, but his voice emerged a muffled croak, more plea than shout.

"I decided to spare you," Naqi said. "I killed her, so you could live. Yet here you are."

He lunged to grab the handle of the slider, but her leap carried her there ahead of him. An animal odor mingled with the reek of blood and for an instant, he endured the sight that Maisie Kent in her last moments must have seen, the essence of Naqi's feral soul, all fangs and sinew and claws.

There was no choice. He leaped for the railing and plummeted over, head first. The world upended. Above him loomed the water, a foam-flecked, obsidian sky, while from below the howling nightmare rushed up to slash his face. Then all reversed, and scarlet claws scraped scalp from skull.

The last sound reaching Hugo before the frigid water filled his lungs was the thunder of nearby glaciers starting to calve.

The roar of destruction and collapse echoed up and down the fiord while, from the shore, there rose an ecstasy of yipping, an infernal glee infused with bone-deep knowing, that the Great Thaw had finally begun and untold legions of their kind were soon to be released upon the world.

the butsudan

Hiroshi-san died at the start of the New Year. Now, nine months later, it is the beginning of Obon, the festival of the dead in Japan, and he is due to come home for a visit.

As I trudge back from the market, I can sense the happy excitement and anticipation of the people around me, many of them already wearing yukatas, lightweight summer kimonos, in preparation for the dancing that will start tonight, but all I feel is a profound, stomach-turning dread.

As a Westerner, I don't share the Japanese belief, based in Buddhist legend, that the dead are allowed to leave the underworld to visit once a year, that they are guided back to their earthly homes by bonfires and candles. And yet, this morning I took extra care as I arranged the little bowls of dumplings and noodles on the butsudan, the family altar where the ancestors are worshipped. I set sake and plum wine on the second shelf and arranged a mixture of chopped eggplant, rice, and cucumber on a lotus leaf beside it. I played the pious hostess preparing the symbolic feast. Despite myself, I thought of my dead husband and murmured a brief prayer that, if there should be an afterlife, it finds him well and happy.

I doubt it.

Hiroshi-san was as stingy with a kind word or a smile as he was with the small allowance of yen he doled out to me every week. He was a dour and miserly man in life. In death, why should he be different?

The festivities are already starting in the town park, where the Bon-Odori, the traditional dances, will take place. A young man climbs the platform in the center of the dance space and begins pounding a taiko drum. I see families lugging coolers filled with beer, ice tea, and shaved ice—it is the hottest time of the year.

As I pass the torii gate that marks the entrance to the Shinto shrine up the hill, some children scamper past me. One of them, a little girl with jet hair and huge black eyes, stops to gape at me, then hurls the one word I learned very quickly upon coming to Japan. "Gaijin" she shrieks and points at me. "Gaijin, gaijin!"

Foreigner. A woman, apparently the girl's mother, grabs the child's hand and yanks her along, but the girl stares back at me over her shoulder, taking in my yellow hair and green eyes as one would an exotic butterfly pinned to a board. It has happened so many times, you'd think I would get used to it, but I never do. I was married to Hiroshi-san for five years, but still I am a stranger here. Still an object of curiosity, my height and coloring an invitation to stare, my halting attempts to speak the language ever a source of bewilderment and amusement.

It wasn't supposed to be like this.

When I came to Japan to marry Hiroshi-san, shortly after meeting him at an art gallery in Chicago where I worked as a receptionist, I imagined an exotic, romantic life in a foreign land. I envisioned tea ceremonies and Noh dramas, Zen gardens where red-lipped kimono-clad geisha performed classical dance. What I got were bitter winters and steaming summers, gangs of sullen teenagers with spiked hair and iPods, subways full of salarymen who leered first at me and then at their porno mangas, and a language as incomprehensible as the chattering of crickets on a summer morning.

And along with that, side by side with the kitschy and the profane, an astonishing array of festivals that link the human and the divine, all aimed at invoking the good will of the deities and ancestors.

Now Obon.

Already I can see fires burning—candles flickering in windows and on porches, bonfires tended by bare-armed, sweaty men on open lawns and along the riverbanks. People stand in their open doorways, silent reception committees for the spectral guests. Fireworks explode on every corner, and squealing, giggling children wave glowing pinwheels in the darkening air.

The heat is stifling, suffocating, full of smoke from the fires and the fireworks. Sweat pours down my face and puddles between my breasts. There is no heat in the world like the heat of a Japanese August. It clings to the skin like a hot, damp rag and pastes the hair to the scalp. In such a swelter, all movements seem to require extra effort. In this world supposedly aswarm with ghosts, it feels as though everything is underwater, that I wade along the path as much as walk.

When I reach the wooden house, known as a minka that I once shared with my husband, I see a pair of men's brown Gucci loafers outside the door and know that Katsuro-san, Hiroshi-san's son, has come to honor his father and the other ancestors. I leave my sandals beside his shoes—only the dead wear shoes indoors—and put on a pair of slippers before I slide back the door and go inside.

Even in the smaller towns, a traditional house like this, with tatami mats on the floors and shoji screens dividing the rooms, with bedding that is rolled and stored in a cupboard during the day and unrolled at night, and a hearth for making fires in the winter, is a rarity. In the older minkas the roof is thatched, but ours is tile, the ends of the tiles decorated with images of deities thought to provide protection. The butsudan, or spirit cabinet, with its intricately carved lotus leaves and sutras, occupies a grand alcove in the largest of the rooms. It is the first thing one sees upon entering the house.

This butsudan, handed down through Hiroshi-san's family through generations, is a massive, imposing cabinet made of cherry and cedar wood, hived with a multitude of alcoves and cabinets and cubicles in which to store the dishes, incense, candles, and writing implements which are part of the daily rituals. A gold Buddha rests at the top, presiding over the many shelves and a desk that folds out for copying Buddhist texts.

I call out to Katsuro-san, but apparently he doesn't hear me over the raucous babble of a game show blaring from the TV set in the back of the house. I find this annoying, but not as much so as the fact that Katsuro-san has lit the candles on the butsudan, then left them unattended, a dangerous practice on a sultry evening with a hot breeze coming through the windows.

But then, where money or pleasure's not concerned, Katsuro-san isn't one for details. After Hiroshi-san died, Katsuro-san spent less time grieving than he did visiting banks, exploring the possibility of land deeds, overseas funds, secret stock portfolios. In his younger days, as an importer of antiques and art, Hiroshi-san had reputedly amassed a fortune, not all of it honestly made. Some of his associates were art smugglers and forgers, a few were members of the feared yakuza, Japanese organized crime. Then, after his first wife died, Hiroshi-san apparently woke up to the brevity and fragility of life. He renounced his criminal connections, left Tokyo for this small town in eastern Kyushu, and became a fervent meditator and student of the sutras. After a few cups of sake, he often boasted of a fortune hidden away, but in reality, he lived a life of almost obsessive frugality, deeming even the most minor luxury a reckless extravagance.

Katsuro-san remains convinced a secret fortune exists, if only it could be found, but so far, nothing has turned up. In Hiroshi-san's will, I was left the house and a meager stipend of cash, and Katsuro-san, whose profligacy with money was a constant source of embarrassment and outrage to his father, got even less.

Not enough for either of us to live comfortably.

Certainly not enough to leave Japan.

As I'm frowning at the candles on the butsudan, I notice something else—Katsuro-san has placed fresh flowers on the bottom shelf and, next to that, an exquisite porcelain bowl filled with dark red liquid. I dip a finger into it and touch it to my lips. In the overheated room, cold travels up my spine like an unwelcome kiss.

"Carolyn-san?"

I look up to see Katsuro-san watching me from the doorway. He's taller than most Japanese, with regal cheekbones and a thin mouth that always looks ready to leave teeth marks in something. I walk across the room, and we bow to each other formally, me dipping a bit lower as is customary with women.

"Good-evening, Katsuro-san."

"Good evening, Carolyn-san."

The smallest of smiles, like the flick of a whip, crosses Katsuro-san's mouth. Then we are in each other's arms, kissing, grabbing each other like starving people finding food, his hands tangled in my hair, inside my blouse, my fingers working at the button of his trousers.

Suddenly he pushes me away. "No, we can't. Not at Obon. It's disrespectful."

Such things have seldom concerned Katsuro-san before. His very wantonness has always been the greatest source of his appeal.

With the spell of our reunion broken, my irritation returns quickly. "Why did you light the candles if you were going to watch TV? And what the hell was the idea of putting this on the altar?"

I show him the bowl of thick, red liquid.

He shrugs. "Red bean soup. So what?"

"I haven't prepared red bean soup since Hiroshi-san died. Did you think it was clever to offer it for Obon?"

"I didn't put it there."

"Then how—?"

"Maybe one of the relatives or neighbors stopped by while you were out."

He takes the small dish, lifts it to his mouth, and drains it. "There. All gone. What is it, Carolyn-san? Are you afraid of bean soup now? It wasn't bean soup that killed my father. He choked to death on mocha. It was an accident. You know that."

Do I? Is he testing me? I try to read his expression, but inscrutable is not an adjective applied to the Japanese for nothing.

"It's Obon," he continues, "and you feel guilty, so your mind is playing tricks. It's understandable. But what happened between us didn't really begin until after father died. It isn't like we were sneaking off to Love Hotels behind his back."

No, we sneak off to Love Hotels now—in Beppu, a larger city up the coast. It would not look good before the neighbors if Katsuro-san spent too much time here, and the three Meiji brothers, who live across the street and raise silkworms, are ever at their windows. So Katsuro-san comes and goes with utmost discretion, often living in a tiny apartment he keeps in an adjacent town.

"Blow out the candles before you go to bed," I tell him sourly as I leave the room.

"Fine," he says. "And by the way, I didn't light them."

«« — »»

We sleep in separate rooms that night, or try to sleep at least. The fireworks explode till well past midnight, the teiko drums pound like punishing blows. I'm wet all over, furious at Katsuro-san yet, at the same time, longing to pull him against me, inside me.

He lied about the candles and the red bean soup—or did he? Was it intended as a joke? If so, it was a cruel one.

No, it wasn't red bean soup that killed Hiroshi-san, but the sticky rice cakes, called mocha, that were in the bean soup. It's a traditional New Year's dish, mochi and red bean soup, eaten for good luck. Ironically, it sometimes brings death rather than good fortune. When baked, the mochi becomes extremely sticky and almost impossible to chew. Every year, several elderly people suffocate when the mochi they are eating gets stuck in their windpipes, but every year those seeking good luck ignore the danger.

At two a.m., unable to sleep, I get up from the futon. My intention is to go to Katsuro-san's room, crawl into his futon, and make him forget the ancestors. Then I realize he must have had the same idea, because he's standing in the doorway, holding a candle, watching me.

Except it isn't Katsuro-san.

Hiroshi-san regards me with a stricken stare. The candle flame illuminates the shifting shadows from which his face emerges. His mouth gapes and he gasps for air. His voice is the painful sound of a dull knife scraping bone. "Hell," he rasps, "I am in hell."

Then he lifts the candle to his lips and drinks the flame. The fire blazes behind his eyes, giving his wizened face a fierce, demonic countenance. He reaches out for me. I scream, and he is gone.

«« —»»

The next day members of Hiroshi-san's extended family come to visit and pay their respects before the butsudan. I tend the candles and the incense, make sure the food is ample and the sake flows, as aunties and uncles and cousins make their obligatory appearance, bowing deeply before they begin their prayers, engaging Katsuro-san in endless conversation of which I am made no part. Hiroshi-san's family, especially Katsuro-san, resent the fact that in all these years, I've been unable to learn anything beyond the simplest Japanese. They do not appreciate how difficult their language is, how unnatural the construction of their sentences, as though they set out to build a house but did it upside down, the roof being laid down first, followed by the stories in reverse order, then the floor and finally, the basement. They don't understand that reading the characters, the katakana, hirogana, and kanji, is like trying to follow a backwards road map drawn by a blind man and held up to a mirror.

"What did you talk about?" I ask Katsuro-san when the last one finally slips on their shoes and takes their leave.

He gives me the small, sardonic grin of a man who takes for granted his own superiority in all matters. "If you'd only study your Japanese, you wouldn't have to ask."

Ignoring the barb, I press on. "Last night," I begin tentatively, "I dreamed I saw Hiroshi-san. He was eating fire. He said he was in hell."

"A dream, that's all," replies Katsuro-san. "Remember the tradition I told you about, of how Obon began? You were thinking of it, that's all."

The legend goes that one of Buddha's foremost disciples learned his mother had been reborn in hell and couldn't eat, because anything she brought to her mouth would turn to fire. To save her, he was advised to offer food to the monks following their mid-August retreat. The mother was saved, and thus Obon began.

I nod, but remain unconvinced. I may be just a gaijin, but I know what I saw. "We should have left here before Obon. This house is worth a little money, and you have some savings."

The muscles of Katsuro-san's jaw clench like a fist. "Not until I find where father put the money he always bragged about."

He makes a karate-chopping motion with his hand for emphasis. I know we'll talk no more about it.

While Katsuro-san goes to make the obligatory Obon visit to the cemetery, I put fresh flowers on the butsudan and light more incense and candles. The cup of sake on the top shelf looks appealing. To hell with thirsty ancestors—I gulp it down.

A quiver ascends my spine as the strong drink slides down my throat. I feel a wave of dizziness and reach a hand out for the cushion to steady myself. In this stifling room, where despite the breeze, the heat has gathered and intensified throughout the day, the pillow is as cold as if it had just come from a freezer.

I watch as the pale smoke from the incense and the candles trails upward and intertwines, grey yin and dark blue yang, a mating of disparate energies. Hiroshi-san's contorted face stares out from within the smoke like a face peering in through smudged glass. He's smoke himself at first and then he isn't, now shreds of flesh, now thread-thin curls of smoke. The candle flame licks through his phantom flesh like a second, searing tongue.

I blink and flinch away, convinced that I'm hallucinating, but when I dare to look again, the apparition is still there. He shudders, undulating like an image reflected in a pool of water where someone has tossed a stone.

"My wife...forever." I can feel that scraping-bone voice as it rattles its way up my spine. "Mine."

"What do you want, Hiroshi-san?"

"My wife...your duty to the dead."

Duty to the dead? What does that mean? Where I come from, in America, we do not venerate the ancestors. They are the foreshadowing of what we, too, shall be—we do not want to look. We bury them and then move on, to other cities, other states, sometimes to other countries. The past dies and it is gone. Erased from time. Forgotten.

Not here, though. Not in Japan and certainly not at Obon.

The living here are ever captive to the dead.

Hiroshi-san's grey, evanescent hands wave toward the butsudan.

"Clean it," he groans. "Honor the butsudan...you honor me. You free me from this hell."

"Hiroshi-san—"

He opens his gaping, flame-filled mouth: "Wife...do...what I say."

In the overheated room, a deep chill descends. Suddenly I am shivering violently, and the small meal I had for breakfast lurches toward my throat.

I fetch water, polish, and cleaning rags and set to work. The butsudan already gleams, but now I clean it more thoroughly, running the cleaning rag up into every nook and hidey-hole, exploring the junctures where the boards are fitted together, removing the tiniest speck of dust from the creases of the Buddha's robe.

The butsudan has a roof on top, in the manner of a Buddhist temple. Gold paint outlines the ornate filigrees and arabesques that, generations ago, some unknown craftsman carved into the handsome wood. I polish and dust the outer shelves, then reach inside to get at the very back.

I can't see the characters carved into the wooden panel on the inner seam of the butsudan's roof, but I feel them there and trace them with my fingers. At first I think it's just more decoration, but the location is in a place where no one would ever see it, unless, like me, they made a pretzel of their spine to get at it with a dust rag. There are two characters carved into the wood and, below that, a thin ridge where two boards meet unevenly. I fetch a mirror and hold a candle in an attempt to see the characters, but they are too far back, too tiny. I fetch a paper and a pencil with thick, soft lead and, leaning so far back I feel like a contortionist, I make a rubbing of the characters.

Katsuro-san is just returning from the cemetery. Although I want to run to him at once to ask the meaning of what I've found, I realize there is something else I must do first. Besides, I am afraid to know the truth, afraid of what I may learn.

Later that evening, when I hand him the rubbing, he frowns and studies it.

"What's this?"

"It was carved under the roof of the butsudan. What does it mean?"

He shakes his head as though profoundly saddened by my Western ignorance. "If you only would learn Japanese, you could read these yourself."

"Are you going to tell me what it means or not?"

"It's nothing," he says. "Just the signature of the artist who carved the butsudan, that's all."

"But in such an odd place?"

"That's all it is. Really, Carolyn-san, what did you expect?"

What did I expect indeed? The disappointment and hurt takes my breath away, as though I've been kicked in the chest. Despite his sarcasm and subtle disdain for me as his father's gaijin's wife, I wanted Katsuro-san since the first time I saw him, since the first time his hand accidentally brushed my hip as we passed in a hallway, the first time he held my gaze a moment longer than is proper. With Hiroshi-san dead, I've dreamed of leaving here with him and starting a new life far from Japan, far from a language I can't understand and the endless veneration of centuries' worth of ancestors.

For a moment I am silent, absorbing what Katsuro-san has said, listening to the distant throbbing of the drums. I smile as warmly as I can and take his hand. "The Bon Odori is starting. We should take part."

He looks bemused. "I thought you didn't like these foreign dances."

"At least we'll be outside in the fresh air. Change into your yukata. Come on."

While Katsuro-san is changing, I put more food upon the altar, remove the wilted flowers, and light fresh candles and incense, as Hiroshi-san has told me to do. I feel certain that his ghost observes me and is pleased, that in some way I cannot understand, it is my destiny to honor his spirit in this fashion.

On any other night, the sight of Hiroshi-san's son and myself walking together might raise eyebrows, but at Obon it is only fitting that families reunite, both the living and the dead. At any rate, we are soon lost in the streams of people heading toward the Buddhist temple beside the river. The priest has climbed up into the bell tower and begun to strike the bell, the oldest in the Prefecture of Fukuoka. We walk past bonfires ablaze and children holding folded pieces of colored paper, playing a game that involves using paper spoons to try to scoop goldfish from a tub before the paper gets wet and rips. In the sticky heat of evening, almost everyone has changed into brightly colored yukatas with bold geometric designs.

Fireworks explode. Dogs howl and yap. The beating of the taiko drums is frantic, pounding.

Katsuro-san and I push our way into the dance, where dozens of people are already whirling madly, four concentric circles revolving one around the other, the brilliantly colored yukatas blowing and billowing like a giant kaleidoscope being twirled.

The Bon Odori dances vary from town to town, but all depict some local theme or story. Hand gestures mime activities like digging or cutting rice, or the gentle flowing of rivers. As more people join in, the circle expands, then doubles back on itself like a snake eating its own tail, the dancers moving around a central platform festooned with crepe paper. The air is dense and musky with sweat and incense and the smoke from the bonfires. Long past the point of exhaustion, we still keep up the hypnotic, trance-inducing pace. The ghosts returned for Obon celebrate among us—their spectral bodies pulse in rhythm with the drumming. They are with us, the land of the dead superimposed over the land of the living, caught up in an endless unseen mating dance of sweaty mortal flesh and the wraith vestiges of the departed.

The faster and harder we dance, the more clearly I can see them. Like a shimmering mist, they mass along the road between the bonfires, avid for the memory of a time when they were as we are now, possessed of mortal flesh and human lust and joy and greed.

Their hunger, like our own, is vast and insatiable.

It is the hunger of the dead for what they have lost, the hunger of the living for one more taste of what they will inevitably lose. I can feel my own death—whether it comes tonight or thirty years from now—like teeth upon my throat.

"Come with me," I call to Katsuro-san, and when he turns to me, I see the same wild hunger in his face, the greed for life and more life. It is the first time in so long that we have looked into each other's eyes and really seen each other.

We pull free of the whirling mob, fight our way through the outer circles of the dancers. A stone bridge leads across a deep pond filled with koi to a temple dedicated to the scholar and calligrapher, Tenjin. We cross the bridge and duck underneath where the shadows are deep and no light penetrates. Katsuro-san sits with his back against the stone arch, opens his yukata and guides me down on top of him. Above us, the drums are pounding, the dancer's feet stomping out the beat, voices raised in song. The urgent sounds Katsuro-san and I are making go unheard.

It's after midnight as we walk back through the temple complex to the house, our sweat- soaked yukatas clinging to our bodies. My hair is plastered to my faces in a damp cap. Fireworks still explode intermittently and ashes drift in the air from the fires. In the deep darkness, where no one can see us, Katsuro-san slides his arm around my waist and kisses me as silent tears stream down my face.

In his embrace, I start to have a change of heart. I decide to tell him that I know the truth about the writing inside the butsudan. In the heat and passion of our coupling, I have—for a moment—the wild hope that there still might be a future for us, that underneath our lies and pretenses, we could still make a life together. I think of the riches Hiroshi-san claimed to have stashed away and the life of ease and prosperity Katsuro-san and I could enjoy if we could find them.

"Katsuro-san, I have to tell you something," I begin.

But as we round the corner and head back to the house, there is a terrible and ungodly sight. For a moment, I imagine that the Meiji brothers across the street have lit a bonfire, although their yard is even tinier than ours and to do so would put the entire block in danger. Katsuro-san cries out in anguish and breaks into a run.

I wail like a madwoman, "Wait, don't go inside! There's nothing there!"

He doesn't hear or, if he does, my words mean nothing to him.

Still pleading with him to stop, I run behind him, but Katsuro-san is already at the door. He heaves it open and plunges inside. Through the thick smoke, I get a glimpse of flaming shoji screens. It occurs to me if any ghosts are still adrift this Oban, they will be lost no longer. Our blazing minka is a gigantic milestone of flame and fury.

Two firemen hauling a hose yell at me in Japanese and shoulder me aside. I glimpse Katsuro-san's writhing silhouette for just an instant before a burning beam cuts short his screams. I don't see Katsuro-san again, but I see his father. Hiroshi-san's phantom form takes shape amid the smoke and cinders. Soot frames his smile and ashes cling to him like scales. A look of vengeful satisfaction contorts his face. In a grim and terrifying way, he looks well pleased.

Unlike Katsuro-san, the butsudan, along with most of the house, survived the blaze. Our ever vigilant neighbors, the Meiji brothers, had seen the flames and called for help. Then they rushed into the house to save the one thing that any Japanese would know is valued above all else. The butsudan sat safely on the lawn where the Meiji men had carried it while Katsuro-san was searching for it in vain amid the smoke and flames.

For nothing.

Like his father, Katsuro-san underestimated me. It's true I failed to learn much Japanese and my attempts to speak are still pitifully inept. But I can use a kanji dictionary well enough to know that he was lying when he told me the words carved into the butsudan were the craftsman's signature. What I found were the characters for 'discovery' and 'prosperity' and in the hidden compartment behind them was a key that I removed before I ever tested Katsuro-san's loyalty by asking him their meaning. The key was inside an envelope and, on it, in both Japanese and English, were instructions.

«« — »»

On the last day of Obon, while Katsuro-san's body is being held waiting a final burning in the crematorium, I take the key to the Buddhist temple and wait while an officious young monk scurries to find the priest.

The priest is a portly, broad-faced man with a bald dome and a belly that would do credit to Gautama himself. When he learns that I am Hiroshi-san's widow, his smile expands like the wings of a pink bird unfolding and he bows ever more deeply.

"Yes, yes," he says, beckoning me.

He leads me to his office at the back of the temple and presents me with a carved, lacquered box. "Hiroshi-san was a generous and pious man," he says. "Over the years, he gave a fortune to the temple, but he never wanted anyone to know. Merit comes from anonymous giving, he used to say. Hiroshi-san entrusted this to me. He told me you would come for it one day. He said he would make sure you learned of it."

At last, I think, this is what it all was for.

But when I open up the box, there is only this: a small porcelain bowl. In it, a tiny ball of mochi.

And I remember New Year's Day, when I prepared the mochi in the sweet bean soup, cooking it 'til it was soft and rubbery. Katsuro-san had left the house. I came to Hiroshi-san while he was napping, his mouth open, snoring. Almost lovingly, like a mother bird feeding its young, I popped a thick piece of mochi into his mouth. His next snore sucked it down. When his eyes opened in surprise and fear, I clamped my hands across his mouth. The mochi plugged his windpipe. That New Year's Day, he was among four other elderly Japanese men who died eating mochi for good luck.

A tragedy, all too preventable, the newspapers predictably pointed out.

It is the last night of Obon when I walk down to the river to watch the final ceremony. Candles are being lit and set in little paper boats to float downstream from the river to the sea, guiding the departing spirits back to the land of the dead.

As I watch the parade of lights stretching out to the horizon, I know that I will remain here in Japan, that I will tend the butsudan, put out the offerings of rice and pour the sake and plum wine, that I am the keeper of the ancestors, guardian of the ghosts of my dead husband and dead lover.

You are still my wife, Hiroshi-san said.

I know that he is right. One day the candles in their little boats will mark the way for me. One day my spirit will follow them, traveling to my own destiny in the land of the dead.

And when Obon comes around, I will return with all the other ghosts, to remember what I've lost.

how real men die

Eddie Pitrowski hitched up his jeans in a dingy Patpong hotel room and wondered how he could still enjoy sex so much, knowing that in just a few days, he was going to watch his best friend die.

Worse, that he was going to be the one to kill him.

What kind of cold-hearted bastard could compartmentalize such a thing, he asked himself. A sociopath? A sex addict? A nutcase?

All of the above, his ex-wife Annie would have probably said. Their daughter Margaret, too, who according to her mother had become a lesbian purely to spite Daddy and now piloted a Yellow Cab through sections of Detroit that even the cops avoided. The kind of neighborhoods that Eddie had grown up in.

The plump, poppy-lipped girl he'd spent the last twenty minutes bending over the bed collected her clothes, twirled a sequined thong around her finger, and purred, "For a farang, you good fook, Eddie. You ready more boom-boom?"

Eddie thought if had any more boom boom right now his heart might torpedo right out of his chest, but he grinned at the complement, happy to hear he was a *farang who could fook*.

He'd had his fun. Now it was time to get down to business. "Your boyfriend back in Soi Cowboy said you'd bring me something extra. You got it with you?"

The girl wiggled the thong up over her hips and reached for her tote bag which was festooned with sequins and looked larger than the suitcase Eddie'd brought with him for ten days in Thailand. Carefully, she extracted a baggy, which she passed to him using the tips of her nails, as though whatever was inside might try to bite her. Inside was a smaller bag. Eddie unzipped it and shook a minuscule speck of powder onto his finger. Put it to his mouth and got a humdinger of a jolt.

The girl came around behind him, curled her arms around his waist and slithered against his spine like a cobra. "Farang love Thailand," she cooed. "Best sex in world."

"Not to mention the best China White," Eddie said. He resealed the baggy and counted out the girl's money along with what he owed for the heroin. The girl had worked pretty hard, so he added a few hundred baht as a tip, then ushered her out into the steaming, sexed-up, neon-blinding chaos of the Patpong night. He hailed a tuk-tuk, gave the driver some bills, and sent her on her way.

No sooner was she gone than another girl approached, this one a mini-skirted bottle blonde who whispered a menu of obscene suggestions like a hostess proffering a tray of hors d'oeuvres.

Though sorely tempted, Eddie declined.

Ah, true paradise, he thought. Then he did a nimble hop-skip to avoid plunking his foot in a pile of dog shit and almost got nailed by a recklessly swerving songthaew, a green pick-up truck with two benches in the back that served as a popular form of public transportation. The driver screamed something as he careened past, the passengers in back packed in like toothpicks and holding on for dear life.

Okay, so not a perfect paradise. But still... every five feet another beautiful, buyable, fuckable woman.

What the hell could be better than that?

Then he thought about the baggy in his pocket and, even in the sticky swelter of the neon-and-exhaust-fumes-saturated night, a mean chill banged through his ribs like he'd been tongue-kissed by the devil himself. His mouth filled with ashes and his stomach twisted like a wounded snake.

I need a goddamn drink. Now.

He dodged his way across the chaotic traffic clogging Surawong Road and ducked into the tingling cool of the Nang-Klao Club. His buddies Danny and Kurt sat at the end of the horseshoe-shaped bar, quaffing Singha beers, while a pair of diminutive, bikini-clad bar girls fluttered around them like brilliantly plumaged parakeets. Kurt Anderson was a beefy, fireplug of a man with a barrel chest, curly grey hair receding off a broad forehead, and a goofy, lopsided grin that women found irresistible. He was an ardent photographer and clung to his Sony HD video camera with the kind of protective reverence some men reserve for the family jewels. Beside him slumped Danny Pinchero, fifty-eight years old, a couple years short of retiring from the Ford plant where he'd put in three decades. He was pole-thin and sinewy, with bloodshot black eyes that flashed like exposed synapses and seemed to recede deeper into his skull every day.

All three of them had grown up on Detroit's tough east side, surviving on guile, guts, and sometimes, sheer meanness. They'd each seen the inside of a cell more than once, although only Eddie had done serious time—two years for possession and assault in '83 and a nickel in the early nineties for impulsively holding up a Party Store while under the influence of Wild Turkey and a grab bag of pharmaceuticals. He'd been more or less clean since then, working off and on in construction, but his temper still got him in trouble—he'd been 86'd from so many bars that Kurt joked the only gathering of drunks where he was still welcome was the AA group that met in the First Baptist Church across the street from the neighborhood tavern.

"Got what you went for?" said Danny, his eyes glued to a spotlighted stage in the center of the room.

"Yep."

"So it's under control?"

"As planned."

He took the stool next to Kurt and ordered a Mekong whiskey, then turned his attention to the stage, where a splay-legged young woman was popping ping-pong balls from between her thighs like a hen laying eggs. The crowd applauded uproariously. The woman looked like she was mentally filling out tax forms.

The Mekong came and he chugged it, floating away on the sweet burn for a moment before he signaled the bartender for another. That one went down smoother than the first, and he called for a third.

Kurt leaned over and whispered, "You're hittin' it pretty hard, don't ya think? When the time comes, you don't wanna be too effed up to...you know... take care of business."

Eddie was always amused by Kurt's persnickitiness when it came to good honest cursing, but he didn't care for the lack of trust the comment implied. He grunted and hoisted the fresh drink the bar girl put in his hand.

Kurt sighed audibly. "Just saying, man."

A ping-pong ball suddenly beelined in Eddie's direction. He plucked it out of the air, stuck out his tongue and slurped it long and obscenely before tossing it back to the girl.

He turned to Kurt. "Who the fuck you think you're talking to? This is me, Eddie! I'll be fine."

《《—》》

The phone call had jolted Eddie awake two weeks earlier, on a teeth-clackingly cold night in the middle of a bitter winter, snow pelting down on the icy slick streets of Detroit, wind keening across frozen Lake St. Clair like a blade scraping steel.

Roused from an inebriated slumber, he fumbled in the recliner cushions for the cell and got it to his ear in time to hear Danny say, "Eddie, you there?"

"Danny? What the hell! You know what time it is!"

"Time to head for Bangkok, that's what time!"

Having consumed most of a fifth of Jack before dozing off, the laugh track from an 80's sitcom clawing for whatever consciousness remained in his benumbed brain, Eddie was in no mood for a rude awakening. His buddy's declaration, uttered without preamble and made more menacing by the fact that the speaker sounded stone cold sober, knocked him sideways and pissed him off, as if a not at all funny Zen monk had just blindsided him with a koan and then kicked him in the shins for good measure.

He lurched awake, spilling the dregs of his drink onto the soiled, crumb-flecked carpet. "Bangkok? What the fuck you talking about?"

"Bangkok," Danny pronounced the word with hearty, desperate zeal. "Hot girls, cheap booze, sex capitol of Asia—the place you said every real man ought'a party hard before he kicks the bucket."

"I said that?"

"Hell, yeah, you did! Up at Houghton Lake four summers ago. When we signed the pact? Remember?"

Eddie grabbed the bottle of Jack and glugged back a throat full. "Pact? Can't say I recall any pact."

72

"Bullshit you don't."

He remembered, all right. Like yesterday. A scorcher of a night, sitting around in folding chairs outside Kurt's RV, three boozed-up, reefer-toking, middle-aged fools philosophizing about good deaths and bad deaths and in what manner they wanted to exit this world. They'd reminisced about guys they knew who'd gone out in a blaze of glory in motorcycle crashes, bar brawls, and drug deals gone haywire—these were the good deaths, the macho ones—and then the other kind, like that poor son of a bitch Big Jim Earl from Gratiot Street, whose very name used to evoke awe, but who ended up at the VA, frail and ridden with tumors, wearing a diaper and hooked up to a feeding tube, and how the fear of being weak and helpless, unmanned, the fear that had probably dogged each of them since the moment the doctor pronounced them male, had struck them all silent, like Death had snuck up and grabbed each one of them by the balls.

That was when they'd cooked up a plan to cheat the cancer ward and the Alzheimer's wing and go out like the two-fisted s.o.b.'s they knew themselves to be.

Real men to the end! they'd shouted, high-fiving and slamming shots like the Red Wings had just aced the Stanley Cup.

"I dunno, there might'a been some damn fool thing we signed," Eddie said finally. "But next day, after we sobered up, we burned it."

"Don't matter. A deal's a deal."

Eddie hoisted the bottle, but thumped it down again without swigging. A question commandeered the silence, but he was afraid to voice it.

"If you're saying what I think you are, then—who's getting the one-way ticket? It ain't me. So who drew the short straw, you or Kurt?"

He shut his eyes. The television blatted mindlessly. In the distance, a dog howled.

"I got throat cancer that's spreading like crabs in a whorehouse," Danny said and Eddie could hear the click of fear in his voice. "Doc says without treatment I got maybe another good month or two before it crawls up my neck and takes a shit in my brain."

"Aw, fuck, Danny. Jesus Christ. I can't believe it."

For some reason, he'd always had this premonition that of the three of them, it would be Kurt who got done in prematurely by some terrible affliction.

"How long you known?"

"Coupla weeks. I could do chemo and radiation, slow it down for a while, but what the fuck for? I'd rather go wild in Thailand and die with a grin on my face and you and Kurt by my side than hooked up to some fuckin' torture device."

"You told Kurt?"

"He's on the phone with Thai Air even as we speak. Ten days from now, I told him. That give you time to clear your calendar?"

"Danny, look, I'm not sure I can do this."

"Don't worry about the money, this junket's on me."

"It ain't the money."

"What then? The pact was your idea, man! The world's a cold fucking place, you said and we three gotta watch each other's backs! Right up to death's fucking door!"

On the TV Eddie saw a racing hotrod roar off one end of an opening drawbridge, slam onto the other side and keep going as it outpaced a frantic soundtrack.

Danny coughed, cleared his throat. When he spoke again all the bravado was stripped away. His voice sounded small, constricted.

"Eddie? You're with me on this, right? I'm scared, man. I don't know how to die. I'm counting on you."

In the silence that followed, he could hear the wild wind keening like a madwoman across Lake St. Clair, and he wished he were out there, plowing along in the dark and the cold the way he did when life got to be too much, not really caring if the ice held him or not, yelling out drunkenly as the snow pelted his face, just him, Eddie Pitrowski, alone in a black and white universe with a bottle of Jack in his hand.

No, I can't do this. I won't do this. No fucking way.

He took a deep breath. "Fuck yeah, Danny, I'll help you. Hell, what are friends for?"

《《—》》

"Holy shit, how did she do that?" Danny said as Ping-pong Girl winked and undulated offstage.

"A ping-pong show ain't nothing," said Kurt. "Wait 'til we get to Chiang Mai. Then you'll see some effing sights!"

Kurt was always raving about Chiang Mai, a city on the Ping River in the northern part of the country that he'd first visited during his tour in Vietnam. Liked it so much he'd been back a couple of times since. Said Chiang Mai was where the really hot girls were, the hardcore stuff, down n' dirty.

"I see a sight I like right now," declared Danny, sliding off his stool and putting his arm around the curvy, foxy-eyed bar girl who'd been caging over-priced drinks from him all evening. "How about it, honey? Ready to show an old man a good time?"

The girl giggled and made the wai gesture that was familiar by now, palms pressed together, head tilted. She took Danny's hand and they adjourned upstairs, where rooms could be reserved by the hour.

After Danny left, Eddie and Kurt drank their way through the lesbian show and the dominatrix skit and laughed when a ruckus broke out between a blond, Nordic-looking dude who was loudly contesting his bar bill to a couple of hot little numbers in slinky, Day-Glo dresses and matching, drop-dead red lipstick, who'd been glued to him like he was the last lifeboat leaving the Titanic. The guy threw down some baht, which evidently wasn't enough, because the girls pursued him out of the bar, hurling words at his retreating back like poisoned darts.

About that time Danny came back with his girl, who he introduced as Lek. He was grinning as he explained he'd just paid the mama-san for a 'long time' meaning he'd bought Lek's time for the rest of the night and could now take her back to the hotel.

"Isn't she the prettiest little thing you ever seen?" Danny beamed as Lek tee-hee'd and covered her mouth, batting lashes black as squid ink.

When they came out of the club, looking to hail a tuk-tuk, Eddie saw the Nordic guy rolling around on the ground with the two hot little numbers kicking the shit out of him.

"What the hell?" His instinct was to help the poor guy and he started toward them.

Kurt grabbed him. "Leave it alone, man."

"But those bitches are kicking that dude in the nuts!"

"Look at the Adam's apples and the biceps," said Kurt. "Those are katoeys—female impersonators—and they're tough sons of bitches. You do *not* want to eff with 'em."

A couple of foot patrol cops pushed through the crowd then, stocky, grim-faced men whose brown uniforms fit their muscular bodies like sausage skins. They wore badges identifying them as "Tourist Police." When the ladyboys saw them, they took off, sprinting into the alleyway behind the bar.

"Goddamn, that's the best show I've seen tonight," said Eddie, watching them race off in their towering high heels.

«««—»»»

The following day, rain was pouring so hard it felt like the entire city of Bangkok lay at the foot of a waterfall. The four of them cabbed over to the Grand Hyatt on Rajdamri Road where, during a liquid brunch of Mimosas and Bloody Mary's, it was unanimously decided to follow Kurt's suggestion and travel to Chiang Mai.

Lek didn't want to be left behind, so Danny, against all advice from Eddie and Kurt, opted to bring her along. At the bar where they'd stopped for cocktails on the way to the bus station, Eddie tried to ask her if she'd be able to get her job back at the club in Bangkok, but she just smiled like a southeast Asian Mona Lisa and snuggled up to Danny.

"You gotta get rid of her," Eddie said, "She thinks she's your girlfriend," but Danny said, "She relaxes me. I like having her around," and Lek, getting up to visit the lady's, lost her balance and dumped her drink into Eddie's lap, which caused Kurt to laugh so uproariously he blew beer out his nose.

The rain and the drinking slowed down the pace of their departure, forcing them to catch the last northbound bus of the day, a local that lurched to a stop at every village and rice paddy and didn't arrive in Chiang Mai until the following day. Lek had been to Chiang Mai and recommended the Lucky Star Hotel, a neon-drenched silver tower across from the Ping River, but Kurt said the place was a firetrap and looked like it had been constructed out of tinfoil. He checked into a seedy-looking low-rise hotel a few blocks away called the Mandarin Orchid.

After the endless bus ride, Eddie wanted to stretch his legs, so he agreed to meet Danny and Lek later at the hotel bar and moseyed up Lai Kroh Road by himself. He stopped in a club for an eye opener and, several drinks later, found himself in a rent-by-the-hour room with an albino hooker who moved with such lethargy and languor he figured whatever drugs she was on were even better than the shit he'd scored back in Bangkok. Her skin was talcum white, her nipples almost invisible. She ghosted on top of him, weightless as fog, and just as he was going to town, really into it, something shifted and the creamy pallor of her skin, so sensuous at first, began to appear corpse-like and horrifying. His erection flagged and he found himself thinking of the China White and how it would liquefy when heated, the cloudy whiteness of it filling the syringe, the prick of the hypo into Danny's vein, liquid death leaking in, his best friend dying in his arms.

He rolled away from the woman and crawled onto the floor, dizzy and hyperventilating. The air conditioner was blasting away, but he felt feverish, delirious, like he might puke. His girl sat back on her haunches, looking peeved at being so unceremoniously unseated. If he was having a heart attack, he got the feeling she might not be in any hurry to call the Thai version of the EMT's.

After a few minutes, he revived enough to get dressed and splash some water on his face, pay the woman, and head out to meet Danny and Lek, but he'd forgotten the name of the hotel. The streets all looked identical, as similar as the computer generated byways of some generic Asian city in a video game. He meandered past rows of open air stalls selling charcoal grilled chicken, fresh flowers and diamond-shaped dumplings sizzling in grease, and noticed a number of people crunching some insectoid delectable that looked like fried grasshoppers. He passed a bustling arcade full of restaurants and stores and paused to stare in the window of The Numbah One Noodle Shop, where customers hunched before fly-speckled windows, slurping from bowls heaped with tangles of silvery, shoelace-thin noodles.

Unsure which direction to go in, he turned in a circle, feeling like a fool for being so utterly lost.

A stiff drink, he decided, would help clear his head and reorient him.

His hotel might be impossible to locate, but he had no trouble spotting a bar. The nearest one was The Joy Palace, across from the noodle shop. He hurried toward it like a desperado fleeing a posse.

As he ducked inside, a tall, overweight American in his late thirties, wearing baggy shorts and a flamboyantly patterned shirt was barging out. His red-brown hair was shaved down into flat bristles, and his small, furtive eyes darted back and forth under doughy lids. He stared at Eddie openly and rudely, then leaned toward him and stage-whispered, "I wouldn't bother coming in here, I was you. No action."

Eddie took in the array of skimpily attired young women lounging around the back wall and said,—"Well, you ain't me, mister. I think those girls look damn fine."

The guy crowded closer, forcing Eddie to inhale the reek of his garlic lunch. He spoke in a gruff, yet circumspect voice, like he and Eddie were part of the same unsavory conspiracy. "They're not bad—if that's what you're into."

Well, what the hell else would I be into, Eddie thought. Then he remembered the brutal katoeys beating up the guy in Patpong and concluded that this dude must have a predilection for ladyboys. He actually grinned, because the mental image of the pudgy flat top getting it on with some skanky, stiletto-wearing chick impersonator was so hilarious.

"Yeah, well, I'd be careful about that kind of action. Could be dangerous." He started to move on, but the big-bellied dude was now staring at him as though transfixed by some magic words Eddie had unwittingly uttered.

"Yeah, you understand, all right. I can tell. Careful—that's the ticket." He tried to take Eddie's arm. "Let me buy you a drink, and I'll give you the names of some people around here you can trust."

Huh?

Eddie wasn't in the mood for creepy cloak and dagger. He shoved the guy aside—it was like elbowing a Humvee—and rather than proceed into the bar, made a beeline out of it. In his agitation, he glanced upward and suddenly recognized his hotel, the 'Tinfoil Tower', jutting up out of the swarm of low rise establishments surrounding it.

A few minutes later, he found Danny and Lek at a table in the lobby bar, sipping frou-frou strawberry concoctions that looked like something you'd serve to kids after an Easter egg hunt.

"About time you showed up!" Danny said when Eddie lurched in. "I was afraid you got lost!"

"Me? Never! This is me, Eddie Pitrowski you're talking to! I got a G.P.S. hard-wired into my brain." He pulled up a chair. "Where's Kurt?"

Danny pantomimed aiming a camera. "Out trolling for local color. Thinks he's gonna be an I-Reporter for Fox News, go viral on You-Tube or some such."

"You-Tube!" exclaimed Lek.

Danny said, "I been trying to tell Lek about the good old days in Detroit, like when you and me and Kurt stole that crate of .38 specials from the crew of Angels at the Rocking Horse Inn and that time we almost got shot-gunned cartin' off TV sets during the riots in '67."

"Good times, all right," Eddie said, while Lek smiled and nodded. Eddie had the feeling Danny could've said, "Lek, this is the guy who came all this way so he could hotshot my ass to kingdom come," and gotten the same enthusiastic response.

Danny had just launched into a story about the time he and Eddie and Kurt were out ice-fishing and Eddie fell through and almost drowned, when he suddenly stopped talking. His face took on an ashen sheen. He began to cough so violently that his head whiplashed back and forth and he gripped his throat like a man trying to strangle himself.

A couple nearby stared at him, then got up and moved away.

Eddie glared at them. "That's right, don't get too close! Swine flu! Highly fucking contagious!"

"You crazy?" Danny gasped.

Eddie felt like an asshole. He offered Danny a glass of water while Lek tried massaging his back, but he shrugged her away. "Quit pawin' me! Go find somebody who ain't dying."

Lek shrank back, looking like she'd been slapped. "Want help you, Danny," she said, the kindness and sadness in her voice making Eddie feel bad for the way he'd urged Danny to ditch her.

Sallow-faced, eyes streaming, Danny rasped, "There's nothing anybody can do for me." He looked at Eddie. "Shit, I thought this last hurrah in Thailand was a great idea, but I'm sick and tired of feeling like a fucking piano's about to drop on my head. How much more time I got, man? When we gonna fuckin' do this thing?"

Eddie gulped, his mouth so dry he felt like he was swallowing nails. "Tomorrow. But hell, nobody's sayin' we can't postpone it."

"Fuck postponing. Let's just get it over with. *Right now.*"

Eddie felt a stab of panic. He lowered his voice. "We can't, Danny. It's too late for me and Kurt to change our tickets. We gotta be in the air before anybody—"

"Yeah, yeah, I know. Before the maid comes to clean the room and finds a stiff with a needle in his arm."

"You gotta hang in there, man. You got enough pain meds, right?"

"Yeah, but they make me feel dopey. That nurse I used to date, LuAnn, scored me some liquid Valium, but the one time I shot some, I slept for a day. Don't have time now for any twenty-four hour siestas."

"Better be careful with that shit," Eddie said.

"Yeah, don't wanna cut short my promising future."

Eddie gestured to the Pepto Bismol pink cocktails. "There's the trouble right here, this sissy shit she's got you drinking. You need a man's drink." He stuck his hand in the air and waved it at the bar-girl like he was hailing a cab. "Three whiskeys down here!"

"I've had enough," Danny said, with such finality that Eddie wondered if he was talking about more than the drinks.

He took Lek by the hand. "C'mon, honey, let's go back to the room. See can we have some—what's that word you use?—sanuk?"

Her face brightened. "Sanuk!"

"What's sanuk?" Eddie said.

"Means having fun," Danny said. "Least I think it does."

As she passed Eddie, Lek pressed her palms together in the wai gesture and bowed, as though she were expressing gratitude. "Jai dii," she said and touched Eddie's chest.

"Jai dii?" Bewildered, he looked at Danny.

Danny shrugged. "No idea. But she said it to me, too. Probably means dumb white dude."

《《—》》

After Danny and Lek left, Eddie slammed another whiskey, which tamped down the restlessness and quelled some of the anxiety that clawed inside his chest like a caged rat. He thought about visiting a massage parlor—maybe even getting a massage— but didn't think he was good for another go-round this soon, so he ambled out of the bar and swayed up the street, assaulted by the color and chaos. A half-naked man in a blue and green sarong squatted at a table, gutting fish. A flock of dusty children galloped after a soccer ball. An old woman slouched in the shade of the awning next to the Numbah One Noodle Shop, drumming her fingers to the beat of some pop-Thai song while a gaggle of winter pale tourists looked over her stock of knock-off Prada handbags and Armani sunglasses.

The heat plus the alcohol he'd consumed left him feeling transparent and floaty, like everything was underwater and he was drifting along on a warm, pungent current of seawater. He thought about finding a songthaew to take him up into the mountains that rose cool-looking and green outside the city, but the need to distract himself with women and booze was too urgent to compete with such a placid indulgence.

Drawn by a cool gust of air-conditioning, he wandered into a narrow, bamboo-paneled bar with a dancer gyrating on a small stage and a row of girls slouching against the wall. The place looked oddly familiar. When he realized he was back in The Joy Palace, he started to do an about-face, but then a girl at the bar caught his eye. She wore khaki slacks and a blue cotton shirt, and her curves were pleasingly generous. After so many variations on the theme of straight jet hair and boyish hips, she struck Eddie as uncommonly alluring. He claimed the barstool next to her, proclaiming grandly, "Sanuk, sweetheart, when's your turn to shake that sexy tush?"

The woman turned to him. She was a westerner in her early forties, with piercing blue-grey eyes that appraised him scathingly. "Did you just use the word 'tush'?"

"Hey, I was just funnin' with you," he said, embarrassed by the gaffe. "I knew you weren't a dancer. You're too—uh—too—"

"Old and overweight?"

"—nicely dressed, I was gonna say."

"Right." She sighed in that long-suffering way women often adopted around Eddie and began scribbling in a spiral notebook that lay open on the bar in front of her.

He ordered a beer and made small talk. The woman ignored him and continued to write, which puzzled Eddie, since he thought he was being the epitome of charming. He decided a proper introduction was in order and stuck out his hand. "Name's Eddie Pitrowski. Born and raised in Detroit."

She gave his fingers a gingerly squeeze. "Ilsa Jacobi."

"American?"

"From L.A. I live in Bangkok now."

"I just came from Bangkok—helluva place!" The bartender set a Singha in front of him and he took a thirsty pull. "What're you doing in Chiang Mai?"

"Working."

She turned back to the notebook. Eddie leaned closer. "You writing about Thailand? 'Cause if y'are, maybe I could help you with that. Give you an American guy's perspective."

"I'll bet that would be riveting."

He tried to see the page, but it was at an angle and partially covered by her hand. "So what *are* you writing? A journal? My ex-wife used to journal. Women like that kind'a thing."

She put down the pen. When she shifted on the stool to face him, her blouse parted slightly and he could see the swell of a breast, the lacy trim of a black bra strap.

"Not that you'd be interested, but I'm doing an expose on child trafficking for *The Bangkok Times*."

"A reporter, eh?" said Eddie, barely listening. Had she said her name was Ilsa or Elsa? He was trying to guess her bra size. A hefty chest, probably a 36 or a 38C. Bodacious and blonde. His type of gal.

"So what're you up to later, Elsa? I'm staying over yonder at the Lucky Star Hotel. Maybe we could meet for a nightcap, do some clubbing, take in some sights."

She slammed the notebook shut and faced Eddie—who was wondering what the hell he'd said wrong—with tigerish green eyes.

"You may have somehow overlooked this, but along that wall are fifteen or twenty young women who, for a pittance, will accommodate your every stupid, selfish, egocentric whim. So why the hell are you hitting on me?"

He tried his most ingratiating smile. "I'm not hitting on you, honey. I like talking to you is all. Now this thing you're writing, what's it about?"

"I just told you."

"Don't think you did."

She rolled her eyes. "You don't remember because you're drunk on your ass."

He spread his arms. "It's Chiang Mai. Everybody's drunk on their ass."

"I'm not."

He laughed. "Well, there you go. That's the problem. Let's see if we can fix that." He beckoned the bartender. "Another drink for the lady."

Ilsa rattled off some words in Thai. The bartender glanced at Eddie, sniggered, and strolled away flicking her long hair.

"Hey, what'd you say to her? I was just trying to buy you a drink? Pass the time of day with some conversation? Why do you have to be a bitch?"

She gave him an icy once-over that reminded him of a fifth grade teacher he used to be scared to death of. "Oh, it's *talking* you want? Okay, let's start with this: what're you *really* doing in Thailand, Eddie Pitrowski?"

The questioned flummoxed him, seeming to hint at knowledge of something she couldn't possibly possess. What did she mean, *really* doing? Did she suspect something? Was she psychic?

After fumbling for words, he finally blurted, "I'm traveling with a couple of buddies. Here to see the sights."

A smirk jerked her pretty mouth askew. "The sights? You mean like the National Museum and the Wat Chiang Man? Maybe the

Elephant Nature Park or the Baan Haw Mosque? All are famous attractions here."

Museums, mosques, nature parks—this was all news to Eddie, who gestured at the crowded room and said, "I'm here for the same reason as the rest of these guys."

"So for you then, taking in the sights, that means the bars and the massage parlors and the brothels?"

He felt trapped. Why was she pestering him? "I like to raise a little hell, sure. That bothers you, lady, go hang out in a tea house, not a bar."

"You're the one who wanted to talk."

"Didn't expect a lecture. All I did was ask what you're writing about."

He felt his shoulders tense, waiting for her anger to descend on him like a blade, but instead her expression slackened with a melancholy so profound and unadorned that he turned away, her sadness too painful to confront because it mirrored back his own.

"I'm telling the story of a little girl named Tran," she said finally.

"What?"

"You asked what I'm writing, and I'm telling you. Again. A story about everything people like you avoid looking at. The places where children are bought and sold and raped."

Eddie could feel the fury radiating off her like a heat lamp. "Well, that's terrible, that's awful," he managed. "That go on much?"

"Thailand's a hub for child traffickers. Especially in the north."

"Jesus," said Eddie, and he thought about Margaret. Not Margaret as she was now with the shitkicker boots and *Dykes Rule* tattoo on her biceps, but Margaret as he actually remembered her, as a smiling toddler and a mischievous ten-year-old. Before his drinking got out of hand. When she still called him Daddy and hugged him around the waist.

He realized Ilsa was still talking. "My brother and his wife adopted a little Thai girl a couple of years ago. Six months ago, she died of AIDS that she'd contracted while being forced to work in a brothel in Chiang Mai. Her name was Tran. She was thirteen years old."

"That kind of thing, it can't be going on right out in the open?" Eddie was wishing he'd never started this conversation. All he'd wanted was to buy the woman a few drinks, get his mind off Danny. Now she'd gotten his mind on something worse.

"Did you notice the noodle shop across from the arcade?"

"Yeah, Numbah One Noodle Shop." He pronounced the word as it appeared on the sign, so that it rhymed with rumba. "These people can't spell worth a damn."

"Have you been inside?"

"No, don't really care for that khao soi shit." He couldn't believe he was still trying to impress this woman, showing off the name of a regional dish he'd heard Kurt order a few days earlier. "I'm more of a steak and eggs man myself."

She laughed harshly, looking at him like the word moron was tattooed between his eyebrows. He hated women like her, women who just by existing made him feel like a loser. He wanted to get up and leave, but didn't want her to think she'd run him off.

"The noodle shop? You're not telling me it's some kind'a kiddy brothel?" When she didn't answer, he blustered, "That's impossible! It's just a bunch of people sucking down soup."

"Not if you know a guy named Toy, and not if you get upstairs."

"Toy? Guy's name is *Toy*? You're kidding me, right?" He saw she was serious and went on, "Well, what about the parents of these kids? Don't they look for them?"

"Sometimes they're the ones who sold their children in the first place."

"They do that?"

"If the family is poor enough or greedy enough, yeah, they do."

Eddie absorbed this. "Okay, if you know so much, call the authorities. Get the cops involved."

"They are involved. In more ways than one. Some of the police are as bad as the traffickers. Short of finding a dead body on the premises, getting the police to organize a raid is tough. My partner and I have a couple of connections in the police force, but it's not enough yet. The legal system here is unbelievably complicated and—"

"Oh, screw the legal system," Eddie snapped. It was a sentiment he'd frequently expressed before—often in more colorful terms—about the court system back home on the occasion of numerous arrests and arraignments. "People like you, reporters, writers, you find something absolutely over-the-fucking top terrible and get your skirts all in a knot, but then what? If what you're saying is true, kids are being held prisoner in that noodle joint right now and all you're doing is sitting here yakking about it."

"Okay, Captain America, I suppose you'd know what to do?"

"Well, hell, when kids are in danger, you don't diddle around crying about how awful it is, you take action. You get your hands dirty, you do whatever it takes!"

"Easy to talk tough when nobody's gonna call you on it. You're too busy being a sex tourist to do anything more challenging than unzipping your pants."

"Hey, I just came here to have a good time."

She leaned back, appraising him. "I'm sorry, Eddie, but for somebody who came all this way to get drunk and buy sex, you don't look like you're having much fun."

"Listen, lady, if I told you why I really came to Thailand—" He stopped himself just in time. *Jesus, what was he thinking?*

Her mouth crinkled disdainfully. "Yeah, I know, you'd have to kill me."

«《—》»

The sunlight outside hit Eddie in the face like a blowtorch and he almost staggered as he navigated his way up Loi Kroh Road. Across the street from the Numbah One Noodle Shop, he paused, taking the measure of the blank-faced customers who sat at counters in the windows like birds on a line, and watched the customers—mostly men—come and go. After about ten minutes, a side door opened, and a lean, sinewy man with brilliantly tattooed arms sauntered out. He wore boot cut black jeans and a red t-shirt and he walked with a hip-rolling, arrogant glide. He didn't seem in a hurry to go anywhere, but shook a cigarette out of a pack and strolled into a passageway between the restaurant and an adjacent shop full of tourist geegaws.

Just for the hell of it—to have a look-see and prove to himself that Ilsa was wrong—Eddie decided to go in and get something to eat. He pointed to a picture on a laminated menu, but the bowl of yellowish, flat noodles the guy behind the counter gave him reminded him of a mound of worms the vet had once extracted from his hound dog's butt. He'd barely paid for the food before he abandoned it and went plunging back into the mid-afternoon furnace.

The intense heat hit him like a brickbat. He lunged to the edge of the pedestrian traffic, ducked into the passageway where the skinny guy had gone to have his smoke, and heaved up a putrid stew of undigested noodles and beer.

When he straightened up, wiping his mouth on the back of his hand, he found himself looking at an incongruous scene. The passage opened into a narrow street, little more than an alley, where vendors had set up a line of booths, hawking the usual assortment of tourist rip-off's and trinkets. Flat Top was standing there with a little Asian girl, looking over a display of DVD's.

If that's the kind of action you're into…

Suddenly, in light of the conversation he'd just had with Ilsa, Flat Top's words seemed to make terrible sense. Eddie was besieged by a mad impulse to do *something* and do it *now*, an act of expiation for all the grief and rage that was percolating in his soul like what had just been disgorged from his stomach.

He stepped out of the passageway and hollered, "Hey, you!" but in the general hubbub his voice was drowned out.

Flat Top was leading the little girl into the maze of booths. Eddie followed, staying at a distance until the pair turned onto the crowded street and Flat Top raised his arm to hail a cab. At that point, the decision seemed to make itself. He raced to catch up to them and blocked the way.

"Let go of that kid!"

Flat Top looked up, dumbfounded, and barked, "Who the hell are you?"

"I'm your buddy from The Joy Palace, remember? *This* is the kind of action you meant? A kid, for Christ's sake!"

"Lower your voice, you old coot. Walk away. This isn't your concern."

"I'm making it my concern."

"How about this?" He brushed his shirt tail aside, a casual gesture that gave Eddie a glimpse of the lethal-looking knife sheathed next to his waist. "You want to make this your concern, too?"

Big mistake.

Eddie Pitrowski was a man who'd grown up on Detroit's meanest streets, who'd survived gang fights, rogue cops, and five years in prison. In the fight-or-die mentality of Eddie's youth, you never let the enemy see the blade until it's stuck between his ribs.

"Fuck you," Eddie said, and smashed his fist into Flat Top's broad nose. There was a crack like celery snapping, and blood spurted out. Flat Top looked stunned. He threw a sloppy round-house, but Eddie parried the blow and banged a hook off his temple. As he moved to throw another punch, he glanced down and saw the little girl cringing in terror. For a second, he felt bad for scaring her, then realized that her reaction wasn't directed at him, but at something behind him. He turned too late—a blow that felt like a mule kick slammed his lower back, a second, harder one pounded his kidney. Pain razored through him. His lungs emptied, and his legs liquefied as the ground swooped up to meet him. Above him, backlit by a supernova of diamonds, the wiry, sinew-and-bones man from the noodle shop twirled a retractable metal baton above his head, grinning like a demented majorette. His eyes blazed with crazed, manic energy as he circled Eddie, snorting and jabbering. "You make trouble here, I fooking kill you. I kill you, moothafooka…

"C'mon, Toy, take it easy," Flat Top said, using his shirt tail to staunch the flow of blood from his nose. His voice was as amiable and conciliatory as a gent in a fine dining establishment recommending a good Merlot. "He's just some drunk thinks I fucked his little sister. He won't bother us again." To make his point, he stepped back and lobbed a kick into Eddie's side. Eddie rolled away, pain gusting through his body like a gritty wind.

By the time he got to his feet, the little girl had disappeared and Flat Top and Toy were going into the noodle shop, friendly as could be.

《《——》》

Rather than pursue the two men, which was his first inclination, Eddie reluctantly heeded the demands of his aching body and hobbled back to the hotel, where he found Kurt fiddling with his camera in the lobby bar. He looked up in amazement when Eddie limped in.

"Jeez, what the heck happened? You piss off the wrong ladyboy?"

Eddie ordered a whiskey and recounted a heavily edited and embellished version of what had occurred.

"Effin' pervs," Kurt said when he'd finished the account, "ought'a be stomped on like roaches."

"Damn straight," Eddie said.

"Man, you can't pull that shit here."

"My sentiments exactly—fuckin' freaks."

"No, Eddie, I mean you can't pull that macho shit, playin' hero and all. You're lucky you didn't get your skull busted open. Don't forget why we came here—to give Danny a smokin' hot send-off, right?"

That rankled Eddie, because Kurt seemed more interested in wandering off to find photo ops than hanging out with Danny, but he didn't say anything. Kurt went on, "This isn't the States, Eddie. You see things don't sit right with you, keep your nose out of it. Walk away."

"Shit, man, you weren't there. I'm telling you, you seen that creep with the little girl, you'd'a done the same thing."

Kurt stared at him as though trying to read his mind. "No, Eddie. I would not. You know why? Because I control my temper, I'm not a hothead who takes crazy risks. Most of all, I do not screw up in foreign countries with prisons that make our slammers back home look like the effing Four Seasons." He drained his beer. "C'mon, you look like you could use some cheering up. Let's go bang on Danny's door and see if he's ready to ditch that clingy chick and put some variety in his love life."

They paid their tab, rolled out of the bar, and were getting off the elevator when the door to Danny's room burst open and Lek sprinted into the hall. Her eyes were huge and wet and raccooned with goopy rings of mascara.

She latched onto Kurt's arm, spewing a rapid-fire hodgepodge of English and Thai.

"Hey, slow down." said Kurt, trying to peel her off. "What's wrong? Is Danny okay?"

Eddie got a bad feeling in his gut, like a fist constricting. He charged up the hall into the room, barking Danny's name. No Danny, so he tried the bathroom door and found it locked, yelled at Danny to open up. He had lifted his leg to kick the door, when the lock turned and Danny opened the door. He wore a pair of boxer shorts and an expression of weary disgust.

He looked at Eddie with his leg cocked and sighed. "Jesus, look at this. You're worse than she is. I'm surrounded by goddamn drama queens."

"What the fuck is this?" Eddie said, barging past him. On the back of the toilet was a bottle of Stoli and three prescription medicine bottles. The Vicodin and Oxy were in Danny's name, the liquid Valium was made out to an Oleg Rastinov.

"Who the hell's Oleg Rastinov?"

"No idea. My nurse friend swiped it from the hospital pharmacy."

Eddie picked up the vodka. "And what exactly was the plan here, Danny? The way the girl was carrying on, I figured you were standing out on a ledge."

He shrugged. "Might'a been, if I could'a got the damn window open. I told you my plan. Get it over with."

"How much of this shit did you take?"

"None of it—thanks to you and my nosy girlfriend. So you can hold off on the goddamn stomach pump."

Kurt and Lek came to the door. "It's okay, everything's cool," Eddie said. "Kurt, take the girl down to the bar. Danny and I got to talk."

Lek's eyes flashed fire. "You asshole, Eddie. I not girl. My name Lek. I stay here with Danny."

Eddie looked at Danny. "Guess her English is improving."

Lek hissed something in Thai and gave Eddie the finger.

Danny dampened a washcloth and wiped the mascara streaks off Lek's face.

"I'm okay," he said. "Go on down to the bar with Kurt. Please. I'll be there in a few minutes. "

As soon as Lek and Kurt left, Eddie started in. "What the fuck, Danny, you were gonna off yourself right in front of her!"

"No! I told her to leave! I gave her a whole bunch of baht, enough for the bus back to Bangkok and a lot more."

"What about me and Kurt? Were you gonna send us back to Bangkok, too, so you could die here alone?"

"Wouldn't it be better that way?"

"What about the pact? Friends to the end? We said we'd be there for each other."

"Oh, screw the damned pact. That shit's for kids." He shuffled over to the bed and sat down heavily. When he looked up, despondency drew his face down like a clay effigy crumbling. He looked like he'd aged fifteen years since that morning. "You and Kurt weren't around, so I decided to man up and just do it myself."

"But what's the rush! Look, Danny, you got a beautiful girl here to spend the night with, why piss it away? You know, carpal deity and all that stuff."

"Carpal what?"

"Never mind."

"Look, man, you don't understand. Lek's the reason I decided to get it over with. Meeting her, being with her the past few days, it just makes it all worse! Makes everything from before look so shitty and small by comparison."

"Then get rid of her!" exclaimed Eddie, waving his arms like he was leading a battlefield charge. "Kurt was right about Chiang Mai, this town's overpopulated with hot babes. Let's go get some!"

Then he fell silent, because what he saw scared him and mortified him and touched something so deeply entombed in his heart that decades had passed without his ever admitting its existence, the alcohol doing its part, of course, in the service of this helpful amnesia. Danny was sobbing. The tears slicked his cheeks unashamedly. And Eddie, who on a few occasions had found himself in situations where he was required to bend over, spread 'em, and cough, while a couple of guards watched to see if any sharp objects or dope or maybe a long-stemmed red rose popped out of his ass, squirmed with an embarrassment more acute than any he'd felt in his life.

"I just can't believe my goddamn luck," Danny said. "First time in years I meet a woman I really like, someone I have fun with, and when do I meet her, but when I'm all set to drop the fuck dead!"

Eddie held up his hands. "Hey, whoa, it don't have to be that way. Jeez, Danny, come on back to Detroit. Do the chemo, the radiation, whatever it takes. Maybe somebody'll come up with a miracle cure. Hell, you never know, earth could get hit with a meteor and kill us all."

Danny gave him a blank stare. "Is that supposed to cheer me up?"

"Well, no, but I'm just saying…" He waved his hand. "Aw, hell, I don't know what I'm saying."

They sat in silence for a minute before Danny said, "You know what I hate most? It's not that I'm scared of dying anymore. It's feeling like I never did anything with my life. It all went by so fast—like a dream—and now it's over and I'm like, wait a sec, this can't be all there is to it. I never did anything important or special or even fucking noteworthy—I never made a difference to anybody."

"That's not true. You raised some great kids—"

Danny rolled his eyes. "Cut the bullshit! My son Jimmy's doing fifteen to twenty for his third felony. Benjamin, he just got another DUI and moved back in with his mother. And Angie—shit, I don't know what the hell Angie's doing and I'm scared to ask!" He gave a sour smile. "Prob'ly make for a drama-filled wake, though. Wonder if any of 'em will show up."

Eddie couldn't come up with a reply. He was thinking about Margaret and her mother, asking the same question about himself.

Kurt stuck his head in the door. "Hey, you two old sad sacks. I thought this was supposed to be a party." He held up the camcorder. "C'mon, boys, let's make some memories."

"Of what?" Danny said. "Me croaking?"

"Shut the fuck up before I kill you myself," Eddie said, shoving Danny out the door ahead of him with one hand and pocketing the drugs with the other.

《《—》》

As they bar-hopped that evening and into the night, Eddie discovered a terrible truth: no matter how much booze he slugged back, he couldn't get drunk. Since the age of twelve, when he figured out the combination to the lock on his father's liquor cabinet, alcohol had been his reliable life partner and friend, amping him up when he required bravado, mellowing him out when he needed calm. When things got really crazy, sufficient amounts of it delivered him into the promised land of sweet, pain-free Oblivion.

Now he felt betrayed and furious, because the drinks delivered only a gut-wrenching clarity, his thoughts brutally sharp. Danny's words rat-tatted through his head like a drumroll. What had he done with his own life, for Christ's sake? No wonder his daughter hated him—he was a loser, a low-life, a drunk.

So outwardly, for Danny's sake, he joined the party, but inwardly he brooded and fretted and ran himself down in a belittling loop of recrimination.

A little before midnight, Danny, Lek and Kurt called it a night and cabbed back to their hotels, but Eddie wanted to walk. He headed back up Lai Kroh Road and loitered across the street from the Numbah One Noodle, which was closed up tight, the shades drawn down like sleepy lids over the plate glass windows.

A strawberry-lipped girl cooed to him from a doorway in the nearby arcade. She might have been an owl serenading the stars for all the interest he felt. A pair of Tourist Police swaggered by, and from long habit in dealing with the law, he turned his face away and briefly fell into step with a group of Europeans carousing past.

Recrossing the street, he slipped into the alleyway, noticing an area behind some garbage bins that was strewn with cigarette butts. He moved deeper into the alley and decided to wait. He was good at waiting. He'd learned how to do that in prison. The night settled around him, cloying and moist, the air marbled with the aroma of hibiscus and wet earth mingled with the sour smell of the garbage. Out on Lai Kroh Road, traffic hummed and horns squealed and The Joy Palace glowed in pink neon, but the alley was submerged in shadow, purplish and still like deep water.

Presently, a man slouched by, glanced around, and rapped on a side door, which opened to admit him. This pattern was repeated three more times over the next hour. Then Toy strolled outside, ambled around the corner, and lit up a smoke. He began to talk, low and heatedly, which almost rattled Eddie into giving himself away until he realized Toy was speaking into a Bluetooth type device.

Crouched on aching knees, Eddie fought the urge to grab the pimp by the throat and bash his head to bloody mush against the wall. He argued himself out of it. Still, the arrogance of a man who exploited children, yet felt safe to loiter in the darkness, puffing on a smoke, presented some possibilities.

He was considering this when a taxi pulled up and disgorged Flat Top, who much to Eddie's satisfaction, sported a butterfly bandage across his swollen nose. Toy greeted him, but instead of going into the noodle shop, the two men crossed the street and disappeared into the neon-veiled Joy Palace.

As soon as Toy and Flat Top went inside, Eddie straightened, brushed himself off, and knocked on the side door.

A bulky man with gelled hair and a face as flat and expressionless as a plank opened the door. He wore jeans and a black muscle shirt under a loose sport coat. His prolonged, silent scowl exuded such menace that Eddie figured he must practice it in front of a mirror.

If there was some kind of profile for perverts, he must have passed it with flying colors, because the plank-faced guy gave him the most cursory once-over and admitted him.

Inside, a stairway led to a green-paneled lounge and a dinky bar where a couple of solitary drinkers nursed Klong beers. Pornography featuring western actors played on a big screen TV.

A petite, buxom woman, dimpled and round as a dumpling, perched behind a counter. She stood up when Eddie approached, made the wai gesture, and proposed a few ethnic specialties.

"You want Thai? Cambodian? Vietnamese?"

For a crazy instant, Eddie almost thought she was talking about food.

The woman misread his hesitation. "You want boy? We got boy, too."

"No, no boy." His voice boomed in his ears. Was he shouting?

"A girl. Toy told me you have them young." He put his hand down as though patting a child on the head. "Like so."

"You know Toy?"

"Yeah, friends. Guy at a bar introduced us."

The woman cocked her head and considered him like a banker about to turn an undesirable customer down for a loan, then touched a taloned finger to her chin and chuckled softly, a prickly sound that scurried up Eddie's neck like a spider. He shook off his desire to flee and fumbled his wallet out.

"I want her for all night."

"No all night. Two thousand baht, one hour."

"I'll give you ten thousand baht, and I take her with me. Have her back here tomorrow morning. That's a good deal, lady. I'd take it, I was you."

"You not me." A derisive smile gashed the woman's face, but her eyes remained dull and impassive as a freshly-swept floor. She must hear this kind of pitch all night, Eddie thought.

"One hour," she said. "Two thousand baht. You have problem with that, talk to your friend Toy."

"No, no problem. An hour's fine.

The woman smiled and nodded enthusiastically. They were buddies again.

She led him behind a gold curtain and up some stairs into a low-ceilinged hallway lined with numbered doors. An air-conditioner whirred somewhere, but the air was stagnant and moist, swirling with dust motes and smelling of disinfectant. Thai pop music blatted loudly over tinny speakers.

The woman selected a door, unlocked it using a clutch of keys, and motioned Eddie inside. The room was minimalist sex club chic—a bamboo floor lamp with a low wattage bulb, a flat screen TV, and a queen-sized bed covered in blue silk sheets with a drip pattern of stains in the center.

"Stay," she said as though addressing a pet.

Eddie waited, wondering if the next person to come to the door would be Toy or maybe the police. He wondered what Ilsa would say if she saw him now and then quashed the thought of her, because he was cat-nervous and needed to focus.

The door opened gradually and the shadow of a child flowed into the room, silent as water. As the girl moved into the light, Eddie could see she wore pajamas with a black and red triangular pattern and red rhinestoned sandals. Her hair hung in a long pony-tail, and she stared at her pink-painted toenails.

He squatted before her, knowing he reeked of liquor and sour sweat, and tried his best to communicate by his tone of voice that he meant to help her.

"Hi, honey. I'm Eddie. What's your name?"

She didn't answer. The floor riveted her attention.

"I'm not going to hurt you, understand? I'm getting you out of here. Okay? Speak English?"

She looked up at him, her tiny round face so lacking in emotion that she might have been a life-like doll. "You want boom-boom or lick-lick?"

Eddie recoiled. "Jesus, no, nothing like that." He put his finger to his lips. "Shhh. You be quiet, and we'll get out of here, okay?"

He scooped her up and checked the hallway. Empty. The dis-cordant music had stopped, leaving a disquieting silence in which all sounds seemed amplified. His own breathing boomed in his ears. From behind the eggshell-thin walls came the sounds of squeaking bedsprings, shuffling feet, murmured voices.

At the end of the hall, a metal door opened into a stairwell. Descending it, he entered another corridor, narrow and poorly lit, that reeked of grease and cooked vegetables. He thought he must be near the noodle shop kitchen and began searching for a door con-necting the two sections of the building. Worse case scenario, he figured he could break a window to get out. He tried a likely-looking door. It opened to reveal a small, gloomy room where a half dozen young girls lay curled on mattresses on the floor.

An older girl, who appeared to be in her mid-teens, sat up and gaped at him. Eddie started to close the door, then saw the raw fear in her eyes and tried to reassure her.

"I'll send help," he said.

Her eyes flicked to the child in his arms. For a second, there was crystal cold silence. Then she threw back her head and screamed.

From overhead came a staccato burst of voices. Feet trampled the stairs.

Desperate for a means of escape or a place to hide, Eddie raced back down the hall, grabbing at doors along the way, finding them locked. The last door that he tried was poorly latched and gave when he put some muscle into it.

There was a grunt and the banging of bedsprings, then a male voice like a wild beast roared, "Shut the effing door, we're busy in here!"

Eddie reeled, the scene before him stabbing his eyes like ice picks. His mind struggled to process the images—a camera mounted on a tripod, a child's skinny legs, the white, thrusting rump of a man—and something cracked in his chest like a bone breaking.

When he turned around, his face was inches from Toy, who bared his teeth and shoved a snub-nosed Glock .22 against the side of Eddie's mouth.

"Put her down," said Toy, and when Eddie did so, bending slightly to lower her, he lifted the gun and hammered the butt into Eddie's skull like a wrecking ball into a wall. The world receded to a pinpoint. A massive roaring filled his ears, and he felt himself sinking into red darkness.

Suddenly Toy yelped and jerked up on his toes. A knife blade scraped so roughly into his neck that blood oozed out in a thin crimson line.

"Drop the gun or I'll cut your fucking throat," Flat Top said.

《《—》》

Ilsa paced back and forth in the living room of the Thai-style wooden bungalow near the Ping River where Flat Top had brought Eddie, piling him into a tuk tuk, tipping the driver extra because of the blood he left on the seat. She wore a flowered silk robe and slippers and paused to only to light another Gauloise from the pack she'd been chain smoking ever since Eddie and Flat Top arrived. Between puffs, she'd furiously explained that Flat Top was her brother, David Abbott. Since the death of his daughter Tran, they'd been working for Child Rescue International, with Abbott trying to win Toy's trust by playing the role of a pedophile attempting to buy a little girl.

"I kept an eye out for pedophile johns and tried to buddy up with them," Abbott interjected into her tirade. "Then I'd send their pictures and data on to Interpol."

"Now wait a minute," Eddie said, wincing as Ilsa pressed a fresh ice pack to his throbbing head. He was lying on a sectional sofa, a painful lump that he tried to ignore jabbing his lower back. "You mean you thought I was one of *them*. I ought'a kick your ass."

"Hey, you looked the part," said Abbott. "I saw you staring in the window of the noodle shop like a man trying to come to a decision about something, and whatever it was seemed a lot more important than what you were gonna have for lunch. You looked— I don't know—haunted, freaked out. Sometimes the ones who still have a conscience, that's how they look."

Eddie turned to Ilsa. "What about when you and me met at the bar? Had this guy here told you to bust my balls?"

Ilsa exhaled a thin twist of smoke. "No, that was just me busting your balls. On general principles. I didn't know you and David had already had a magic moment." She paused to crush out her cigarette. "What you did tonight was incredibly stupid, Eddie. Nobody steals a kid from a Thai brothel, and certainly not Toy's! He's obsessed with protecting what he considers his. He doesn't even sleep at night, just wanders around guarding his little house of horrors. He wouldn't 've thought twice about killing you."

"She's right," Abbott said. "They'd be fishing your body out of the Ping."

"I still don't get it," Eddie said. "I saw you and Toy waltz into that bar, the two of you thick as thieves. I figured you'd be in there all night. Why'd you come back?"

"Toy got a text from the Dragon Lady," Abbott said. "She told him some weird guy claiming he was Toy's friend wanted a young girl. I had a feeling it might be you, so I followed him back."

"What about the kid you were with yesterday? Toy let you take her?"

"She isn't one of Toy's," Abbott said. "She's a girl Ilsa and I helped free from another brothel a few weeks ago. I wanted Toy to see her with me, then tell him I was making a porn flick and try to persuade him to sell me one of his girls. If he went for it, I'd be taping the whole conversation, which would be enough to get the police to organize a raid." He glared at Eddie in disgust. "But that's not going to happen now. I'll never get near Toy again. In fact, now *I'm* a target. I may have to leave Chiang Mai."

In the silence that followed, the only sound was the tiny whoosh of Ilsa's lighter and the soft scrape of her slippers on the polished wood floor.

"So what do we do now?" he said.

"There is no 'we'. Now David and I try to figure a way to deal with the mess you've created." She lit another cigarette and inhaled so deeply the smoke must have blackened her toenails. "Best case, Toy thinks you're just a loony crusader on a misguided mission—which I guess pretty much sums it up, doesn't it?—or maybe you were trying to kidnap a child for your own nasty purposes. I might have chosen otherwise, but David felt he couldn't just stand there while Toy pistol-whipped you to death. So as far as infiltrating the brothel, he's useless now."

"But the guy tried to kill me. David here's a witness to that."

"Unfortunately another way to look at it is you're a guy who was trying to run off with a kid, and David pulled a knife on the man who was trying to save her."

"What about the johns? There was a guy—" Eddie gulped and had to pause to collect himself. "—a guy in the room right behind me who must've seen or heard what went on."

"You think a man who has sex with children is gonna admit to it?" said Abbott.

"Well, hell, I'll go to the cops myself."

Ilsa sighed and sank down heavily into an arm chair. "Just know that if you go there with some wild story about Toy, odds are better that you'll end up in prison than he does."

"So he just gets away with it?"

"He does for now. Thanks to you getting involved in something you know nothing about."

Eddie figured he'd swallowed his ration of shit and then some. He got up gingerly and aimed his aching body at the door.

"Hey, sorry, lady. Sorry I tried to make a difference." He looked at Abbott. "Too goddamned bad you didn't cut the bastard's throat when you had the chance. If you had, I'd'a been happy to put my prints on the knife and say it was me done it."

He let himself out into the moist, fragrant night and found himself in a garden fringed with frangipani and hibiscus, redolent of perfume. He heard his name called and Ilsa appeared in the doorframe, a darkly Rubenesque silhouette punctuated by the orange flare of her cigarette.

In the ink-drop darkness of the garden, her low, throaty voice washed over him.

"You tried to do a good thing, Eddie, there's no shame in that. But no more heroics, okay? Go back to your friends. Whatever you saw tonight, let it go. Forget about it."

She had no way of knowing the effect her words had on him, but they acted like kerosene on the fire of his rage. For a second, his vision purpled and he had trouble drawing a breath.

"That's what you don't get," he said finally. He stood facing her so she wouldn't notice the bulge that the .22 made under his shirt. In the confusion after Toy dropped it, he'd managed to palm the gun without Abbott noticing. "You don't know what I saw. You got no idea. And if I don't do something about it, I'm gonna to keep on seeing it 'til the day I die."

«« —»»

A few minutes after leaving Ilsa and David's house, a tuk-tuk dropped Eddie at his hotel, where he went to his room, popped a couple of Danny's Vicodin and collected what he was going to need. Rain had begun to spatter the windows, so he put on a slicker and rain hat, which made it easier to conceal his battered face when he strolled past the snoozing desk clerk at the Mandarin Orchid and took the stairs to Kurt's room.

He banged on the door, and Kurt opened it, clad in boxer shorts and an undershirt. A TV bolted to the ceiling in one corner of the room blared, but Kurt appeared to have been sleeping through the commotion, his eyes sleep-encrusted, pillow marks indenting one cheek.

"What is it?" he said, backpedaling as Eddie shouldered his way past him. "Hey, you're dripping water on the floor!"

Eddie took off his rain slicker and threw it over a chair. He checked the bathroom, the closet, and under the bed, then he started pulling out drawers, throwing Kurt's meticulously folded t-shirts and trousers and underwear every which way.

"What the hell, Eddie? What are you doing?"

"I wanna see your camera."

"Are you blind, you damn fool?" Kurt pointed to the camcorder on the dresser. "It's in front of you."

"The *other* camera. The one you use to film yourself when you rape little girls." He started ransacking the closet, tossing clothes onto the floor. "I *saw* you, asshole. That was *me* opened the door on you tonight. I saw you, I heard your voice, and now I get why you needed to be in a different hotel than Danny and me—you needed privacy."

Cunning and fear flared in Kurt's eyes, twisting his face into something hateful, unrecognizable. Then it vanished as fast as the memory that spawned it and he was Kurt again, with his loose, crooked smile, easy-going, unfazed. "Well, shit, Eddie, you had me going there for a second. I thought this was something serious."

"I find out a man I grew up with, a man I've known all my life, a *real* man, I thought you were—you're out there raping babies and you don't call that serious!"

"That's the second time you've used that word *rape*, and that's effing enough. Nobody's raping anybody. And let me ask you this, what were *you* doing in Toy's joint? Looking for some young stuff yourself?" He made a show of yawning and scratching his ribs. "It's Thailand, Eddie, it's an effing foreign country. Our rules don't apply. So the chicks you've been doing look like they're eighteen— maybe they are, maybe they aren't. Who's to say? I like 'em young, always have. So what? Eighteen or eight-years old, man, they're all effin' whores."

The sound that exploded from Eddie's throat was guttural and choked, a combination war cry and moan. He plowed into Kurt, driving punches into his face and gut, pummeling him onto the floor and pounding his face until there was a fine mist of blood on the carpet. He forced Kurt's arms back, whipped off his belt and tied his wrists. With another belt from Kurt's closet, he secured his legs.

Meantime, Kurt's eyes were coming back into focus. Eddie grabbed the .22 and jammed the barrel under his chin.

"One chance or I swear, I blow your brains out. The other camera, where is it?"

Kurt's eyes clicked to the TV set bolted to the ceiling. "Up there. On the strut behind the TV."

Eddie pocketed the gun, climbed onto a chair, and retrieved the second camcorder. He didn't watch much, just enough to verify what was on it and that Kurt's face was clearly revealed. After seeing it, he figured he had no choice, hadn't really had one since he opened the door to that room. He fished in the pocket of his slicker and went into the bathroom for a minute or two. When he came out, Kurt had flopped off the bed and was inch worming his way across the floor toward the door. Eddie resisted a powerful urge to kick in his head.

Instead he hauled him upright and threw him onto his back on the bed.

He held up the hyperdermic he'd prepared in the bathroom. When Kurt saw it, he started babbling desperate, weepy promises, but Eddie wasn't listening. He stuffed a wash cloth in Kurt's mouth.

"Guess I'll owe Danny an apology for taking this," he said, "but I think he'll understand. Way I recall, we agreed that if one of us was too far gone to be saved, we'd put him out of his misery with a smile on his face. So this is better than you deserve. And this is me, Eddie, putting you out of your misery."

«« — »»

The rain had begun to pour, obscuring his departure, when Eddie descended the fire escape into an alley behind the hotel. A few blocks away, he found a pay phone in a 24-hour convenience shop and called the Tourist Police, using the emergency number he'd seen plastered on posters in touristy sections of town.

There was still a couple hours of darkness left that he prayed he could make use of. He headed off toward the Numbah One Noodle Shop.

《《—》》

It was mid-morning by the time Eddie returned to his hotel, after briefly detouring to toss Toy's .22 into the river. He thought how nice a drink would go down right now, but instead fortified himself with a cup of coffee from the pot brewing on a counter in the lobby. When he knocked on Danny's door Lek opened it clad in one of Danny's shirts, her long hair damp and glistening around her shoulders.

Danny was slouched in a chair, watching a kickboxing match on TV. He saw Eddie and scowled, "Where the hell've you been? You forget what day it is? Danny Pinchero's Grand Exit Party!" He took in Eddie's beaten up face. "Holy shit, you look like ten miles of bad road."

"Tough night," Eddie said.

"And where's Kurt?" Danny leaned forward, craning his neck as though Eddie's body was a scrawny shrub Kurt might be hiding behind.

"He's not coming."

Danny's face crumpled like a wadded up tissue. "What the fuck? What kind of friend doesn't show up for a buddy's last day on the planet?"

Eddie swallowed. His hands were twitching so bad he was scared to take them out of his pockets. "Kurt wasn't the man you and I thought."

"You mean he chickened out? He couldn't even come to shake my hand and say good-bye?"

"He can't be here, take my word for it."

Eddie expected a barrage of questions, but Danny absorbed the news with surprising stoicism. He waved his hand. "Fuck him then, fuck Kurt Anderson. Let's get down to business."

"Look, Danny, I..."

"You gotta catch the bus to Bangkok in a couple of hours to make that flight back to the States, don't you? So let's do this. I'm ready, man, I'm so ready. You know why? Cause while you were off paintin' the town, I stayed here and, you know what, I prayed. First time in years. Lek prayed with me. Oh, we couldn't understand each

103

other, but she's got a real soothing presence, know what I mean? Now I'm right with the Lord. I'm ready to haul ass and go."

The shivers weren't confined to Eddie's hands now. They were traveling up his forearms into his shoulders. Pretty soon he was gonna have to pull his hand out of his pockets or Danny was gonna think he was diddling himself.

"Danny, I don't think I can do this."

"What?" Danny stood up and poked a finger into his chest. "You can't back out now, buddy. Man-up, for Christ's sake! We signed a pact!"

Eddie looked down at the finger jabbing his chest. If the offending digit had belonged to anyone but Danny, he'd be swinging at the guy's jaw. But now his throat felt like it was closing, and he had to gather himself to speak.

"Listen, Danny, I did something, okay? Something real bad. And I know we made a deal, but don't ask me to do this—"

"Wait just a damn minute!" Danny gave his forehead a theatrical slap. "I get the picture! The smack's gone, is that it? You snuck off and had yourself a little party last night. Kurt, too, I'll bet. That's why he's ashamed to show his face."

"No, no, Danny, you got it all wrong. Something else happened—just let me explain—"

"Shut the fuck up, you sorry-ass liar!" He stared hard at Eddie and then he started to laugh. The laughter began low in his chest and then deepened, rumbling up from his belly, like a volcano suddenly coming alive after decades of dormancy. His face turned splotchy red and tears spilled from his eyes.

Eddie felt a new kind of terror now. He thought Danny was losing his mind.

"If you could see your face," Danny said finally, still guffawing. "Jesus, Eddie, you look like you're about to keel over. Don't sweat it, bro. I'm just yanking your chain."

When Eddie looked uncomprehending, he went on. "You're the one who said I'm allowed to change my mind, right? Well, I fuckin' changed it. Forget the China White. I don't give a shit what you and Kurt did with it. I got a better plan."

He glanced at Lek and then looked quickly away, as though not wanting her to know she was to be the topic of conversation. "This girl here, Eddie, she tells me she's twenty-two, but I think she's closer to thirty. Over here, kind of life she's living, thirty's like Methuselah. It won't be long before she's used up and worn out and then what's she got? Nothing. Most of the money she makes goes back to her family in the mountains."

"Jesus, they all say that," Eddie said, but Danny silenced him with a look.

"I'm not an idiot, Eddie. I know she's a hooker and practically everything she says is a lie, but what choice does she have? It's a shit life. I just met her, I don't love her and I sure as hell don't think she loves me—but she seems to like me a lot or pretends to and she's sure given me a good time so far. The thing is, I'm on my way out and she's not. And I've got a little money and not too bad of a house and I got American citizenship which still means something here and there. So what the fuck, I'm gonna stick it out. I got a translator to discuss it with her and it's all set. She's gonna go back with me to the States and we're gonna get married. I leave her what I got, which isn't much by our standards, but it's a fortune to her. After I kick the bucket, she can stay or she can go, but now she's a little bit ahead of the game and I get to die feeling like I did something good in this world. I think that's important, you know? To feel like before I croaked I made things better for somebody."

"But you don't even know her, Danny. It's not like she's family or anything, she's just a—"

Danny held up a hand. "Don't say it. I want to do this."

Eddie started to stay something, but stopped when he heard footsteps approaching. Someone knocked on the door to his room across the hall from Danny's. Before he could stop her, Lek opened the door and said something in Thai.

The boy from the front desk stood holding a folded piece of paper, which he handed to Eddie. "Lady who called said it was important, to make sure I give you the message in person."

As Eddie read the note, his mind went into overdrive, trying to figure out how fast he could get out of Thailand, what he'd do if cops were waiting for him at the airport, and what kind of alibi he could establish with Danny and Lek to prove he'd been with them in the wee hours of the morning. Then he decided that was the old Eddie's way of thinking. He'd done what he had to do. If Ilsa was planning to turn him over to the police, then so be it.

"I gotta go, Danny." Impulsively he leaned over, bear hugged Danny, and bussed Lek on the cheek. "If I'm not back in time to catch the bus to Bangkok, you and Lek go on without me. Don't miss that plane."

"Wait a second! What's going on? You didn't tell me what happened to Kurt!"

"He decided to stay in Thailand."

《《—》》

Outside a light drizzle fell, warm as spittle.

As he got close to the noodle shop, traffic was gridlocked, pedestrians darting every which way, the satellite dishes from a couple of news vans gleaming like giant toadstools in the rain. He pushed his way through the crowd of onlookers until he spotted David Abbott conferring with a squat, stern-faced guy who had the look of a plainclothes detective. Behind the noodle shop, a bus was loading up kids, some crying, others looking blank-faced and stunned. Ilsa was squatting down, saying something to each one as they boarded the bus, a safari hat shielding her face.

Eddie stood to one side, grateful for the rain, which transformed the scene before him into a monochromatic blur of smeary outlines and indistinct faces. The warm rain running down his back felt icy now, as though mere proximity to the noodle shop had caused some kind of thermal shift. In the torrid humidity of the Chiang Mai morning, he realized he was freezing.

Abruptly Ilsa looked up, her gaze uncanny in its accuracy, as Eddie tried to pretend he hadn't seen her. But it was too late now. He held his ground as she stepped under the police tape and strode over.

"Jesus, Eddie. You look like death's leftovers."

"Thanks. Got your message. Can't believe you remembered where I was staying." He tugged down his rain hat as a couple of policemen passed by. "Looks like the police decided to raid the place after all."

106

"That they did. David got a call from a cop friend at eight this morning telling him it was going down."

He made a show of looking around. "Don't see that son-of-a-bitch Toy. Did they haul his ass off to jail already?"

"No, they hauled it down to the morgue."

"Well. A morning full of happy surprises."

Ilsa said nothing, and Eddie shuffled his feet as the silence expanded uncomfortably.

"I didn't think you'd show up," she said finally.

"Why's that?"

"You had a busy night. I figured you'd either be sleeping in or fleeing the country."

"That some kind of joke?"

"Am I laughing?" She pulled out a pack of cigarettes, shook one out, and ducked her head down to light it. Exhaling, she said, "Aren't you even curious what happened to Toy?"

"Not really. Dead's dead."

They stood watching as the bus pulled away, the rain rat-tatting off the roof, streaming down the windows, obscuring the heads of the children that Eddie imagined must have their faces pressed to the glass, wondering what would come next. Or maybe not. Maybe they were like him, and they stared straight ahead, pretending none of it was happening.

"Amazing the way coincidence works," Ilsa said. "The other day at the bar I told you the police would need to find a dead body on the premises to get motivated to do anything—for the record, I was being sarcastic, not issuing instructions. This morning, a street cleaner finds Toy's body stuffed between the garbage cans behind the shop. Apparently he came outside in the early morning and somebody shot off the top of his head at close range."

Eddie shrugged. "Guess God answers prayers."

"If God's in the vigilante business."

"Cops find the gun?"

"I'm guessing it's in the river. I know that's what I would have done with it."

"Yeah, me, too. Think they'll send divers down?"

"Why? You worried?"

"What would I have to be worried about? After I left your place, I went back to my hotel and conked out. Slept like a baby."

She groaned like he'd told a lame joke. "I'm surprised at you, Eddie. I figured you'd have the lying skills of an accomplished sociopath, but you sound like a little boy explaining how the cat threw up on his schoolwork."

"Don't know what you mean."

"Well, first of all, David's sources with the police said that early this morning someone called in a tip that a pedophile was sleeping off a bender in room 216 at the Mandarin Orchid and that the guy's camcorder was there full of child pornography, a lot of it shot at the Numbah One Noodle. So they go there and find the guy beat up, with ligature marks on his ankles and wrists, sleeping off some kind of tranquilizer."

"Sounds like someone with a guilty conscience."

"So he beat himself up, then shot a needle full of sedatives into his neck?" She flicked rain from her face. "Pretty strange, huh? Just a perv and his Camcorder, taking a nap. They said the name on his passport was—"

Her words struck him like a barrage of stones; he felt stunned, annihilated. He whirled on her. "I don't want to hear the asshole's name! I don't need to know the details! A bad guy got what was coming to him, that's not good enough for you? Why you got to keep yapping about it?"

They stood in silence after that, the lights from the police cars shedding streams of color into the slate rain as the remaining children straggled onto the bus. When finally it pulled away, Ilsa tossed down her cigarette and said, "Something's wrong with you, Eddie."

He tried to feign the calm detachment of a man who had nothing to hide, all the while feeling as though his guilt glowed as brightly as bloody hand prints sprayed with Luminal.

When he didn't reply, she squinted and tilted her head like someone trying to puzzle out a riddle. "It's almost noon and you're sober. Shouldn't you be shit-faced?"

"Felt like giving my liver a day off."

"Right. And what happened last night, you had nothing to do with any of that?"

"You kidding me? I'm just an old drunk who got his ass kicked trying to play hero."

She studied him and in that gaze Eddie saw sadness and resignation but also something else that might have been a grain of acceptance—or gratitude.

"If you say so, Eddie. But you don't want to be having this conversation with the police. That being said, aren't you getting homesick for Detroit?"

"You got that right. I'm taking the bus back to Bangkok in a few hours and flying home tonight."

"Then you better get going."

He wanted to kiss her, but settled for shaking her hand. "You take care of those kids, Elsa."

"Ilsa," she muttered as he trotted off into the rain.

《《——》》

The spring that Danny Pinchero died was the coldest in seventeen years, and Lake St. Clair remained frozen deep into the spring. A freak snowstorm came in early May, an arctic blast slamming down out of Canada, whiting out the skyline, the lake, the world. Eddie drove down to the ice and stepped off into white nothingness, the snow gusting so heavily that his boot prints filled up almost as fast as he made them. He thought about Danny and Kurt and he let himself rage, cursing and crying out there in the bluster and screech of the wind, his voice drowned out by the storm, his tears frozen.

With Danny gone and Thailand behind him, his whole life felt out of whack and confused, like a jigsaw puzzle missing key pieces. His emotions ran the full spectrum from pissed off to really pissed off to murderous, but he was running out of furniture to smash and slugging walls just bruised his knuckles. He'd tracked down Ilsa's email address through the rescue group she worked for and wrote to ask her what happened to the guy at the Mandarin Orchid. He was hoping to hear that the bastard would be out of prison about the time Detroit ran out of cars, but she never responded, so after some resentment over being ignored, he let it go. He tried to feel good about the fact that he'd chosen to dose Kurt with Danny's liquid Valium instead of the lethal smack, but he still nursed a dangerous fury—Kurt had grown up with him and Danny on Gratiot Street, how could he have turned into a monster and how could he, Eddie, not have known?—so that snowy spring afternoon, all he could do was stomp out onto the ice and scream his rage into the cold, howling white.

After a couple of miles, though, he ran out of steam. Here was where the idea had been to guzzle down the bottle of Jack he carried inside his parka, stretch out on the ice and fall asleep or fall through, whichever came first, but that plan, like everything else in his life, had changed recently. He set the bottle down unopened—a prize for some ice fishermen if they were lucky enough to find it—mumbled a few words to Danny or God or anybody out there who might be listening and trudged back to the safety of the shore. He wondered idly if this failure to follow through on the original plan meant he'd lost his nerve or his cojones, but figured if Danny could change his mind, so by God, could he.

When he got back to his truck, he sat for a while running the heater, getting warmed up and gritting his teeth at his cell phone, which he'd laid out beside him on the passenger seat. It irked him no end how nervous he felt, because a real man ought not to be scared to call his own daughter any more than a real man ought to need those damned fool AA meetings he'd dragged his ass to a couple of times.

Then again, he was starting to wonder if he had any idea what a real man really was.

What the hell, he thought, and picked up the phone.

Maybe there was still time to find out.

Sanguma

Don't disrobe, he'd told her. *Whatever you do, don't even think about wearing a bikini or a thong. It's not like that here. You'll see. The local women go into the water fully clothed. But if you must, at least wear a laplap, show that much common sense.*

So said Milt. And Milt was the one reading the guide books, so Milt must know.

The day before, in Lae, she'd worn a yellow two-piece to the beach and removed the colorful laplap from around her waist before entering the water, charging into the surf with abandon, diving deep and wantonly into the green, curling waves. When she came out, a group of local men, chugging stubbies and chewing betel nuts at a beachside bar, had stopped talking to stare at her—not appreciatively as she was accustomed to being viewed by men, but with faint disdain, even malice—the way her mother used to stare at the scars on her arms—*stupid girl, how could you be so careless*?

Now she was lounging on the balcony of the Paradise Hotel in Goroka, an East Highlands town inland from Lae, with Milt and their young guide Harry Ingube. They were drinking beer, trying to cool off in the relentless heat after a sweaty, teeth-rattling ride on the Public Motor Vehicle that had brought them to Goroka that morning. Milt had been reading an article in the local paper about three woman in Mt. Hagan who were dragged from their homes, tortured and burned as witches, so the talk had turned to sorcery.

Charlotte found it sobering that in the twenty-first century, even in the Highlands of Papua New Guinea, such atrocities occurred. She said to Harry Ingube, "Is it always women they burn?"

Ingube was a brown-skinned young man with a wide mouth full of startlingly white teeth and jet black, sparkling eyes under curly lashes. He smiled constantly, infectiously, as though his was a festive and merry heart always in secret celebration.

Now the dazzling smile lost some wattage as he took a swig of beer and leaned toward her, so near that for a moment, his meaty lips looked kissably, disconcertingly close. "No, not just women, men, too!" He said this with an enthusiasm akin to pride, as though burning people alive for sorcery was merely a minor rip in society's fabric as long as it lacked sexist overtones.

"It happens like this, you see. A healthy man dies suddenly for no reason, so people believe it is witchcraft. Then a gang of rascals comes looking for the sanguma—the witch—who caused the death and they burn the witch alive."

"Rascals?" said Charlotte, thinking a word she associated with mischievous children to be a tad mild.

"In New Guinea, it means thugs," said Milt in his twangy Aussie drawl. "These rascals, they're the reason it's not smart for you to walk alone or show too much skin." Milt was a gangly, narrow-shouldered man with a neatly trimmed goatee and hooded, melancholy eyes.

Contrasted with his small, cherubic mouth, the pensive eyes gave his face an inscrutable Cheshire Cat quality that might hint at deep and brooding thoughts or perhaps no thoughts at all. He and Charlotte had met in Singapore at the Mandai Orchid Gardens, he on holiday from his job as an assistant principal at a secondary school in Melbourne, she taking a break from teaching English in Hokkaido. It wasn't mad love, exactly, but as Charlotte had observed in her peripatetic life, loneliness could be a hell of an aphrodisiac.

"The people here," Ingube said, "many of them have no education. They believe in sangumas and ghosts and shape-changers. I was lucky. My aunt raised me in Port Moresby, and I was sent to a Lutheran school. But up in the Highlands where we're going—they say that when a plane lands, people still check the exhaust pipes to reckon if it's male or female."

He flashed that bright, captivating smile again and held Charlotte's gaze.

"Bloody hell!" Milt gave his biceps a ringing slap, mashing a mosquito the size of a dime to a bloody smear. He used a napkin to wipe the mess off his arm and said, "Look here, Ingube, what I want to know is whether you'll be able to take us to a singsing. Not one of those staged shows put on for tourists, but the real thing. Our first guide said he could find one, but now that he's dropped and abandoned us..." He left the statement hanging on an accusatory note.

This time, Ingube's smile tried to hide his embarrassment over the fact that Bob Okibo, an older man who'd come recommended as a top-notch guide, had failed to show up that morning, when he was supposed to meet Milt and Charlotte in Goroka. Not so unusual, apparently. An over fondness for Jungle Juice and a certain lackadaisical approach to commitments were endemic to the lifestyle here, or so it said in *Lonely Planet*. While Milt was frantically trying to track down Okibo, smooth and smiling Ingube had approached Charlotte outside the hotel to offer his services.

"Yes, tomorrow we'll go to a big singsing with many tribes," Ingube said. "No problem."

"What about the Mudmen of Asaro? Will we see them?" The famous Mudmen were high on Milt's lists of reasons to visit New Guinea.

"Mudmen, yes, yes" said Harry, though Charlotte had the feeling he knew as much about the likelihood of the Asaro Mudmen showing up as she did. Still, she added a request of her own, "Harry, I'd like to visit a spirit house where they keep the sacred masks. What's it called, a haus tambarans?"

Inguba picked at the label on his bottle of beer, not meeting her eyes. His evident discomfort prompted Charlotte to ask, "What's wrong? Aren't there any here?"

"No, no, there is a spirit house klostu—nearby," Ingube said, "but, women, they are tambu. Long time back, if a woman went inside a spirit house, the penalty was death."

"Tough place to be female" said Charlotte, chugging her South Pacific Lager. She remembered seeing a red and white pamphlet published by the police department in the give-away rack of a shop back in Port Moresby. The title "It's Illegal to Beat Your Wife" had seemed like a put-on at the time. Now she was starting to realize such information was put forth with dead seriousness.

As she pondered this, a commotion came from the street below. A battered Toyota pick-up careened around the corner, two-wheeled it over a curb, and braked with a sound like a pig having its throat slit. The bed of the truck was packed with young men, all shabbily dressed and armed with clubs and bush knives. They jumped down out of the truck bed and jogged up the street like a posse. People scurried to get out of their way. Vehicles U-turned.

"Don't look at them, get down," hissed Ingube. He grabbed Charlotte's arm, yanking her below the level of the railing, and squatted beside her, his face so close that she could see the diamonds of sweat glistening in his furrowed eyebrows. His fingertips brushed her bare arm, leaving in their wake a sensation of electrical energy, of silver sparks cascading through her blood like neon fish.

"What's going on?" said Milt, who was crouching inside the door to the lobby.

"Stay down," Ingube said, "Police will be here soon."

Through a gap in the railing, Charlotte could see the gang fanning out down the street, entering the stores and hostels along the block. A pair of them approached the hotel. They wore bright bandanas and filthy-looking shorts and their bare, coppered chests gleamed in the sun.

To her amazement, the desk clerk, a scrawny old man with skin gnarled and brittle-looking as tree bark, hobbled outside to confront them. The young men shouted at him and the old man hollered right back. Charlotte tried to understand what they were saying, but they were using the Pidgin dialect that was nearly incomprehensible to her. One of them kept rubbing his thumb over the hilt of a mean-looking knife. She was sure the old man was going to be gutted like a mackerel right there in the street, but amazingly, after more yelling and gesturing, the two rascals turned away.

Behind her, Milt exhaled audibly. "Bloody hell! Remind me to buy that bloke a beer."

«« — »»

"What do you suppose that was about?"

Charlotte sat on the edge of the bed, looking out the window onto the street below, where a woman at an open-air stall was serving up plates of fried sweet potatoes, taros, and yams to a trio of Westerners on bicycles. Farther on, beyond the post office and

114

the row of shops and budget hotels, she could see the roof of the Goroka Market, the Raun Raun Theater and in the distance, the outline of the improbably named Mt. Kiss Kiss, with its steep trek to the look-out at the top.

Beside her, Milt was paging through a "Guide to Flora in New Guinea," trying to identify some plant specimens he'd picked earlier that day. All was quiet. As Ingube predicted, police had shown up, but only after the gang of rascals had piled into their truck and screeched away.

"Maybe they were just fired up, celebrating payday," said Milt.

She twisted to face him. "No, they were looking for someone. I don't feel safe here. I think we should leave."

He put the book aside, stroking his goatee as though that simple action might somehow coax forth erudition. Not for the first time, Charlotte thought he was either very wise or adept at feigning it. Finally he said, "Tell you what, after the singsing tomorrow, we'll come back, get a good night's sleep, and catch the first flight to Port Moresby the next morning." He put a hand at the small of her back and leaned forward to kiss her neck.

She wriggled away like a skittish cat. "It's too hot for that. Doesn't it ever cool off here?"

"Apparently some of us are already cool." He added petulantly, "Ugabe's keen on you, you know. I've seen him looking at you."

"What is he, all of nineteen, twenty? At that age, a boy's keen on any woman who gets within fifty feet of him."

"And at your age, a woman can be keen on any man who shows interest."

"At my age?" snapped Charlotte, who was not yet forty and hardly considered herself a crone. Never-the-less, the words stung. She found herself reverting to an old form of self-soothing, crossing her arms and stroking her forearms with either hand, cradling them like small animals in need of comfort.

Milt coughed and looked embarrassed. He took her hands away and held them still. "I'm sorry, Char. I didn't mean to say that. Come on, it's been a long day. Let's get some sleep."

《《—》》

Sleep was a struggle. The bed was narrow, the mattress lumpy as undercooked porridge; the relentless heat gave no quarter. It was as if all day the earth absorbed the heat only to exhale it in sweltering waves after dark. Mosquitoes whined round her ear and she thrashed on sheets slick with sweat.

To her annoyance, Milt fell asleep at once and began to snore deeply. That he could sleep under such circumstances was alone reason to hate him.

Had she been less fatigued, Charlotte might have sensed what was happening and woken herself up before it was too late, but by the time she caught the cloying, giddy fragrances of citrus and spiced plums and ginger, she was deep in the den of her nightmares.

Candles—how she had loved them, the ceremony, sensuality, and drama implicit in their use.

In the kitchen of her childhood, fist-sized chunks of tallow, rainbow colors, were lined up on the sink—lavender and tangerine and dandelion gold. In the window sill, the finished product: some stumpy and sawed-off as gnomes, others skinny as broomsticks, a few obvious failures where the candle ended up crooked as a bent back or listing tipsily to the side—the ones she privately labeled "Mom Staggering Out of the Alibi Lounge," chuckling as she fed those back into the bubbling saucepan on the stove to be melted down again.

As always, she was alone, which had frightened her when she was young, but thrilled her now that she was almost ten and had discovered her own company to be more interesting and entertaining than that of most adults and certainly all children. She was creative, she could sew dresses and bake brownies that she slathered in German chocolate frosting from a can, she could fill the sink with soapy water and give her Barbie dolls a bath, dunk their blonde heads under until they drowned, then hold a pretend funeral from which they resurrected as alive as they had been before. These elaborate and somber Barbie funerals required candles—hence, her current project.

The front door slamming startled her—she thought it was her

mother coming home, leaning like a tipsy candle. She turned too fast. Her elbow struck the handle of the pan, the molten tallow sloshing upward, an elegant red arc of languid, airborne lava. As she flung her arms up to protect her face, it splattered onto the stove and across the counter, in search of something soft and living to adhere to and finding what it sought. Had she been designing a batik, the imprint of fiery scarlet semaphores and teardrops and stars might have been stunning. But as it was…

Stupid girl, you could have set the house on fire!

She found herself sitting bolt upright in bed, clawing at her arms, teeth clenched against remembered pain. She gasped Milt's name and reached for him, flailing empty air.

Outside the window, shreds of rose and saffron dawn illuminated the rooftop of the post office and YMCA hostel. She got up and checked the bathroom, found it empty, then dressed and padded downstairs to the lobby. The desk clerk was bringing out a pot of coffee and some paper cups. She asked if he'd seen Milt leaving the hotel. He said he hadn't, but looked at her oddly, as though merely to voice the question was to implicate herself in something unsavory.

"Maybe he went for a walk," she muttered weakly.

The old man filled a cup with coffee and handed it to Charlotte. "Now why would he do that?" he said, shaking his head. "It's dark. Not safe out there."

Charlotte sipped the coffee "That was very brave, what you did yesterday, confronting those thugs."

The old man snorted and waved off the compliment with a boney hand. "Them rascals drink, think they big men. They sober up, find out they still no 'count."

"What did they want?"

The wizened desk clerk studied her, then shrugged and turned away. Charlotte thought the conversation was at an end when suddenly he said, "You had a different guide before you come to Goroka, no? Man named Bob Okibo."

She nodded, "Yes, Okibo showed us around Lae and Mt. Hagan. He told us he'd meet us in Goroka, but he never showed up."

"That's cause he dead," the desk clerk said.

Charlotte's voice came out a scratchy whisper. "My God, was there an accident?"

"No accident. One minute he's getting off the PMV, next he go bugarup, get the chills and die. He from Goroka, his clan is here. Them rascals think somebody used witchcraft to murder him. They looking to get payback—money, blood, or both."

Charlotte struggled to keep her expression from betraying her. It was she who had hired Okibo in the first place, when she and Milt had just flown into Lae from Port Moresby. She'd chatted with him outside the hotel for half an hour, negotiating a fee and an itinerary, while Milt was upstairs studying his guidebook. How many people had seen her talking to Okibo, she wondered, feeling a minor frisson of fear which she dismissed as ludicrous. She was a tourist, for God's sake. Okibo guided tourists for a living. How many other foreigners had he talked to in recent days?

"These men, do they know who they're looking for?"

"Right now they don't know for sure, but don't matter to them as long as they find somebody they decide be guilty. When they do, they torture that person until they confess. Then they kill them."

"And if they don't confess?" asked Charlotte.

"They kill them anyway."

《《—》》

She went back to the room to compose herself and try to think. Milt was missing, Bob Okibo had dropped dead, a gang of thugs was trying to track down a sorcerer: if the various events were not so dire, she'd have laughed aloud. She decided to give Milt another hour. If he didn't return by then, she'd hire a taxi and visit the police station, the hospital, the Australian Embassy. In the meantime, she'd try to find Harry, who—assuming he was not with Milt—must have an idea where he could be.

Enough, thought Charlotte. She grabbed her brimmed hat, doused herself in mosquito-repellent, and was heading for the door when her eye caught sight of something odd outside the window: having already risen once, the sun appeared dissatisfied with its performance and, like an actor asking to make another entrance on the stage, had gone back to cross the lip of the horizon for a second time that hour. Not only that, but it had chosen for its curtain call, a location more southeasterly than east and was now a livid siena smear at the end of Kundiawa Road.

Mystified, she hurried outside and ran up the street to where a group of people—some weeping, others cursing, cheering—were witnessing, not a sunrise, but an ungodly spectacle. The stench of singed meat assailed her nostrils. Her eyes watered from the smoke.

Before her, a bright and hideous flower bloomed, its malignant petals formed of flame, the scarlet stamen made of human flesh, and in its center, the charred mask of what had once been a face, but still, improbably, alive, eyes gone but mouth thrown wide to emit the screams of hell itself. The woman's legs were V'd, her huge belly convulsing as though the fire had slid down her throat and was burning through from the inside. It took Charlotte a moment to realize the woman was already dead; it was not her screaming, but the tar-black and bloody thing that now emerged between her legs and dangled from her corpse.

The sight and stench felled her like a blow. She bent double and began to wretch.

One of the men turned toward her with a reproving glare. She recognized the long-lashed eyes and rictus smile of Harry Ingube.

The sight of him was like a vicious slap, shocking her awake. The baby and the burning woman vanished. She was on the bed in the hotel room and feet were pounding up the stairs. Someone tried the door. A key rattled in the lock.

Milt dashed into the room, tossing his daypack on the bed, babbling like a game show contestant who just won a microwave. "My God, Charlotte, what an amazing night! I got to witness an initiation ceremony! You should have seen the masks—hundreds of them, generations old! I felt like I was—Char, are you okay?"

"Of course I'm not okay! I've been worried out of my mind. Where the hell were you?"

"A spirit house. Harry said there was one *klostu*, remember?"

"He took you there?"

"No, no, nothing of the kind. He mentioned where it was, but I was the one who got it into my head to go. Honestly, Charlotte, I wanted to take you with me, but you heard what Harry said, that women aren't allowed." When her expression didn't change, he added peevishly, "I thought you'd be pleased for me."

"Oh, I'm tickled to death, that you got to go on your bloody adventure while I thought maybe your head was going to show up on a pike."

"Come on, Char, don't carry on. Look, Harry's downstairs. He says if we leave now, there's a PMV can take us around Mount Michael to within a few miles of the singsing, and he knows a short cut through the forest will get us the rest of the way. Why don't you take a shower, throw some things in your pack and meet me downstairs in half an hour?" He said this as he retreated out of the room, closing the door behind him with exaggerated care.

"Oh screw you!" yelled Charlotte. She reached for the object that was nearest, which happened to be the pillow on Milt's side of the bed, and flung it at the door. As she did, something fell on the floor—a delicate white blossom with a yellow stamen and waxy, pale green leaves along the stem. Insects had apparently been at it; a cluster of tiny, ragged punctures were nibbled in the centers of the leaves. Was it something Milt had brought back to identify? She started to pitch it into the waste can, then reconsidered and slipped it into the side pouch of her daypack.

«« — »»

They caught a rattletrap PMV south to Lufa and part way around Mount Michael, grassy valleys alternating with steep peaks that jutted above densely forested hills. When they exited the PMV, Charlotte saw no trail at all, but Harry's eyes were falcon keen. He led them unerringly up narrow, winding trails where, under a thick canopy of vegetation, a tree-kangaroo observed their passing from on high, gravely, with black button eyes, like a small but dour judge, and birdwing butterflies the size of saucers fluttered among the trees.

Long before they reached the singsing, they could hear the distant thunder of the Kunda drums and the unearthly ululations of the singers summoning ancestral spirits to the festival. Smoke snaked above the trees as the forest gave way to open spaces where neat clusters of low walled, round huts were built among the rolling kunai-grass covered hills. As they approached, the singing picked up in intensity, chanting interspersed with yips and trills more suited to the repertoire of jungle birds than human throats.

Energized by the din, Harry picked up the pace and led them to a slightly raised area between two of the huts where they could view the dancing and take pictures, but Charlotte didn't know what to focus on first. The scene before her was a kaleidoscoping whirl of riotous color and furious sound, a weird cacophony of glottal grows and a hollow, almost metallic keening made by the women dancers on the periphery of the throng.

The drumbeat picked up speed, became a single wild, primeval heartbeat that held all other hearts in thrall. The ground shook with the stomping of feet as painted bodies slick with pig grease, bedecked with cowrie necklaces and bird of Paradise plumes, offered up their incantations to the spirit world.

As time wore on, there was no lull, no pause in the dancing. Charlotte began to feel queasy and light-headed. She looked for a place to sit down and was suddenly surrounded by a group of nearly naked figures caked in white mud, their heads covered in grotesque, gourd-shaped masks.

She looked around for Milt, knowing what it would mean to him to see the famous Mudmen of Asaro. With their fearsome appearance, it was easy to understand how, generations ago, they could have terri-fied an enemy tribe who saw them rising from the muddy river bank and believed they were ancestral spirits returning for revenge.

One of the Mudmen danced closer, his grey mask looming over her until it almost scraped her cheek. Hard, enamel-bright eyes gleamed through the holes in the mask. The Mudman's gyrating body blurred and reconfigured, the arms branching into a multiplicity of grasping limbs. She tried to shove away the leering mask and felt it dent and squish between her fingers, sloughing off like lizard skin, until she looked into Harry Ingube's rakish, grinning face. She screamed, but the sound was smothered by the rumble of the drums.

The world blinked out for a moment and when it returned, she was peering through the viewfinder of her camera again. The Mudmen of Asaro were still caught up in their ferocious dance, their masks intact, their limbs the normal number. A hand clasped her shoulder. Harry beckoned urgently. "Hurry! He's over here!"

He led her to an open area behind the huts. A circle had formed around a greased and feathered harlequin with a black and yellow face who knelt on the ground, bent over a pile of rumpled clothes. Only when she realized the man was administering CPR to the unresponsive bundle on the ground did she realize it was Milt.

"What happened?" Pushing her way through the onlookers, she grabbed Milt's wrist and felt for a pulse, but the very inertness of him, the limp density, told her this was not a living body. The harlequin gave up his ministrations and said gravely, "He began to shake. I think that he is dancing. Then his eyes roll up, he falls down, and he dies."

"But he can't be dead, it isn't possible!" cried Charlotte. "He wasn't even sick, he was fine"

She looked up and saw Harry eyeing her. Then she realized all the men were watching her. In a strange, detached way, her mind pushed grief aside, to be dealt with later, and began to calculate the degree of danger she might be in. She was with Milt. Now Milt was dead. She'd talked at length and in public to Bob Okibo, and he was dead, too. Had any of the men here been among the group of rascals in Goroka the day before?

As if reading her thoughts, Harry said, "Charlotte, we must go back to Goroka. We must go now."

His tone brooked no nonsense. With the help of some of the men, they wrapped Milt's body in a heavy cloth and secured it with rope, so that his body resembled a giant silkworm cocoon. Two men then hoisted the body between them and followed Harry and Charlotte back along the trail to the dirt track where the PMV had left them hours earlier. They didn't linger, but dumped Milt's body like a load of trash and made haste to return to the singsing.

When the green mini-bus finally pulled up, the driver was unwilling to take a dead body on board, and the passengers inside grumbled and shot Charlotte and Harry dark looks. Finally, after some negotiations and a hefty bribe from Charlotte, the body was secured atop the vehicle and they rumbled off.

They were half-way to Goroka—Charlotte had seen the signs for a coffee factory and a trout farm that were popular tourist sights—when suddenly Harry yelled "Stop!" at the PMV driver. He grabbed Charlotte's hand and pulled her toward the exit.

"No, we can't get off! We can't leave Milt!"

"The driver will drop his body at the morgue," said Harry, muscling her off the bus. "But now I need to show you something important—so that you will understand."

"Understand what? What are you talking about?"

In the bruise-colored twilight, his incandescent smile looked wolfen, feral. "Charlotte, this is where I used to live. Don't argue, you come with me now, please."

Was it her imagination or did people watch her surreptitiously as they passed, children smirking behind their hands, women muttering in Pidgin? They were on the edge of a shanty town, tiny corrugated shacks cobbled one atop the other. Women squatted over cooking fires, mottled pigs rooted in the garbage. Although Charlotte could barely see where she was going, Harry threaded his way effortlessly along the narrow, littered passageways, pulling her by the hand. Occasionally, looking back, she thought she glimpsed the shadowy images of men moving stealthily behind them, keeping pace but not trying to catch up, but she said nothing to Harry. They reached an open area where a grove of wind-whipped trees wrapped bare limbs around each other like frightened children.

"Here," said Harry. "This is what you must see."

She saw nothing: an open area, stunted trees, the bald earth littered with lager bottles, crumpled food wrappers. What she felt, though, was far more tangible and menacing—hostile gazes pricking her skin like poison darts and the tang of danger, imminent and deadly, wafting in the sultry air.

That's her, she imagined hidden onlookers were whispering, *the one who bewitched those men! Sanguma!*

"Please, let's go," she said, "It isn't safe."

But Harry, having brought her to this stricken, terrible place, was in his element now, focused on his own thoughts only, oblivious to danger.

"Years back," he said, "a pregnant woman—a sanguma—was brought here to be burned. At first the fire, it will not start, but when it finally begins to burn, she struggles so hard the baby, it pops out between her legs. The baby's auntie grab him quick, bundle him up, and run."

"And the woman?"

"She died."

"The baby?"

But she knew the answer already—she'd seen it in her dream, the infant, wet and screaming, expelled between the legs of its dying mother.

"This is what happened to the baby," Harry said. He turned his back to her and peeled his shirt off. The seared skin covered most of the region between his shoulder blades and waist, curving pink-white deltas against a nut brown field, smooth and rubbery as a carnival doll in some places, puckered and peppered with haphazard pigmentation in others. Repulsive in its glossy slickness. Like a blind woman reading a map in Braille, she ran her palm across the pale peninsulas and continents and atolls that described his injuries.

"I watched you on the beach in Lae," he said. "I saw your arms and recognized you from my dreams—a burned woman who searches for her spirit-mate, but doesn't recognize him."

He turned and tried to pull her to him. She shrank away, not so much appalled by what he'd said than by the fact that she was not sufficiently repulsed. Excitement, lurid and terrible, thrilled through her like a fatal poison.

"We're two parts of the same person, you understand me, Charlotte? Even in death … together."

He looked past her then and saw something that caused his smile to petrify like a mask nailed to his face, so much so that when the four men rushed at him, screaming, brandishing clubs, he never flinched or cried out. Even as they beat him to the ground, the smile, now bloody, missing teeth, remained carved upon his face.

So intent were they on beating Harry that Charlotte went almost unobserved—until she tried to run. Then one of them, a squat, flat-eyed man, skin black as lava rock, came after her. He whipped his fist into the small of her back and sent her sprawling.

"You want to live?" he said, mildly and conversationally as a waiter asking how she liked her tea.

"Yes. Yes!"

"Then you were never here. You did not see this. The *sanguma* who bewitched our kinsman Bob Okibo did his work alone."

What happened next she watched in sick disbelief and horror, crouched down behind a tarp someone was using for a wall. One of the men broke a tree branch off and lit it while the others dragged Harry to the trunk and bound him tightly. And while she hid there, seeing his flesh blister and blacken and his face dissolve, listening to the terrible howls that came from his still living form, she became aware of others with her. Some emerged from the shanties to watch what they would later, under interrogation by the police, deny ever having seen. Others came from other realms entirely, ancestors who'd suffered through their own horrific deaths and waited to welcome Harry as their own. They nudged and nuzzled against her, familiar as family, grey and evanescent as ash.

«《——》»

It was dawn by the time she found her way out of the shanty town and caught a PMV going to Goroka. She sat by the window, watching the light cascade across the lush hillsides, tasting tears. For the first time since she'd come to New Guinea, she saw its fierce and mysterious beauty for what it was—a doorway into things she didn't understand.

Back at the hotel, she ignored the desk clerk's somber stare and started up the steps, then turned back. Digging into her pack, she pulled out the leaf she'd found underneath Milt's pillow.

"You will dispose of this for me?"

He stared a moment, his nostrils flaring like a panicked mule, and made the sign of the cross across his chest while murmuring several verses from the Psalms.

Satisfied that her suspicion was correct, she softly said, "Tell me what it is."

"The leaf, it is the heart," he finally said. "The holes are punctures made by a sorcerer to bring about a death." He crossed himself a final time and said, "Your guide, the man Ingube—"

"—is dead," said Charlotte, and only then the desk clerk seemed to draw a proper breath.

She went upstairs to her room. Gooseflesh rippled her skin like rain dappling the surface of a pond. She had to hold her right hand steady with the left one so she could unlock the door. She staggered inside, shut the door and slumped against it.

The heat of the room failed to penetrate the sudden chill on her skin, as though within her flesh a frozen skeleton had moved to life, pieces of it chunking off, tiny glacial bits of bone floating in her bloodstream.

Something shifted and reformed in the corner where the open bathroom door blocked off the thin light seeping through the windows and cast a dense rectangle of shade. The shadows slid like panels in a Chinese puzzle box, as something that had once been Harry crabbed its blistered limbs along the wall. His voice echoed clearly in her mind, at once imperative and plaintive.

Even in death…together.

She did something then that, before the events of the last twenty-four hours, would have been inconceivable—she turned to the wobbling, reshaping thing massed in the corner and addressed it as though it could understand.

"There's nothing here for you. Leave!"

The faceless head shook slowly, like a sea anemone responding to the motion of the tides. For some reason—there was no mouth that she could see—she had the terrible sense that the wretched thing was smiling.

The ice in her blood probed behind her teeth and stunned the air out of her chest. Red flares hissed behind her eyes. A great weight compressed her heartbeat and pinched her lungs to the size of seeds.

Marshaling all her waning strength, she reached for the pillow on her side of the bed and turned it over.

Knowing even before she did, what she would find there.

 tivar

Graham's whisper was harsh with fear. "Did you *hear* that?"

I had almost drifted off to sleep, no easy feat in early summer in the interior of Iceland. At that time of year, the sun finally goes through a facsimile of setting around one a.m., when it teases a brief dip below the horizon, but the resulting night is a pale, anemic mockery of true darkness, more a ghostly half-light that turns the world into a sepia-tinted photo and conjures shadows that tempt the eye to trickery.

Perhaps the ear as well, I thought, as I rolled over and pushed the sleeping mask off my eyes.

"What?" My voice was thick and gravelly, my muscles painfully sore. We'd been in the saddle almost eight hours a day for the last five days, herding the horses from Stolli's farm in southwest Iceland into the northern Highlands.

"Stallions," Graham said. "I heard them screaming."

I reached over and patted the lump in Graham's sleeping bag that I took to be his shoulder. "All the horses we're herding are mares and geldings and foals. You were dreaming."

"I *heard* them, Ellen."

"It was probably that story Stolli was telling us."

Stolli Sorenson, a horse breeder and rancher whom we knew from the Landsmot Horse Festival that Graham and I attended every summer was also our guide on this adventure. I'd wanted to do a cross-country ride before Graham and I flew back to the States, and Stolli had come up with the suggestion that, following the old Icelandic custom, we'd drive his herd up into the Highlands for the summer. We'd started out from Stolli's farm west of Gullfoss, then headed north following the Pjorsa River between the glaciers Hofsjokull and Vatnajokull into the desolate Sprengisandur. Even the name Sprengisandur is ominous, deriving from the Icelandic word for exhaustion. In earlier times, so afraid were riders of the ghosts, elves, trolls, and outlaws who supposedly populated this barren region that they'd run their horses almost to death in an attempt to make the fastest possible crossing.

Stolli was also an enthusiastic student of Icelandic history and the events described in the sagas. The night before, he'd been telling us about the brutal custom of goading stallions to fight each other, sometimes to the death, and wagering on the outcome. The idea must have stuck in Graham's mind.

Graham was silent for so long that I thought he'd fallen asleep. Then he surprised me by whispering, "Ellen, do you think Stolli knows what he's doing?"

"Of course. Don't you?"

"I did until now. Have you looked at the map?"

"Not since we left Gullfoss."

"We're way off track, at least thirty or forty kilometers."

"Did you say anything to Stolli?"

"Not yet. You know Stolli, he'll just give me a look and say he grew up herding horses out here and who the hell am I but a rich American who buys Icelandics as a hobby."

"Some truth to that," I said.

"But either he's lost and won't admit it, or for some reason he's taking us way off the route We should've reached one of the overnight huts by now or at least seen tire marks from the four wheel drives the touring companies use. We've seen sheep, nothing else. We're out in the middle of nowhere."

I ran my hand along the side of his face and studied the thoughtful grey eyes, the brow furrowed with concern. A small, trim man in his early sixties, Graham inherited from his industrialist father a love of fine horses and lusty women and the money to buy plenty of both. Unfortunately, the private detective I'd hired back in Bar Harbor had told me Graham's latest indiscretion was more than a fling; I'd heard a tape of Graham pillow talking with his lady love about his plans to ditch me. He had the lawyers ready, the papers drawn up. He was simply waiting until we returned from Iceland to drop the bomb.

Knowing this, it was with some effort that I caressed his cheek solicitously rather than raking it with my nails.

"The middle of nowhere? But that's the idea isn't it? The interior of Iceland. You don't get more in the middle of nowhere than this."

He continued as though I hadn't spoken. "This canyon Stolli's talking about—he said it was northwest of the Tungnafellsjokull glacier, but it's not on any of the maps."

I patted his hand, not knowing how to answer. I didn't know it at the time, but there are a lot of things in Iceland that aren't on any maps.

"At least I have the Ruger I bought from that Norwegian at the horse show," he went on. "Just in case."

"In case what?"

"I don't know. I just don't think it's smart for the three of us to be out here alone without any protection."

"Go back to sleep," I said.

"I don't think I can." He sounded frightened.

But within minutes he was snoring loudly.

《《—》》

I waited a short time, then opened the tent on my side and crawled out, zipping it behind me and pulling on the paddock boots I'd left outside. No sign of life from Stolli's tent, but he could fall asleep on the back of a bull.

We were camped at the base of a slope leading up into steep hills topped by turret-like formations of rock. To the north loomed a chain of grey, brooding mountains striated with yellow and pink bands of rhyolite. To the east, only the outlines of icecaps and a pair of dormant cinder cones were visible on the horizon. The vastness of it made me shiver, this desolate and beautiful wasteland where it seemed that minds as well as bodies might become lost.

The horses, twenty-two head of piebald, bay, smoky black, and silver dapple, were spread out across the hillside. Small, surefooted beasts with large heads and short, powerful necks, they were perfectly suited to Iceland's harsh weather and treacherous terrain. Their distinctive gaits, the smooth tolt and the flying pace, were easy on the rider's back and ideal for long distances. As I watched them now, they looked unreal, drifting apparitions in the hazy light that might have been sculpted from shadow and fog.

I did a quick count and was relieved to find them all there. I still believed Graham had dreamed the stallions, but I wanted to be sure. We didn't need the added complication of a pair of wild stallions trying to pick off mares from the herd.

I tramped up the slope, skirting a jagged tongue of obsidian rock where sometime in Iceland's recent past, a lava flow had reached this point and halted, hardening into pock-marked rock carpeted with velvety layers of moss. Higher up, the hills gave way to a series of slate shelves strewn with boulders. From here, I had an unobstructed view, but I saw nothing except our tents below and the horses, grazing peacefully.

Peaceful and mindless, ignorant of any world beyond their immediate one of sky and wind and grass. And I thought of my father, a frequently unemployed ranch worker with a penchant for philosophy, who used to lament that most people acknowledged no world beyond their limited experience. He believed our lives were just a tiny scrap in an immense and never-ending tapestry, the depth and breadth of which we could never see or understand completely. Privately, I thought that, since he lived hand to mouth and had no creature comforts to offer me or my three brothers, he tried to pretend material pleasures were of secondary importance anyway—a foolishness I'd always openly disdained.

As far as I was concerned, my immediate experience was the only one that counted. Soon I planned it to include luxury homes in Vail and Grand Bahama, and a fabulous horse ranch outside Reykjavik, where the finest Icelandic horses would be bred.

Too bad for the bitch who thought she was going to be Graham's fourth wife.

After this trip, I'd be his grieving widow.

My pleasant musings were short lived. I felt the hair at the back of my neck prickle as something tripped an inner alarm.

Glancing toward the obsidian outcrop, I saw a nest of shadows that seemed to swarm and thicken. A palette of funereal shades, muted greys and dun and umber, coalesced into the vague outline of a figure creeping slowly toward me in the unnatural twilight. As it got closer, I made out a tanned and bearded man who wore a shabby, long-sleeved shirt, leather boots, and cloth pants cinched with a drawstring at the waist. Had I met him in a city, I would've crossed the street or looked for a cop. As it was, I held my ground and noted with sick dismay that he was brandishing a knife.

My mind emptied of thought like an overturned bowl. All was instinct. *Never let them know that you're afraid,* was a rule I knew from a lifetime of working with horses.

In as calm a tone as I could manage, I said, "Who are you? What's your name?"

At the sound of my voice, he flinched and looked perplexed, but he didn't lower the knife a single centimeter.

I stretched a hand out in what I hoped to be a soothing gesture, while with the other, I scrabbled behind me on the rock wall for a chunk of loose stone.

"How about putting that down? You're scaring me."

His brows furrowed into a single bushy bar. He squinted with suspicion and befuddlement, shaking his head like a man trying to awaken from a terrible dream.

"Please," I said, but he kept approaching, the knife still held aloft but less surely now, as though the option of severing my arm at the shoulder was no longer entirely certain.

"Asgerd," he growled, barking out the word in the voice of one unused to speech, whose tongue and lips formed only with difficulty around the syllable. "Asgerd."

"Asgerd? Is that your name?"

He was so close now I could see the beads of sweat on his forehead, the dirt in his beard. There was something else, too, something even stranger than his appearance, but I couldn't quite identify what it was—or wasn't—and I let it go. My attention was on the blade, which he finally sheathed with what seemed like some reluctance. Suddenly his right hand grabbed for my throat, but only to drag the back of his fingers slowly across the skin, like a blind man learning Braille. His touch made my flesh heat and prickle, as though his fingers gave off a mild electric charge. He stared at me, but I knew he didn't see me. Whatever it was he looked upon was distant as the stars, though he'd evidently found its likeness in my face.

131

And while he studied me, I studied him—the matted beard that looked like it might provide a nest for mice, the dried blood streaking his temple, the look of bereavement and bewilderment in his eyes. For a moment, his neediness reflected back to me the child I once was, angry and lonely, scared there would never be enough to go around, always wanting more. Like looking into a mirror that transcended time or perhaps foretold the future.

"Don't!" I cried out and jerked away.

His hand withdrew. Pain flashed in his eyes and he fled from me as though I carried plague.

«««—»»»

My first thought was to wake up Graham and Stolli and tell them what I'd seen, but I knew Stolli would be skeptical and Graham would want to launch a search, since it would be virtually suicidal for a lone man to be hiking in this area. Because no sane person ventured alone into the Sprengisandur, with its swift, glacial rivers, unpredictable weather, and harrowing emptiness. The danger of becoming lost, hypothermic, or injured was just too great.

And really, then, what had I seen—a bloodied and bedraggled man in peculiar clothing, a man who looked at me with first with rage and then with sorrow, a man who'd touched me as though we knew each other?

I lay awake through the remainder of what we still called night, although the sun dimmed but never set completely, and tried to come to some rational conclusion. The man was real, I told myself, I hadn't had a waking dream or conjured a phantom. A hiker lost out here might well be mad from exhaustion, dehydration, and terror. He'd be desperately in need of help and I had offered it.

So why had he run away from me, I wondered. *Why had he run?*

«««—»»»

Why did it never end, this torment?

Sometimes his head cleared enough that he could stitch memories together, but they unraveled like the fraying threads of a poorly woven cloak. Time, if it still existed, had become a hellish labyrinth, corkscrewing and spiraling, a snake devouring its own tail, or freezing solid as the rivers of winter.

He knew this: that he was Gunnar, son of Thorkel, and that his life had once included a bounteous farm and able-bodied kinsmen, a proud lineage of sturdy farmers and sailors who'd plundered the coasts of Ireland and Britain for treasure and slaves.

Now time had ceased, but he ran unceasingly, pursued by fragments of memory and his enemy Thorir's vengeful kin.

War horses screamed inside his skull and tore at each other with their teeth: a contest between his own stallion and Thorir's. His own horse had been killed. By way of recompense, he had demanded the hand of Asgerd, Thorir's cousin, in marriage, but Thorir had laughed, telling him Asgerd scorned his offer and that Gunnar was of low birth, hardly better than the son of a slave-woman.

Here memory lapsed, but his aching forearms retained the jolt of impact when, in a rage, he'd planted an axe between Thorir's eyes.

In the summer, the matter of Thorir's killing was brought before the Althing, to be judged by the Lawspeaker and the local chieftains. Witnesses appeared, including Asgerd, who denounced Gunnar as a scoundrel. She demanded he be put to death or sentenced to full outlawry, which amounted to the same thing. To be outlawed meant that a man was to be given no protection or aid by anyone, not even his own kin, and could be killed with impunity.

The Althing decided in favor of Asgerd and her family, declaring Gunnar an outlaw. He fled to the farm of his brother Egil, hiding in the shieling, where the cow herders and shepherds lived during the summer, but Thorir's kinsmen eventually learned where he was staying. He fled into the Highlands for a time, but when he to Egil's farm, he was greeted by a ghastly sight—his brother's head impaled upon a scorn post. A curse on Gunnar and his entire family was carved in runes into the post.

Now he was deep in the Sprengisandur, and Thorir's kinsmen were still in pursuit; he'd seen the glow of their campfire in the distance. He'd seen Asgerd, too, and now brooded bitterly over that encounter, wondering what she was doing here and how he should deal with her.

«《——》»

I awakened to the aroma of bacon frying and coffee brewing—
Stolli was up, making breakfast. He was a broad-shouldered,
ruddy-faced man whose Nordic good looks were marred only by
swollen nose and broken veins of the chronic alcoholic. When he
saw Graham and me emerge from our tent, he proffered two mugs
of steaming coffee, making a point to hand the larger one to
Graham, and grinned, "Big day today."

"You say that every day," snapped Graham.

"Every day's a big day when you're out on an Icelandic horse,"
said Stolli, with a cheerfulness I had to concede was a bit much to
take at this hour. And what hour was it anyway? My body clocked
somewhere around five a.m. but the sun said afternoon. Hard to
believe that, come winter, the light would be in exile once again
while pitch darkness ruled the day.

Over breakfast, Graham brought up the subject of our location.
"I think we've gone off track, Stolli. This canyon you keep talking
about, I can't find it on the map. Where exactly are we anyway?"

"Whatsa matter, Graham? You think we're lost?"

"It looks that way."

"Nice to know you've got faith in me," said Stolli, scowling in
a way that made his eyebrows appear to do push-ups. He turned to
me. "What about you, Ellen? You think we're lost, too?"

I bit into a piece of hardfiskur and pretended to chew it thought-
fully. "I think we must be taking the scenic route. If the canyon's
not on the map, that just makes it more mysterious."

Graham shot me a look that said I must have lost my mind.

"We'll be there in another day," said Stolli. "Then you'll thank
me. And wait 'til you see the valley beyond the canyon. Lush,
green, it's why I bring the horses up here every summer, wild-
flowers everywhere."

"I'm sure the horses love it, but I've seen a lot of valleys,"
Graham said. "Missing this one isn't going to kill me."

"And what do I do with the horses, leave them here without
adequate pasture?"

"Take them back to your farm. They're better off there anyway.

It always did strike me as ridiculous, this custom of driving the horses into the Highlands for the summer."

"Like you'd know about Iceland or the horses," Stolli said.

Graham clutched his fork like he was thinking of shoving it through Stolli's eye. "I own some of the best Icelandics in the world."

"Because you've got money to buy them and fly them to the States. Doesn't mean you know a goddamn thing about them."

I raised my hands. "Stop it, both of you. I won't have breakfast ruined by your bickering."

Stolli glanced at me with those pristinely clear blue eyes, eyes I could at one time have gotten lost in until I realized the lethality that lurked behind them. He looked benign, but I knew he must have teeth marks on his tongue. "Sorry Graham, I was out of line. Go on, drink your kaffi."

"I don't want coffee," said Graham, who typically consumed at least three cups to start the day. "My stomach's upset already."

A few minutes later, while Graham walked off to find a private place to squat, I cornered Stolli. "We aren't alone. I saw a man out there last night."

"One man? On a horse or in a four wheel drive vehicle?"

"None that I saw."

"On foot? Impossible."

"I saw him, Stolli. He was carrying a knife. He scared me wit-less."

"Did you talk to him?"

"No, I was too focused on the knife. But he was injured and dis-oriented. I offered to help him, but he ran off."

A sarcastic grin stretched thinly across Stolli's mouth. "Outlaws used to hide out here. Maybe you ran into a tivar, one of our moun-tain spirits."

"Don't start, Stolli. This guy was as real as I am."

Stolli shrugged. "Makes no difference what you saw. The plan's been set. We stick with it."

"We can't! Not if there's someone out here."

He took a deep breath, expelled it. I smelled the remnants of last night's—or maybe this morning's—gin. "It's too late to change your mind, hon. I'm not going back without earning my two hundred thousand."

"What two hundred? We agreed on one fifty."

"I want more for the aggravation of having to put up with Graham's bitching."

"Fine then, just do it."

"That's more like it. I earn my money, you get your widow's weeds, and everybody—well, almost everybody—goes home happy." He ran the back of his fingers across my cheek. Nothing like the way the strange man had touched my face the night before. It was a gesture of smug arrogance and power, with no a hint of anything resembling affection. Not that I expected any. For a long time, I'd thought Stolli was gay—and concealed the fact with his hard drinking and over the top machismo. He wasn't. He liked females all right, but I had a terrible suspicion they weren't the kind you find in centerfolds. At the horse shows in Reykjavik, when he thought I wasn't looking, I'd seen the way he watched the young girls up on their pretty ponies. When we'd talked about the money, he'd told me his plan was to move to Cambodia where "a man can have anything he's ever dreamed of."

I shrugged off Stolli's hand and turned to collect the breakfast plates.

"And by the way," he added, "I need some more of those veterinary tranquilizers you swiped back at the horse show. He didn't drink his kaffi."

《《—》》

An hour later, we set out again across terrain so desolate we might have been on the moon, a comparison not altogether far-fetched since the Apollo astronauts had actually once trained here. We skirted a thermal area, where the earth puckered and spat up globs of boiling mud, then followed an icy river that twisted like a convulsing snake along frozen banks. Driving the herd ahead of us, we forded it at a point that appeared shallow, but frigid water still splashed up to our knees. In the distance a stretch of basalt cliffs rose up like the silhouette of a great city, but I knew that when we reached it, the only inhabitants, if any, would be plump, brown-feathered ptarmigans.

When we stopped to rest the horses and have lunch, I busied myself frying up the last of the potatoes to go with the strips of haddock and cod that were a staple of our meals. Graham scanned the cliffs with his binoculars and reported there was a wooded bluff above a gorge, but that the entrance appeared too narrow to navigate with the herd.

"Is that the canyon you've been raving about?" he asked Stolli.

Stolli had just made coffee. Now he set down the pot and brought Graham a full mug.

"No, it isn't, my friend."

"Then what canyon is it? Where the hell are we?"

"Know what, Graham, I don't know. You were right. You're always right. I've got us fucking lost."

"Oh that's just great," said Graham. "Now what do we do?"

Stolli let out a booming laugh. "You should see your face, Graham! I was only kidding. That's the canyon, all right. We made it."

He tried to give Graham the mug of coffee. "Drink this, perk you up."

"Dammit, I'm nervous enough," said Graham.

"No kaffi?"

"I couldn't stomach it. Not 'til we're back in Reykjavik."

"Right you are," said Stolli. He set down the mug, grabbed the iron skillet I was using to fry the potatoes and, wielding it like a tennis racket, smashed it across the back of Graham's skull, crumpling him instantly.

"Jesus!" I shrieked. "You didn't have to do that!"

But Stolli only shrugged and smiled. "What was I supposed to do, he wouldn't drink the fucking kaffi!"

《《——》》

We tied Graham, deeply unconscious, to the back of his horse. I stayed behind while Stolli rode toward the canyon, driving all the horses except my own ahead of him. I hoped Graham would remain unconscious, that he wouldn't wake up at the last moment and see

137

what was about to happen. It was a terrible way to die, but Stolli and I agreed the authorities would never question it.

As I watched Stolli ride away, I felt alone and suddenly vulnerable, aware of a solitude so profound and vast one might sink down in it and never resurface. Tears welled in my eyes. I thought about Graham's gun and wished that I'd taken it from him before Stolli rode off.

Raising the binoculars, I scanned the cliffs at the highest point, where the basalt columns rose up like the pipes of a massive cathedral organ.

The man I'd met the night before was standing high up on the canyon wall, balanced on a ledge. His arms were folded on his chest and he was staring toward the mouth of the gorge, the direction from which Stolli would come. How he'd managed to cover the same amount of ground that we had, I couldn't imagine. Even if he had a horse, we couldn't have missed seeing him on the bleak, dark-sanded lava desert we'd traversed.

Saddling my horse, I galloped toward the canyon to warn Stolli. I was still a quarter mile away when I heard loud noises and the sound of Stolli yelling. Pulling my horse up short, I took out the binoculars and scanned the entrance to the canyon until I spotted him. He was using a chunk of lava to bang on a metal pan, spooking the herd into flight. I checked the cliffs again, but the man who'd followed us was gone.

I wondered how much he'd seen and what he might do about it.

As I approached the mouth of the canyon, I saw Stolli riding toward me.

"It's done," he laughed. "Heartiest congratulations to the grieving widow!"

"Shut up, you idiot, we have a problem."

"What now?"

"That weird man I told you about—he's here. He must have seen you."

Shielding his eyes from the relentless sunlight, Stolli squinted up at the cliffs. "If someone's there, I'll deal with it. Let's collect our victim of tragic circumstances first. Come on, I need your help."

I doubted that. I thought Stolli took a sadistic pleasure in making sure that I saw Graham's mangled remains. I didn't want to be alone, though, so I rode with him.

At its widest point, the canyon was about three hundred feet across but after that, it veered inward and narrowed sharply. I could see fresh hoof prints in the dirt, where the herd, spooked by Stolli's noise-making, had stampeded through.

A quarter of a mile in, the passage narrowed to the point where we could no long ride comfortably side by side and Stolli took the lead. I kept looking above, half-expecting a hail of rocks or even a boulder to descend on us. The horses were nervous, too, ears back, jittery in such close quarters. We dismounted and continued slowly until the passage began to widen again.

"This isn't possible," said Stolli. "He isn't here."

"You're sure this is where you left him?"

"Of course I'm sure! Right there, where the horses couldn't miss him. He was still unconscious, but I tied him up just in case. Even if he woke up, there's no way he could've untied himself and climbed out. It's too steep."

"It's that man I saw. He moved Graham out of the way."

"For what?"

"He's a fucking do-gooder, Stolli, how would I know?"

《《—》》

He relived the scenes endlessly, but in different order, key moments tossed and gathered up and flung again like bones hurled by a sorcerer.

Thorir's kinsmen had been a savage lot, afire with bloodlust. After decapitating Gunnar's brother, they slung his body across a horse and carried it away, seeking to desecrate the corpse further by denying it a proper burial.

Gunnar had retreated to the remotest part of the Sprengisandur, an area where even outlaws seldom ventured, and he watched his brother's killer's gallop toward the gorge. He knew they were using Egil's body to lure him out into the open, that he was sealing his own fate when he crept into their camp that night, but as a man of honor, how could he do otherwise?

139

Two men were guarding the camp, but Gunnar came upon them so silently that he was able to kill the first one from behind, running his spear clear through the man's chest. The second man came at him swinging an axe, but Gunnar blocked the blows with his shield and plunged his dagger through the man's eye. Then, before the others awakened, he untied Egil's body and carried it on his back up onto the bluff.

«« — »»

As we continued searching for Graham, Stolli raged.

"Where is he? He didn't just walk away." Suddenly he whirled around and screamed in my face. "What did you do, Ellen? You get cold feet? Did you sneak back here, untie him, and hide him somewhere?"

"How would I do that…? Why would I do it?"

"I don't know. But so help me God, Ellen, if you did, you're gonna die here with him."

At that moment, I didn't think anything could have frightened me more than Stolli, but I was wrong.

"Shut up," I shouted. "Listen!"

It was the sound that I thought Graham had imagined, the high-pitched, terrifying skreighing of stallions fighting, increasing in intensity until it seemed the battling horses must be just beyond us, at the other end of the canyon.

Stolli ran to grab the reins of his horse, but it reared and cantered away, my own horse right behind it. Above the sound of the stallions, there rose the dull percussive beat of hooves, as the herd reversed direction and raced back up the gorge.

"Climb!" I shouted, but Stolli was already grabbing at a handhold in the rock wall and hoisting himself up.

I put my booted foot up on a rock, grabbed a ledge above me—and fell back as the rock gave way. I could hear the horses pounding closer, terrified by the banshee-screams of the stallions.

Another handhold—this time, I got some leverage and pulled myself up a few feet off the ground. As I continued to climb, I looked up so I could follow the path Stolli had chosen and saw him already far above me, almost at the top. He was reaching for the

140

final handhold to vault himself up. I saw a face peer down at him, a hand extended.

"Stolli, don't!"

But there was nowhere else for him to go. He hesitated an instant, then reached up and grabbed the proffered hand. The muscles in the man's thick forearm bulged as he gripped Stolli's arm and heaved him up over the edge. When I saw Stolli standing, brushing himself off safely, I let out the breath that I'd been holding and reached for my next handhold. The horses were much closer now. The stallions, the damned stallions that I still couldn't see, went on ripping each other.

Something tumbled from the cliff top—a brown-tipped scarlet bird, I thought, until I saw the bright blood spraying.

A few seconds after his hand passed by, the rest of Stolli followed.

He struck an outcropping of rock, rolled about twenty feet, and fell again, thudding to the canyon floor with a force that must have killed him.

It hadn't. He flopped onto his back, face slack with shock as he stared at his pumping wrist and mangled legs and the horses racing toward him in full flight.

The lead horse instinctively jumped him, but the ones behind were bunched together and pulped him beneath their hooves.

I didn't look again until I'd reached the top and pulled myself over. Below, what had been Stolli was now a gory mush. Except for a gyrfalcon that wheeled overhead, I was alone on a broad bluff forested with thickets of dwarf birch and willow.

I couldn't take time to worry about Stolli's death or Graham's disappearance. I needed to get back to the camp, pack some provisions, and round up the two horses Stolli and I had been riding. My plan was to head north toward Lake Myvatn, which would be swarming with campers, hikers, and four wheel drive tours this time of year. I could get help and report two deaths.

I was already rehearsing what I'd tell the authorities when the man who'd just murdered Stolli emerged from the thicket of birch. At his waist a small axe hung from a leather strap, its blade so recently used that the bloodstains were not yet dry. He looked even more haggard and filthy than before. I realized then what it was that had struck me the first time I'd seen him but that I hadn't been able to place—he was covered in sweat, dirt and blood, yet he had no odor.

As real as I am, I remembered telling Stolli, and yet how could he be?

He stared at me, eyes black with anger, and spat out words I couldn't understand, but whose essence was all too clear—I was guilty, shamed, and stood convicted.

"Please," I said. "Whoever it is you think I am, I'm not. Whatever it is you think I've done, I'm sorry."

I stretched my hand out to him, beseeching leniency, and waited for God or Satan, one, to act on my behalf.

He gripped the axe, but instead of hoisting it to cleave my skull, he merely ran his thumb along the blade so that his thumbnail, when he raised his hand, was slick with blood.

He bared his teeth, part grimace, part deranged grin, the malicious smile of one who can afford to wait, because he has all eternity to do so.

I knew then that he would.

Behind him, the saplings bent and parted.

"Get away from her!" ordered Graham, aiming the Ruger. His forehead still oozed blood from the awful gash. He looked unsteady and demented, like a torn, wind-blasted scarecrow.

I raised my hands in an absurd gesture, as if my palms could deflect a bullet. "Graham, let me explain."

"No need to." His voice quavered and broke with exhaustion. "I know what happened. This madman attacked me in our camp. One minute I remember we were having coffee and the next I woke up here and saw him tossing Stolli off the cliff."

Relief transfixed me. Graham didn't know what really happened, and with Stolli dead, he'd never have to know the truth.

"Stay back!" Graham shouted suddenly, because the man had started inching toward him. His face betrayed no fear whatever of the gun. His eyes shone with bright malevolence as he freed the axe from his belt.

Graham stood rooted, frozen.

"Graham!" I shouted, "Shoot him!"

«‹—›»

Memories of bloody mayhem ebbed and flowed through his being like a lurid tide. He had never feared death, only cowardice.

It was retrieving his brother's body that had proved his undoing. Three of Thorir's kinsmen tracked him onto the wooded bluff above the canyon and cornered him at the edge of a cliff, but so fiercely did he fight that within minutes one of them was dead, the other dying.

The third man dealt such heavy blows with his sword that Gunnar's shield split down the center. He tossed it aside and reached for his axe, but to his amazement, his final adversary had transformed into a withered, elfin man who wielded, not a sword, but a puny, inconsequential object with a round black eye. The strange weapon didn't cause him pain, but the shock of the noise enraged and unhinged him, and he hurled himself at his enemy.

As he did, he saw Asgerd's face and knew all that had happened to him was happening still and ever would be, eternity spent dying in the Sprengisandur, careening through the void.

«‹—›»

I stood immobile at the cliff's edge, unable to comprehend what I'd witnessed.

As the man lunged toward him, Graham fired the gun over and over into his chest, but for all the damage it did, he might as well have flicked him with a feather. The huge man never faltered. With a roar, he flung away the axe and seized Graham in his massive arms, twisting, and then lurching backward as in a drunken pirouette. One minute he and Graham spun together in a bizarre embrace, teetering at the cliff's edge. Then gravity took them and they were gone.

I was the only one who screamed.

I didn't look right away and when I finally did, I saw what I feared seeing most—Graham's body, but only his.

«‹—›»

In the end, I got everything I wanted and much that I did not. The deaths of Stolli and Graham were deemed accidental—it's understood that those who venture into the harsh interior of Iceland sometimes meet grim fates. With the money I inherited from Graham, I bought Tolting Pony Farm, where I raise Icelandics, but it's near Madison, Wisconsin, not outside Reykjavik. I travel widely, obsessively, but I've not returned to Iceland.

At least not physically.

In dreams, I go there nightly, fleeing through the infernal bleakness of the Sprendisandur, pursued by something pitiless and savage. I cry out and try to run, but find myself ensnared by clumps of shadows that seethe like snakes around my feet. They slither upward toward my throat and I awake sweat-drenched and screaming.

I can't see the one who follows yet, but I can sense him nearby, patient and implacable.

I know I don't have long to wait.

Lately, just before I fall asleep, I hear the stallions screaming.

nikishi

Seasick and shivering, Thomas Blacksburg peered out from beneath the orange life boat canopy, watching helplessly as the powerful Benguela current swept him north up the coast of Namibia. For hours, he'd been within sight of the Skeleton Coast, that savage, wave-battered portion of the West African shore stretching between Angola to the north and Swakopmund to the south.

Through ghostly filaments of fog that drifted around the boat, Blacksburg could make out the distant shore and the camel's back outline of towering, buff-colored dunes. To his horror, the land appeared to be receding. Having been brought tantalizingly close to salvation, the current was now tugging him back out into the fierce Atlantic.

A leviathan wave powered up under the boat, permitting Blacksburg a view of houses strung out like pastel-colored beads. Impossible, he thought. This far north, there was nothing but the vast, inhospitable terrain of the Namib desert, an undulating dune scape stretching inland all the way to the flat, sun-blasted wasteland of the Etosha Pan.

Blacksburg calculated his options and found them few. So suddenly and fiercely had the storm struck the night before that no distress call had gone out from the ill-fated yacht Obimi. With the captain knocked overboard and the boat taking on water, Blacksburg and his employer, Horace DeGroot, had been too busy trying to launch the life boat to radio for help. The Obimi wasn't expected in Angola until the following Friday. No one was looking yet. And when they did look, there would be nothing to find. And now it was just him.

The settlement in the dunes appeared to be his only chance.

Checking to make sure the leather pouch strapped across his chest was still secure, he dove into the water.

145

«« —»»

Hours passed before finally he hauled himself ashore and collapsed, half-dead, onto the sand. The fog had lifted, revealing a narrow beach hemmed in between two vast oceans—to the west, the wild Atlantic and, to the east, an unbroken sea of dunes that rose in undulating waves of buff and ochre and gold. Silence reigned. The hiss and thunder of the surf was punctuated only the cries of cormorants and the plaintive lamentations of gulls.

Believing that he'd overshot the settlement he'd glimpsed from the boat, Blacksburg trudged south.

Fatigue dogged him and acted on his brain like a psychedelic drug. Retinues of ghost crabs, fleet translucent carrion-eaters with eyes on stalks, seemed to scurry in his footprints with malevolent intent. Once he thought he glimpsed a spidery-limbed figure traversing the high dunes, but the image passed so quickly across his retina that it might have been anything, strands of kelp animated by the incessant wind or a small, swirling maelstrom of sand that his exhausted mind assigned a vaguely human form.

The hyena slinking toward him, though, was no trickery of vision. A sloping, muscular beast with furrowed lips and seething, tarry eyes, it angled languidly down the dune face, its brown and black fur hackled high, its hot gaze raw and lurid.

Blacksburg took in the clamping power of those formidable jaws, and dread threaded through him like razor wire.

He bent and scooped up a stone.

"Bugger off!" he shouted—or tried to shout—what emerged from his parched throat was a wretched, sandpapery croak, the sound a mummy entombed for thousands of years might make if resurrected.

The hyena edged closer. Blacksburg hurled the rock. It struck the hyena with a muted thunk, laying open a bloody gash on the tufted ear.

The hyena's lips curled back and it uttered a high pitched whooping sound so eerie and wild that the temperature on the windswept beach seemed to go ten degrees colder. He heard what sounded like a Range Rover trying to start on a low battery, but this false rescue was only the guttural cough out of the spotted hyena's broad muzzle. With a final saw-toothed snarl, the pot-bellied creature—which was 70 kilos if it was 10—wheeled around and loped back into the dunes that had spawned it.

«« — »»

Exhaustion had so blunted Blacksburg's senses so that he almost sleepwalked past the grey, wind-scoured facade of a two-story house whose empty window frames and doorway stared down from atop a dune like empty eye sockets above a toothless mouth. Climbing up to investigate, he found a gutted shell, the bare interior carpeted with serpentines of sand, roof beams collapsed inward to reveal a square of azure sky. Gannets nested in the eaves. On the floor, a black tarantula held court atop a shattered chandelier.

Spurred by a terrible intuition, he struggled up another dune until he could look down at the entire town—a pathetic row of derelict abodes, a sand-blasted gazebo where lovers might have lingered once, a church whose steeple had toppled off, the rusted carcass of a Citroen from some forgotten era.

The hoped for sanctuary was a ghost town. A graveyard of rubble and stones.

Stunned, despairing, he roamed amid the wreckage.

The wind shifted suddenly and he inhaled the mouth-watering aroma of cooking meat. The hot, heady aroma banged through his blood stream like heroin. Saliva flooded his mouth. Half-dead synapses danced.

Stumbling toward the scent, he crested another dune and looked down upon the beach to see a sinewy, dark-skinned old man using a stick to stir the enormous cast-iron potije that rested atop a fire. The old fellow wore frayed trousers, a yellow ball cap, and a short-sleeved pink shirt. His left hand did the stirring. The right one, flopping by his side, was lacking all its fingers.

Behind him, a girl in her late teens or early twenties was pulling a bottle of water from a canvas backpack on the ground. She uncapped the bottle and poured it into the potije. She wore an ankle-length tan skirt, battered high-tops, and a billowy red blouse.

A brown bandanna around her head held back a crown of wind-blown dreads. An old scar zigzagged like a lightning bolt between her upper lip and the corner of one eye.

With feigned heartiness, Blacksburg slid and trotted down the dune, crying out, "Uhala po." It meant good afternoon in the Oshiwambo tongue, but judging from the old man's reaction, it might as well have been a threat to lop off his remaining fingers. The old man's eyes bulged and he let loose a shriek of mortal fear. The woman had considerably more sang-froid. She held her ground, but snatched up a sharpened stick.

"My name is Blacksburg," he croaked, holding up his hands to show he meant no harm. "I need help."

The old man commenced a frenzied jabbering. The woman chattered back, and an animated exchange took place, virtually none of which Blacksburg understood. Finally the old man fell silent, but he continued to appraise Blacksburg like a disgruntled wildebeest.

"Excuse my uncle," the woman said, in meticulous, school book English. "You frightened him. He thought you were an evil spirit come to kill us."

"No, just a poor lost wretch." He gestured at the empty water bottle. "You wouldn't have another of those, would you?"

The woman took another bottle of water from the backpack and handed it to Blacksburg, who gulped greedily before eyeing the potije. "Fine smelling stew there," he said. "What is it, some kind of wild game, stock, chutney, maybe an oxtail or two?"

Using her stick, she speared a dripping slab of wild meat. Blacksburg fell upon it like a wolf. The meat was tough and stringy as a jackal's hide, but, in his depleted state, he found it feastworthy.

Between mouthfuls, he gave a version of his plight, detailing the sinking of the Obimi and the loss of her captain, but speaking only vaguely of the one who had chartered the boat, his boss Horace DeGroot. The woman told him that her name was Aamu, that she and the old man were from an Owambo village to the east.

"We'll take you there tomorrow. A tour bus stops by twice a week. You can get a ride to Windhoek."

DeGroot's largest diamond store was in Windhoek. Blacksburg had no intention of showing his face there.

"But what are you doing in a ghost town cooking up a feast," he said to redirect the conversation. "Did you know that I was coming? What are you, witches?"

The girl snorted a bitter laugh. "If I were a witch, I'd turn myself into a cormorant and fly up to Algiers or Gibralter. I'd never come back."

Something in her vehemence intrigued Blacksburg, who was no stranger to restlessness and discontent. "Why do you stay?"

The bite in her voice was like that of a dust storm. "Do my uncle and I look rich to you? We live in a tiny village where the people raise cattle and goats. A good year means we get almost enough to eat. A bad year…"

Blacksburg saw no evidence of food shortage in the overflowing potije, but saw no need to point that out.

With greasy fingers, he gestured toward the forlorn remnants of the town. "This place, what is it? What *was* it?"

Aamu foraged deeper inside the backpack, bringing out a couple of Windhoek Lagers. "No ice," she said. "You drink it warm?"

He grinned. "I'll manage."

"Come walk with me. I'll tell you about the town." She took off at a brisk pace, high-tops churning up small clouds of sand, hips fetchingly asway.

Walking was the last thing he wanted to do, but Blacksburg wiped his hands on his trousers and headed up the dune behind her. It was a star dune, one of those sandy forms created by wind blowing from all directions, and it had Blacksburg's eye. Suddenly, with an agility and vigor that caught him by surprise, the old man lunged and seized his biceps in a fierce, one-handed grip, babbling wildly while pumping his mutilated hand.

"Nikishi!" he repeated urgently.

Blacksburg, a head taller and twenty kilos heavier, shook him off like a gnat.

"What's wrong with him?" he asked, catching up to Aamu.

"He's warning you about the evil spirits, the ones that take animal and human form. They like to call people by name to lure them out and kill them." She rolled her eyes. "My uncle's yampy. In our village, people laugh at him. Last week he grabbed a tourist lady's iPod and stomped it in the dirt, because he thought that evil spirits called his name from the earbuds." She took a swig of Lager, grimaced. "Can't stand this stuff warm."

She took off abruptly again, climbing nimbly while Blacksburg labored to keep up. They navigated a surreal dunescape, where decaying buildings pillaged by time and the unceasing wind stood like remnants of a bombing. The larger buildings, the ones the desert hadn't yet reclaimed entirely, indicated a degree of bourgeois prosperity that must have, in its heyday, seemed incongruous, perched as the town was on the edge of nothing, caught between the hostile Namib Desert and the pounding surf.

Aamu must have read his thoughts. "Forty years ago," she said, "this was a busy diamond town called Wilhelmskopf. Water was trucked in once a week. There was a hospital, a school, plans for a community center, even a bowling alley. Everybody lived here— Afrikaners, Germans, Damara and Owambo tribesmen."

"What happened?" Blacksburg said, although he could guess. Many of the smaller diamond towns had petered out by the middle of the previous century, eclipsed by the huge discovery of dia-monds in Oranjemund to the south. Of these, Kolmanskopf, a ghost town just outside Luderitz, and now a major tourist attraction, was the most well-known.

Aamu's answer shocked him. "In the late 60's, there were a lot of violent deaths, people found with their throats ripped out, torn apart by animals."

Blacksburg thought of the hyena that had menaced him on the beach. "Hyenas? Jackals?"

"Certainly. But fear spread that a nikishi and its offspring lived among these Wilhelmskopf people, changing into animal form at night to prey on them. A few superstitious fools panicked and turned on one another, accusing each other of sorcery. Eventually the town was abandoned. Can you believe such bosh? Now it belongs to the ghost crabs and the hyenas."

Blacksburg finished off his beer and flung the empty bottle across the threshold of a faded cobalt house with sand piled inside up to the turquoise wainscoting. Lizards stern and still as ancient gods stared down from a piano's gutted innards and perched atop a cracked and broken set of shelves. A shiver rustled his spine. He looked away. Down below, in the purpling twilight, he could see the old man reaching into the potije with his stick, stabbing slabs of bloody meat and flinging them out across the sand.

"Hey, he's throwing away the food!"

Aamu looked away, embarrassed. "I told you he's mad. Years ago, my uncle was here collecting drift wood after a storm when he was attacked by what he thought was a nikishi. He claims it called his name, and when he answered, it bit his fingers off and ate them while he begged for mercy. His mind hasn't been right since. He says the nikishi told him he must come here after every storm and make a spirit offering of meat and beer. To thank the nikishi for not eating all his fingers."

"Waste of good food," scoffed Blacksburg. "This transforming rot, you believe it, too?"

She looked affronted. "Of course not. I'm educated. I was sent to Swakopmund Girls' School. I studied German and English, some science, learned about the world. That's why it's hard for me to live in an Owambo village. I know something bigger's out there."

Blacksburg bit back a sarcastic jibe. What would someone who considered schooling in Swakopmund to be a cosmopolitan experience know about the wider world? This Owambo girl inhabited the most barren region of one of Africas least populated countries. In Blacksburg's view, she was a half-step above savagery.

"How did you and your uncle get here? Trek across the desert?"

She arched a kohl-black brow. "No, we rode our camels. Look!" Grabbing his hand, she pulled him along a passageway between a debris-strewn house and a derelict pavilion and laughed.

For a second he almost expected to see two tethered dromedaries. But it was a black Toyota Hilux, sand-caked and mud-splattered, that was angled on the slope behind the buildings.

Blacksburg gave the Hilux a covetous once-over.

"Nice-looking camel, this. Where do you gas it up?

"There's a petrol station for people going to the Etosha Pan about forty kilometers from here. And the safari companies that fly rich tourists in from Cape Town and Windhoek, they have way stations through the desert. Before he became ill, my uncle used to guide for one. That's how he got the jeep."

"I need to get to Angola," Blacksburg said. "What say I buy it from you?"

She eyed him scornfully, his ragged, salt-caked clothes, bare feet, disheveled hair. "And use what for money? Shark's teeth? Ghost crabs?"

"No need to mock me. Let me explain…" He felt a sudden, irresistible urge to touch her, as though some electrical energy pulsed inside her skin that his own body required for its sustenance. A few strands of hair had whipped loose from under the bandanna and he used that as an excuse, reaching out to tuck the hair back into place. To his dismay, she flinched as though he'd struck her.

"Sorry." He held up his hands, contrite. "Look, about the jeep, I can pay you well."

"The jeep isn't mine. It belongs to the village."

"Loan it to me then. Go with me as far as Luanda. After that, I'm on my own."

"But why should I help you?"

"A fair question that I'd expect of you, a graduate of Swakopmund Girl's School. Here, let me show you something." His smile was confident, but his stomach corkscrewed at what he was about to do—betting everything on this girl's gullibility and greed.

"You say you want to see the wider world. What if I told you, you could go anywhere you wanted and live like a movie star? What would you say to that?"

"I'd say maybe you swallowed too much seawater, Blacksburg. That you're as crazy as my uncle."

"Crazy, huh? Look here."

With a showman's flair, he reached inside his shirt, unhooked some clasps and pulled out a leather wallet protector. Unzipping it, he produced two plastic baggies.

"Cup your hands."

He unzipped one baggy and spilled into her palms a treasure trove of uncut stones. Even in the dimming light, they glittered like a fairy king's ransom. Aamu's breath caught. She cradled the diamonds as though she held a beating heart. Her voice, when she finally spoke, was a reverential whisper.

"*Ongeypi?* What are you, a jewel thief?"

"I'm a diamond dealer," he corrected brusquely. "I was transporting these to a buyer in Luanda."

He scooped the stones back into the baggy and opened up the next. These were a few museum quality pieces from DeGroot's private collection, several of which had been loaned out over the years to South African celebrities headed to New York and Cannes. Enjoying himself now, warming to his role, he plucked out a dazzling yellow diamond on a platinum chain. When he held it up, the sunlight put on a fire show, the facets blazed.

Aamu's dark eyes widened as he fastened it around her neck. In her inky irises were gold glints, a few grains of sand out of this Namib desert.

"It must be worth a fortune!"

"A bit more than a used jeep, I imagine. If you get me to Luanda, it's yours to sell. Do we have an arrangement?"

She frowned and chewed her lower lip. "What about my uncle? We can't let him go back to the village. Everyone will know I took the jeep and went off with an *oshilumbu.*"

Blacksburg cringed a little at being called 'white man," and looked down onto the beach, where the flames under the potije still danced. The old man paced a furious circle around the pot, raising his arms in wild supplication to whatever dark gods fueled his imagination. Silhouetted against the blood red sun, the mutilated hand looked like a misshapen club.

He took Aamu's hand and brought her fingers to his lips, tasting the meat and salt under the nails. "Right then, let's leave your uncle to his demons."

She laughed and pulled away, trotting along an alleyway between a half-dozen tumbled-down buildings, beckoning him to follow. When he caught up with her, she was framed in the empty doorway of a small stone house where, with a dancer's grace and the lewdness of a seasoned whore, she slowly peeled off the scarlet top and beige skirt.

"At the school in Swakopmund," she said, letting the blouse fall, "the priest said I was too wild—too hungry for excitement, for boys and beer, for freedom. He said it's wrong to want too much, that it's a sin to be too hungry." In the fading light, her black eyes made promises both heartfelt and indecent. "What about you, Blacksburg? Are you too hungry?"

For the first time in months, Blacksburg permitted himself a laugh of real delight. For a giddy moment, he actually romanced the notion of the two of them leaving Namibia together, a fantasy that Aamu's reckless passion only fueled.

She rode him with a mad abandon Blacksburg had experienced in only a few women—and then always prostitutes high on serious street drugs. If it was sex she'd been talking about when she asked him if it was a sin to be too hungry, then both were surely hell bound.

Their rutting was as much attack as ardor. Blacksburg, glorying in pain both given and received, rampantly devoured her. His mind stilled, past and future fell away, until all that remained was her thrashing body and feral moans, the sea-salt scent of her and the fierce and biting sweetness of her teeth and tongue. He drank in the musky sweat that ran between her breasts and down her prominent ribs and tangled his hands in the lush snarls of her dreaded mane, and when they rested, panting, sated, knew only that he wanted more.

Later, she spooned her limber body around his and chuckled in his ear, "Where will you go after you sell your diamonds? Don't lie to me. I know you're running. You wouldn't be so quick to trade a diamond for a jeep if you weren't a desperate man."

He was surprised when truth slipped out. "England, maybe. My mother always said we had relatives in Cornwall. I might go there."

"Cornwall." She pronounced the word like one uttering an incantation. "Maybe I'll go with you, Mr. Blacksburg."

And, for a few ecstatic moments, the idea of an impromptu adventure with this exotic woman moved Blacksburg deeply, fed into his desire to see himself as noble, heroic even, a survivor conquering the world by dint of ruthlessness and valor and self-will. The man he truly was, rich and powerful like DeGroot.

Later, as he drifted toward sleep, he saw filaments of moonlight slant through the empty window and spill across her face. She was lovely, even with the scar, but what mesmerized him, what he could not tear his eyes from, was how the yellow diamond glimmered around her dark as bitter chocolate throat.

Blacksburg dreamed about his mother. She stood outside the cottage in Cornwall before a running stream that he had seen in photographs. No longer gaunt, used-up and grey as he remembered her, but young and spirited. Her voice was high and lilting, clear as birdsong, infused with a calm serenity that in her life he'd never known her to possess. She called to him, not in the sharp haranguing style that had been her nature, but with a serenity and sweetness. Blacksburg almost loved her then, an alien emotion he had seldom felt for her in life, for this woman who had been an Afrikaner whore.

He woke up to the unholy cackling of hyenas and the taste of charred meat on his tongue.

Aamu was gone. For a second panic gripped him. But the diamonds, still secure in their plastic baggies, were undisturbed.

He pulled his clothes on and went outside into a night no longer flecked with stars, but murky, swimming with long, damp tresses of fog. He felt like a diver floating along the bottom of the sea, enveloped in an endless, choking school of pale grey, tubular fish.

Peering down onto the beach, he tried to spot the old man's fire and thought he glimpsed the orange flare of a few remaining embers, but no sooner had he started to descend the dune, than a low, contralto rumbling halted him. The sound came from a dozen yards away, where the fog-swathed columns of the pavilion jutted from the gloom like a ghostly Parthenon.

As he approached, he saw a nest of shadows, low to the ground, diverge and reconfigure, then caught a glimpse of a pink shirt and let himself exhale. The old man was asleep in the pavilion, the noise he'd heard undoubtedly was snoring. More movement— undulating, languid. He saw what looked to his uncertain eyes to be a wild crown of Medusa dreads whipped back and forth—a host of unwelcome images besieged his mind—but it was the hyena's glaring eyes and not its mane-like, ruffled tail that finally made the scene before him recognizable.

The hyena's eyes flashed, then vanished into the fog only to reappear a few feet away. The grumbling, growling intensified. Blacksburg, shocked motionless, counted five sets of eyes.

A frightful snarling commenced as two of the hyenas, snapping wildly, fought over a choice morsel. Bits of skin and gristle flew. Blacksburg glimpsed a ragged nub of bone attached to a scrap of pink cloth.

His breath caught in a stifled gasp. A hyena's head jerked up, and it raised its gory snout to test the wind.

Blacksburg shoved away from the pavilion and plunged head-long into the fog. He tried to remember the location of the jeep, thinking he might be able to lock himself inside, but the drifting mist cast a surreal opaqueness across the dunescape. Nothing that he saw was recognizable, the blank facades of the buildings as alike as weathered tombstones.

Ahead the murky outline of a crumbling two-story building floated up out of the fog. An empty window gaped. He hurled himself through it, tripped, and landed atop the piano he'd seen earlier—its ancient keys produced a wheezing bleat.

Behind him a sagging door led into a low hallway. The darkness was crypt black. He groped his way along, stumbling over obstacles—a plank, an empty drum of some kind—until he half fell into a small enclosed space, a storage room or closet. He huddled there, heart galloping, listening for the murderous whoops of the converging pack.

Blacksburg?

His own name sounded suddenly as alien and frightful as a curse. It floated on the hissing wind, at once as distant as the moon and close as his own breath, Aamu's voice or maybe just the scrape of windswept sand. He cleared his throat to answer and found that he was mute.

They call people by name to lure them out.

Although never in his life had Blacksburg been superstitious, now some atavistic fear crawled out of his reptilian brain and commandeered all else.

He tried to tell himself his frantic mind was playing tricks, but an older knowledge told him what he feared the most, that what called to him was no hyena but a shape shifter, a nikishi, that would split him open like the old man, from groin to sternum and feed while he lay dying.

Blacksburg!

The piano suddenly coughed out a great, discordant cacophony, as though four clawed feet had leaped onto the keyboard and bounded off.

The door he'd come through creaked, and then a single animal sent forth its infernal wail into the hollow building. At once other hyenas, some inside, others beyond the walls, took up the ungodly cry.

Knowing he was seconds from being found and trapped, he bolted from his hiding place, raced up the hallway and hurled himself through a window that was partially intact, crashing to the sand amidst a biting drizzle of shattered glass.

Without pause, he got up and pounded down the duneface, arms pinwheeling, skidding wildly.

The hyenas converged around him.

The largest, boldest of the beasts feinted once before going for his throat. Its teeth snagged his shirt, taking with the fabric a strip of flesh from Blacksburg's ribs. He fell to one knee, one arm up to guard his jugular, the other to protect the pouch across his chest—even knowing, beyond all doubt, that both were lost to him.

The ecstatic yips of the hyenas were suddenly drowned out by the roar of an approaching motor. The Hilux teetered at the top of the dune, then careened straight down the face, sand spewing out behind the tires, high beams punching through the fog. It slammed onto beach, suspension screaming, bounced off the ground, and veered toward the hyenas. The pack scattered. Blacksburg staggered to his feet, as the jeep skidded to a halt beside him.

"Get in!"

Aamu flung the door wide, and Blacksburg launched himself inside, the jeep lurching into motion while his legs still dangled out the door. A hyena leaped, jaws snapping. He screamed and kicked out. The hyena twisted in mid-air and fell away. Blacksburg muscled the door closed.

Aamu gunned the engine and the jeep tore away through the fog.

She drove like a witch, outdistancing the pack by many miles, before she turned to Blacksburg and said gravely, "I looked for you on foot at first. I called your name. I knew you were close by, but you didn't answer."

"I didn't hear you," Blacksburg said, shame making him curt, resentful of her. They both knew he'd been afraid to answer, that in that desperate moment, rationality had failed him. He'd believed the hyena pack to be nikishis and one of them was mimicking her voice. He was a fool and a coward, just as all along he knew his boss DeGroot had judged him privately to be. In that moment, when he felt as though she'd seen into his soul and found him wanting, he made a harsh decision.

He told her to stop the vehicle and switch places. He would drive.

«« — »»

Later, when the mid-day sun was high and blazingly hot, Blacksburg decided they'd come far enough. He'd been driving for hours while Aamu slept. Now he halted the Hilux in the middle of a sun-blasted stretch of desert bleak and desolate as a medieval rendition of hell, shook her by the shoulder, and said, "Get out."

She sat up, blinking groggily. "What…what are you talking about?"

"It's simple. End of the line. Get out."

"I don't understand." She looked around at the miles of barren, retina-searing whiteness. "Is this a joke?"

He barked a bitter laugh. "Did you really think I was taking you with me? I can get to Angola on my own."

"But…I'll die out here."

"Yes, I imagine so."

For a woman contemplating her very short future, she appeared strangely unmoved. "But we are going to Luanda."

"One of us. Not you." He held his hand out. "And by the way, I want my diamond back."

"Then take it and be damned!" Before Blacksburg could stop her, she yanked the diamond from around her neck and hurled it out the window as casually as if she were discarding a wad of gum.

He swore and struck her across the head. The bandanna came

158

off. He saw the dried blood in her hair, the fresh blood flowing from the wound at the top of her ear. He stared at his hand, where her blood stained it.

She dragged a finger pensively along the scar that ran along her cheek. "You know how I got this? My uncle cut me with a knife. But I was merciful and let him live. Last night I was merciful again. I killed him before I fed his flesh to the hyenas."

Using sheer force of will, Blacksburg hauled himself back from the brink of panic. "You think you scare me? You're crazier than your uncle was. If I can kick my old boss into the ocean when he was trying to climb into the lifeboat, I can damn sure get rid of you. Now get the hell out of my jeep."

She didn't budge. Wild hunger, wanton and insatiable, raged in her eyes. Her lips curled in a soulless smile. "Yesterday I could have killed you on the beach, but I was curious about what kind of man you were, about what was in your heart. Now I know. And now, you know me."

Her voice was lush with malice. Her face, as she commenced her changing, was radiant with cruelty.

"See me as I am," shrilled the nikishi.

At once, her slashing teeth cleaved the soft, white folds of his belly. She thrust her muzzle inside the wound, foraging for what was tastiest. The salty entrails were gobbled first, then the tender meat inside the bones, his life devoured in agonizing increments.

Hours later, a hyena pup following a set of jeep tracks came across a human skull. It seized the trophy in its strong young jaws and headed back to its den where it could gnaw the prize at leisure.

going north

"Why do you want to go to the North Pole?" asked Aunt Gish as she and Pruitt waited in line at the Galleria Mall to see Santa Claus.

Pruitt shrugged, wishing she'd never said anything about the North Pole. She didn't know if she could trust Aunt Gish with something so important. In her seven years, Pruitt had learned not to trust anyone, to play along with what the adults wanted when she had to, but better yet, to stay out of their way.

Pruitt wasn't even sure if it was okay to talk to Santa, but she figured she had to take the chance. Even a mall Santa was more than just an ordinary grown-up. He was someone who might be able to help her.

The Galleria Mall in Fort Lauderdale was crowded with shoppers, adults carrying packages and scurrying around so frantically they reminded Pruitt of roaches carrying off crumbs when you turned on the light in the kitchen at night, and little kids, some excited, some shy, one or two bawling like babies, who were standing in line to see Santa.

Pruitt Nelson and her Aunt Gish were near the middle of a line that stretched from Santa's big, star-dusted throne all the way to the WalMart at the end of the mall. They'd been waiting almost an hour already and Pruitt was worried: was Aunt Gish going to become impatient and drag her out of there before she had a chance to talk to Santa? Especially since Aunt Gish hadn't even gone to the ladies' room to do a joint or a line or anything. Neither Miriam nor Daddy could have put up with the Mall for five minutes without a smoke or a snort.

Aunt Gish seemed to be doing just fine, though, and Pruitt was grateful, if a little surprised. She'd already heard Daddy telling Miriam that Aunt Gish was crazy, that the reason she hadn't come

161

to Mom's funeral two years ago was that she was locked up in the loony bin in New York City after getting hysterical and threatening to shoot herself right there in the principal's office of the school where she used to teach second grade.

The line inched forward. Pruitt could see the shine on Santa's nose, the fake snow on his knee-high black boots. *Help me*, she thought. *Please help me*.

"It's real cold at the North Pole," Aunt Gish said, long after Pruitt had assumed the subject was dropped. "Why would you want to leave Florida, where it's warm and sunny, to go live in a place that's so cold?"

"Because I *hate* it here," said Pruitt, crowding up behind a fat toddler with a lollipop stick protruding from his mouth like a very thick hypodermic syringe. "I hate the Palmetto bugs and the hot weather, and I hate…" Pruitt started to say "Daddy and Kenny and Miriam" but decided against it. Aunt Gish was Momma's older sister, after all, and she might repeat what Pruitt was getting ready to say, and Pruitt might get smacked around.

"And what makes you think the North Pole would be better?"

But Pruitt didn't answer. She just clamped her lips shut tight against her teeth and waited while the line crept forward, inch by inch, toward Santa.

Pruitt knew perfectly well that this red-suited, lumpy-looking man with the white beard and the crinkly brown eyes wasn't the real, the one and only, Santa Claus. She'd already seen one Santa ringing a bell next to a kettle outside the Sears store on Federal Highway and still another waiting at a bus stop, leaning up against a lamppost, looking puffy-eyed and hung over. She figured, however, that these assistant Santa's probably reported back to the *real* one at the North Pole and that they probably filed their information (which Pruitt imagined like a kind of police report) with the Big Man himself.

So when she was settled on Santa's lap and he asked her what she wanted most for Christmas, Pruitt told him, and Santa laughed and said that wasn't possible and Pruitt, who didn't think what she'd asked for was the least bit funny, punched Santa in the eye with her small, knobby, fist and then burst into frustrated howls.

"Are you gonna beat the crap out of me?" asked Pruitt as she and Aunt Gish drove out Sunrise Boulevard toward the subdivision in Lake of the Pines where she lived with her father and his girl-friend Miriam. It was the first time that she'd spoken since the disaster with Santa Claus, when Aunt Gish had come swooping down like an enraged falcon and snatched Pruitt away, demanding to know what Santa had said or done to so distress the child.

"No, of course, I'm not going to beat you," Aunt Gish said. "Why would you ask such a thing?"

"When I'm bad, Miriam always says she's gonna beat the crap out of me and that she wishes I was dead."

Aunt Gish fumbled in her purse on the seat between her and Pruitt, pulled out a Bic and a pack of Winstons, and lit a cigarette. Pruitt noticed that her fingernails were so badly bitten they looked red and infected, and her hands were trembling. She figured that must be because Aunt Gish hadn't gone to the ladies room to smoke or snort or inject anything during the whole time that she and Pruitt were out.

"Pruitt, I need to ask you something. When you hit Santa Claus, was it because he did something to you? Did he touch you where he shouldn't have? Your private parts, I mean."

"Between my legs?" asked Pruitt.

"That's right."

"You mean the way Daddy and Kenny touch me when Miriam's not around?"

A delivery van was backing out of the driveway of a Furniture Warehouse and Aunt Gish almost broadsided it, swerving out of the way just at the last second and making the tires of her Plymouth squeal. She pulled into the parking lot of a convenience store at the next corner and shut the motor off.

"What do you mean, Pruitt? Who's Kenny? What do he and your Daddy do?"

Pruitt realized that she'd said too much, but Aunt Gish kept asking questions, so finally Pruitt told her a little bit, that Kenny was one of Daddy's customers who came around a couple of times a week with lots of cash, but she left some things out because Aunt Gish got very white and started biting on her lower lip and a drop of blood leaked out that she didn't even seem to feel. Pruitt thought what Aunt Gish probably needed was a very stiff drink, as Miriam would say, but she was scared to suggest it.

"Santa didn't hurt me like Daddy and Kenny do," said Pruitt, deciding it was time to change the subject. "I hit him 'cause he laughed at me when I said I wanted to go to the North Pole."

Aunt Gish poked at her weepy eyes with a Kleenex and lit another cigarette, holding it outside the window so the smoke didn't get in the car.

"You want to go to the North Pole really bad, don't you?"

"Yeah," said Pruitt. "I have to."

Aunt Gish started up the motor again. "It's still light. We can't go to the North Pole, but do you want to go to the beach?"

"What about Daddy and Miriam?"

"Fuck 'em," said Aunt Gish.

Pruitt was impressed that her geeky-looking aunt would say such a thing and thought maybe she'd been wrong to think Aunt Gish was just a nerd and a weirdo. It was an easy mistake, though. Aunt Gish was enormously fat and looked frumpy and old in a candy cane blouse which was meant to look Christmasy, but really just looked dumb, and a brown polyester skirt and ugly brown shoes, and her hair (which was the same color as the shoes except for a thick streak of white at the top) tucked up like a huge mushroom that was sprouting out of the top of her head. She'd seen Miriam snicker when Aunt Gish first waddled in the front door and Daddy had muttered to Miriam that Aunt Gish's clothes must be "nuthouse chic" and that maybe it was the shock treatments that had caused part of her hair to go white.

"Yeah, fuck 'em," whispered Pruitt under her breath, and if Aunt Gish heard, she pretended not to.

They drove over one of the bridges crossing the Intercoastal Waterway and parked in the lot of a motel across the street from the ocean. Aunt Gish took off her clunky shoes and her hose and Pruitt took off her Keds and they walked down onto the sand, which was still warm even though the sun was now almost down, the light slanting off the waves so fiercely that it looked like someone had tossed a million silver coins onto the water.

Aunt Gish was very quiet and after a while, Pruitt looked up and said, "Are you mad at me?"

Aunt Gish looked surprised. "Of course not. Why would you think that?"

"You're crying."

"Because I'm sad," said Aunt Gish, "and I'm angry. Oh, Pruitt, I'm so angry I could...I'm just very angry, but not at you. You haven't done anything."

They continued up the beach together, passing beneath a pier where people were casting poles off into the silvery water and pelicans swooped and rose against the glitter of the sea. At one point Aunt Gish reached to take Pruitt's hand and lead her around a jellyfish, but Pruitt pulled her hand away and stepped around the jellyfish herself. She didn't want to hold hands with Aunt Gish or anyone else. It made her feel trapped, like her hand was being molded into a part of the adult's body and no longer belonged to her. Of all the scary feelings that Pruitt had known in her short life, the feeling of not belonging to herself was the scariest of all.

After they'd walked in silence for a while, Pruitt got her nerve up to ask the question she'd been wondering about ever since Daddy first told her that Momma had had an older sister who'd moved to Florida and bought a house trailer in Delray Beach.

"Daddy says you were locked up in a place for crazy people in New York. Were you *really*? Or was Daddy just making it up because he doesn't like you?"

Aunt Gish laughed and almost reached for Pruitt's hand. Then she must have remembered that this was something Pruitt didn't seem to like, and she let her hand fall back by her side.

"Your Daddy's right. I had what they used to call a nervous breakdown, but really that just means I cried all the time and couldn't eat or sleep or work and I didn't want to live."

Pruitt remembered when her mother was alive and acted that way every time she couldn't get her crack. She'd gone out one night, very late, leaving Pruitt with her father, and she never came back. There'd been a stabbing, said the policeman who came to the door the next day. Something about a drug deal gone bad that Pruitt's mother got in the middle of.

"When you didn't want to live no more, was it because you couldn't get drugs?" asked Pruitt, kicking at what looked like long strands of foamy spit hawked up by the ocean.

"No, nothing like that." Aunt Gish said. "I used to teach school, and a few years ago there was a little boy in my class, a wonderful little boy, named Timmy Anderson, and he kept coming to school with bruises so I called the people who're supposed to look out for children like Timmy and said I thought someone was hurting him. Someone in his home. But those people were very overworked and they didn't really have time to visit Timmy's house more than once and, well, one of his parents beat Timmy very badly soon after that and he died. And then a year later there was a little girl named Angie Myers and she had blood in her underpants one day, and I reported it to the same people who were supposed to help Timmy and you know what, they were still really busy, and somebody misplaced Angie's file and one day she didn't come to school at all and..."

"She got killed, didn't she?"

"Oh, honey, I'm sorry. I shouldn't be telling you such awful things. It's just that, after Angie, that was when I didn't want to live anymore. It just seemed like there wasn't any point, like children were dying right under my nose and all I was doing was making stupid phone calls. I felt so bad, I bought a gun and decided to shoot myself. But then I thought, maybe I wasn't ready to die, maybe that was too easy a solution, so I went to a hospital for a while and then when I got better, I decided to come down here to Florida. Take what they call early retirement. Because I couldn't stand to see anymore Timmy's or Angie's. I just thought it would kill me to see anything like that again."

"Come to the North Pole with me."

"Why the North Pole, honey?"

"It's safe there," said Pruitt, kicking the water ahead of her in long silver arcs. "It's cold and quiet and empty so you can just walk for miles and not run into anybody else. And the sun shines and the ice sparkles all the time and it's...safe."

She kicked at the water. A long time ago, back when her mother was still alive, she remembered seeing a cartoon about a pair of children who went to the North Pole to visit Santa. She remembered cliffs of white ice rising straight up into a cold, sunny sky and herds of reindeer moving across frozen, empty plains where you could run forever and no one would ever see you or hear you or hurt you or cause you pain, and when Daddy or Kenny were hurting her or when Miriam was screaming at her, she would go to that cold, clear place of endless, empty space and she would roam among the ice castles and watch the polar bears play and she would be safe, so safe…and free…and she would belong to herself.

"The North Pole is a long way off," Aunt Gish was saying. "You'd need a map to get there."

"No I won't," said Pruitt and she told Aunt Gish her plan.

《《——》》

The beach was brown with shadows, the horizon just a purple streak, like grape jelly smeared over silk, when Aunt Gish said they'd better turn back.

"I could stay with you at your trailer tonight," Pruitt said and Aunt Gish told a deep breath and said, "Oh, honey, I wish you could. But your Dad and Miriam were expecting us back a long time ago. I have to take you home now."

"Please?" said Pruitt. "Don't make me go back there."

"I can't," Aunt Gish said. "I'm sorry, Pruitt, I can't help you. I can't do anything at all."

She shook another cigarette out of the pack, but her hands were shaking so badly now she couldn't light it and finally she said a long string of bad words and threw the cigarette into the sea.

《《——》》

The pink house where Pruitt lived was in the middle of a block of two-story stucco houses in various pastel shades. All the houses had chimneys, built more for looks than for function, but useful during South Florida's occasional winter cold snaps. Pruitt's house had the additional decoration of a trellis extending up one side of the house to roof level. When Pruitt's mother was alive the trellis had been covered with morning glory vines. Now it resembled empty scaffolding, badly worn and in need of a paint job.

A man was knocking on the front door when Aunt Gish and Pruitt drove up. Pruitt's heart sank as she recognized Kenny.

He was darkly tanned with very short, baby fine blond hair and skin the color and texture of alligator hide, and he drove an expensive car with New Jersey license plates. His fingers were long and slender and Pruitt hated the tickly, spidery way they crept over her body.

"That's Kenny," Pruitt whispered. "The one who touches me."

When Kenny saw Pruitt and Aunt Gish approaching, he stared at Pruitt, at her bare feet, the wet legs of her jeans, and a very pale, sickly glow seemed to shine behind the dark brown of his tan that reminded Pruitt of the yellow eyes in a battery-powered triceratops she'd once seen.

Aunt Gish guided Pruitt ahead of her as if they were crossing a very dangerous intersection.

"Pretty kid," Kenny said to Aunt Gish as they came up on the porch, although his eyes never left Pruitt. "Gonna be a real looker when she fills out a little."

The silence following that remark was the loudest Pruitt had ever heard.

Kenny reached down as if to ruffle Pruitt's hair.

Aunt Gish snatched Pruitt backward out of his reach. She put her red, fatty face an inch away from Kenny's tanned, plastic-looking skin and said, in a voice so close to a whisper that Pruitt could barely hear her, "You ever lay a hand on this child again and you'll be in prison paying for your drugs with blowjobs, you fucking pervert."

Kenny took a step back, almost stumbling off the top step of the porch, just as Pruitt's father opened the door. He was a short, wiry man with a boxer's build and blue eyes iced over with perpetual rage.

"Who is this bitch?" Kenny hissed, looking at Aunt Gish. "What does she mean calling me a pervert and accusing me of buying drugs? Who the hell *is* she?"

Pruitt's father apologized to Kenny, who smirked and went inside the house. Then he started screaming at Aunt Gish.

"Get out of here! Go back to New York or the funny farm or wherever the hell you wanna go, but don't you ever come back here, you fat, fucked up cunt." He smacked Aunt Gish hard across the face and she fell backward onto the grass with a loud thump. "Don't you come round here makin' trouble for me, insultin' my friends. You ain't no family of mine. Now get the fuck outa here! Go!"

Pruitt got a glimpse of Aunt Gish before Daddy shoved her ahead of him into the house. She was getting slowly to her feet and her candy cane blouse was all streaked with dirt and her eyes looked like little black dots sunken into the centers of soft, doughy rolls with a splotch of clown red on each cheek.

"Don't make her go" Pruitt said, "she didn't do anything."

Daddy slapped Pruitt in the side of the head and then picked her up off the floor and slapped her again and gave her a kick in the butt for good measure.

"Get your ass upstairs and outa my sight. You'll prob'ly grow up to be as crazy as she is."

Pruitt ran upstairs and threw herself across the bed and cried and after she finished crying she prayed for help. She prayed for Christmas Eve to come and she prayed to Santa Claus.

On Christmas Eve, Pruitt was allowed to play outside until it got dark, then Miriam called her inside and fed her pizza and orange juice in the kitchen.

Around nine o'clock Kenny came over with a couple of bottles and Pruitt went up to bed. "I'll be up later," Daddy said and gave her a wink, and Pruitt felt her stomach constrict into a sharp little fist.

In her room, she opened the window wide and climbed out onto the ledge. The trellis, which was only a few inches away, suddenly looked very distant, the wooden slats rickety and spindly. Pruitt got a foothold and then grabbed it with her hands. The wood made cracking sounds, but it held her weight, and she put the other leg up and started to climb.

Climbing up to the roof wasn't so bad. Getting over the edge was the hard part. She had to get her feet up as high on the trellis as possible and then throw herself forward onto the roof and kind of snake-shimmy onto the roof and then she had to take care to avoid the skylight that looked down over the living room.

But finally she made it to the very top and sat with her back against the chimney, listening to the cars pass on the street below, waiting. The air was warm and muggy, humid with the promise of rain. Presently Pruitt's head lolled and she slept and dreamed...of ice palaces and bright, clean cold.

Then Santa Claus was bending down beside her. Ice crystals gleamed in his beard and frost spilled from his mouth in white puffs. Behind him she could see the dark outlines of reindeer, blowing steam from their nostrils and stamping their hooves.

"Take me with you," said Pruitt. "Please."

Santa Claus lifted her up in his arms and set her down inside the sleigh. Then there was a sharp jerk and the scraping of deer hooves on tiles and the sleigh lifted off. Pruitt leaned out and saw the house getting smaller and smaller, all the bad people and memories receding, and she screamed with joy and excitement.

She screamed...and woke up. The night seemed darker now, starless. Pruitt felt the soft stirrings of panic. She wondered if Santa Claus had come and gone already, if she'd missed her one chance to talk to him.

Downstairs she could hear voices—peering cautiously through the skylight she saw Daddy and Miriam and Kenny. They were gathered around the card table playing poker. A bottle of bourbon was in the center of the table and Miriam, for some reason, had taken off her t-shirt and bra and jeans and was sitting there stark naked, but neither Daddy nor Kenny seemed to notice this. They just kept on playing cards.

From below, Pruitt heard heavy footsteps. She looked up the block and was astonished to see Santa Claus approaching. He wasn't riding in his sleigh at all. He wasn't landing on the roof like he was supposed to. His pack was slung over his shoulder. It looked lumpy and not very full. Once Santa glanced up, almost like he was looking at the roof, and Pruitt waved her hand wildly—*up here*—but he didn't seem to see.

When he got closer, Santa turned and marched straight up the walk. Pruitt heard the doorbell chime. She couldn't believe it.

Santa was ringing the bell and coming in the front door. He had it all wrong. He'd fucked up. Santa Claus had fucked up!

Angry tears over spilled Pruitt's eyes. Frantically she lowered herself over the edge of the roof and started to climb down the trellis.

She heard Daddy answer the door. His voice was slurred and he had that don't-fuck-with-me growl to it, but then he shouted back into the house to Kenny and Miriam, "Hey look what the fuck we got here! Santa Claus says we won some kinda Christmas lottery. Hey, Miriam, did you…?"

The popping started just about the time Pruitt reached the window and was climbing back into her room. She thought: Daddy and Kenny are killing Santa Claus, and then she was running down the hall toward the stairs, and she heard the popping sounds again and again and then everything got very still.

The first one she saw was Miriam, leaning up against the big screen TV Her eyes were wide open, but in place of her mouth was a red, running hole, and a bib of blood was spreading slowly across her bare breasts and stomach. Daddy lay sprawled a few feet away in the hall. The front of his forehead was missing, and gobs of yellow and grey muck, like pudding, could be seen oozing between the bone.

Pruitt's mouth dropped open and she uttered a soundless "O," but she felt neither grief nor fear, just a strange, fluttery sickness in her stomach.

She moved on into the kitchen, where Kenny lay on this back with three bullet holes going up his abdomen like buttons. A cigarette was still between his fingers but it had burned all the way down and the flesh of his fingers was smoking. He didn't move.

From the bathroom, Pruitt heard the sound of someone throwing up and a toilet flushing. She tried to run, but her legs felt wobbly, like she'd already run a hundred miles. Then Santa came out of the bathroom wiping his beard and carrying what Pruitt recognized to be a Glock .9mm.

"Don't be afraid," said Santa, but even before she heard the voice, Pruitt recognized the small white hands with the fingernails chewed down into the quick. "It's okay, honey, they can't hurt you anymore."

Aunt Gish tucked the pistol back into her sack, which was stuffed with what looked like foam rubber. "Come with me?," she said.

Pruitt looked at the bloody bodies all around her and at Santa/Aunt Gish and she knew Daddy'd been right about one thing, that Aunt Gish was crazy as hell, but maybe that was okay, maybe crazy was the best way anybody could be.

Aunt Gish squatted down and looked into Pruitt's face.

"Listen to me, honey, listen hard. I killed three people tonight, so the police will be looking for me. For you, too, because they'll want to protect you from me. If they find us, they'll take care of you, they'll find a family for you to live with, but they won't let you see me anymore. You'll have to find your way to the North Pole alone. Do you think you can do that?"

Pruitt thought about the dangers and possibilities ahead: the chance to find a place to be free, to be safe, a place to belong to herself.

She reached up and took Aunt Gish's hand.

They left the house and walked up the street together and around the corner to where Aunt Gish had hidden the Plymouth behind some dumpsters.

"It's not easy getting to the North Pole," said Aunt Gish. "It may take years and years and all your courage. Not many people get there. I didn't, Pruitt, I never did, but I want you to have a chance."

Pruitt nodded, believing that it could be done, knowing that, with Aunt Gish or without her, she would find her way to the North Pole someday, even if she had to make the map herself.

the high and mighty

and me

I'm over the speed limit by 25 mph, heading west on Highway 55 between McComb and Brookhaven, Mississippi, when the clock on the dashboard clicks over to 12:00 a.m. on the first of July. I spit out a curse. Another day gone, another four hundred miles in the rearview mirror, stopping at fireworks outlets and stands, talking to vendors and customers, keeping an eye on the news for stories about young boys gone missing. And nothing to show for it besides a head-banging hangover from too many Jack Daniels swigged down at a bar outside Panama City last night.

Two more days until the 4th of July. If I don't find the man who calls himself Captain KablAM by then, it'll be another year before I get my next chance.

My palms slide on the steering wheel, swampy with sweat, and I can feel a tiny heartbeat in my forehead where a wormy blue vein pulses between my hairline and temple.

A beer would taste great, but now's not the time.

My cell phone warbles, and it's Charmaine again, so I don't answer. I know she wants reassurance that I am where I'm supposed to be, but I can't talk to her now. I've told her I'm taking my usual boys-only trout float on the Little Red River in Arkansas. What she suspects (I'm pretty sure) is that I'm off on a once-a-year fuckfest with some sex-starved, marriage-bored hotty I met on Cheaters.com or some such.

I hate lying to Charmaine, but there's no other way. The truth about what I do in the days leading up to the 4th of July would seem so bizarre to her, so out of character for her normally staid, stick-in-the-mud, high school English teacher husband, it would make the Internet hotty look like a reasonable choice by comparison.

If my childhood buddy Jimmy Limbo were alive, he'd understand why I'm doing this, but that's the whole point—he isn't.

Off to my right a sign that looks like it was constructed from parts of a busted-up picket fence flashes by: TONY'S FIRE-WORKS! OPEN 24/7! EIGHTEEN MILES AHEAD!

As I stomp the accelerator, I think back to the last time I saw Jimmy Limbo alive.

A high point of summer for Jimmy and me was the week leading up to July 4th, when the rumpled old man with the walrus mustache who called himself Captain KablAM would set up his big green and white tent on a spit of land by Lake Pontchartrain. His prices were low, with discounts for kids, and if you spent $30 bucks, he'd throw in a t-shirt with KablAM! in bright red on the back. He sold all you needed to put on your own super fireworks show—mortar tubes in all sizes, punks for lighting them, igniter cords, and visco and Chinese fuses.

Come the night of the 4th, he'd put on a pyrotechnic display of his own, using some of his unsold stock. Jimmy and I would sit on the ground with the other kids or up on the hood of an older guy's car, sucking down beers I'd filched from the 7-Eleven, marveling at the spectacle of all that razzle-dazzle and din as the Captain launched volleys of shrieking glitter-rockets and dazzling multiple explosions of fountains. For the finale, he'd fire off a blistering barrage of the expensive, heavy-duty explosives called High and Mightys, whose massive reports at close range punched the breath out of me and made my ears sing. How he could afford to literally blow up so much of his inventory, I never did know, but what an eye-popping spectacle it was!

Jimmy and I thought that being a fireworks vender, traveling from town to town blowing stuff up like Captain KablAM did, must be the world's coolest job.

Like most of the kids, though, behind his back, Jimmy and I made fun of the Captain, his silly name with the comic book spelling, his bushy, toilet-brush mustache. We mocked his gruff Cajun accent (which we compared to marbles rolling around in a pan), and we'd snigger whenever he bent over, his baggy brown pants sliding down to display an altogether hilarious wedge of hairy butt crack. This was long before the days when this was in style— Captain KablAM was ahead of his time.

For all our laughter, however, it was just boyish bravado. Deep down I was scared of the Captain, and I think Jimmy was, too— never more so than on that sweltering evening when the last customers had drifted away and the Captain had gotten tired of gonging his cow bell out by the road to try to bring people in, but there was still too much light for setting off fireworks. The Captain plopped down in a lawn chair, his KablAM t-shirt rolling up over his ponderous gut. He took a long pull from the flask he kept in his back pocket, and said, "You boys know who invented fireworks, no?"

At thirteen ignorance isn't something you readily admit to, so Jimmy and I remained silent.

"Why the Chinks did," he growled. "They don't teach that in school?" He shook his big head in dismay at the gaps in our education. "You know *why* they invented them, no?"

Except for the buzz of mosquitoes and the glug of bullfrogs down by the water, the evening was pin drop still. The Captain lowered his voice as though getting ready to divulge a dangerous truth. "Why, to scare off demons, of course! Mogui they're called in Chink lingo." He pronounced it 'maw gwey.' "Like tapeworms they are, wriggling around in your head, plantin' evil ideas. Dem Chinks first tried to get rid of the mogui by burning green bamboo that crackles and pops, but the mogui just howled with laughter. So the Chinks stirred gunpowder into the mix to make a helluva hullabaloo, and dat's how we come to have firecrackers."

Jimmy, who was usually so quiet you'd forget he was there, suddenly piped up, "You been to China, Captain? You seen them mogui?"

The Captain leaned closer, waggling the five fingers on his right hand and the three that remained on his left. "Sure I have! Been to Shanghai and Fuzhou and all dem little no-name villages in between where they make firecrackers the traditional way—wrap the powder in paper rolls skinny as chopsticks and tie 'em together in chains half a mile long. Dem tings go off, it sounds like the Battle of Xiaoting! You watch close when they explode, you can see the mogui flyin' back to hell where dey come from. They never fly in straight lines, either—dem evil spirits are afraid of straight lines, that's why the Chinks build their roads crooked—they fly in spirals and corkscrews and look for someplace to hide—" He tapped his temple, shaking loose a droplet of sweat that rolled down to his jaw and dripped onto the grass. "—dat's when they start lookin' to find a way into your head!"

Goose bumps rippled up my arms when he said that.

I glanced at Jimmy and saw, to my irritation, that he was lapping this up, his blue eyes big as dimes. I wanted to ask him where he thought somebody like the Captain would get money to travel to China and learn about demons, for Christ's sake—did Jimmy think he made millions of dollars selling this shit?—but I also knew from observing the adults in my life, that people will believe just about anything if they want to badly enough, no matter how it flies in the face of what deep in their hearts they know to be true.

"How them mogui decide whose head to live in?" Jimmy asked, taking it all so seriously that I wanted to punch him.

A few seconds ticked by while the Captain's expression mimed grave consideration of the question. Finally he said, "Dem mogui can tell when a man wants to do bad tings. They *know* when he's weak."

The Captain's small, squinty eyes roved the purpling dusk over the lake. I couldn't tell if he was looking for mosquitoes or mogui or what, but at that moment, I sensed something important, something I filed away deep within me as truth: the Captain was talking about *himself,* no one else. It was *his* brain that festered with evil, and whether that meant it was mogui infesting his head or just his own wicked nature, I figured it didn't much matter.

I looked at Jimmy, who was doing his part to scare off the mogui by lighting a sparkler and spinning it. "C'mon, let's get out of here!"

"What, Marcus, you scared of them mogui?" Jimmy said, the red sparks shooting off into the dark.

"I tink he is," said the Captain. "I tink he scared the mogui want *him.*" He looked directly at me, baring his overlapping gray teeth in what passed for a grin, making me feel he was stripping me bare— seeing not just a shy, scrawny kid, but the murky secrets, the half-formed inclinations of the man I would someday be.

And even though I knew I was too old to believe in demons, my throat went dry and my stomach clenched. I pictured the mogui like tiny winged worms, skinny as shoelaces, flying in zigzags as they tried to nest in your hair or burrow through your skull. Without thinking, I reached up and probed my head for suspicious fissures, wondering if even now vicious mogui, tiny as nits, might be lurking there and if they were, how would I know until I did something terrible?

I jumped to my feet. "Fucking bullshit, that's what this is!"

The Captain grunted a laugh, heaved his bulk up from the chair and leaned into me, so close that I could smell the bourbon on his breath and the Ben Gay that he rubbed on his knees. He jabbed my forehead with the boney nub of his missing index finger—poke-poke between my eyes. I felt something pass between us, some-thing that later I would remember as both repugnant and seductive, like the nasty cover of a porno mag glimpsed in a stranger's hands on a street corner, repulsive and shameful and utterly alluring. A dark tickle streamed from that maimed hand into me, and a red thread of pain and excitement pinged its way up my spine. I could feel my face turning crimson while something else, much worse than a blush, was happening lower down.

The Captain's voice was a gritty whisper, meant just for me. "Dem mogui know what you want, boy. I do, too. I can smell it on you."

My hands fisted with fury. I wanted to smash in his leering, lop-sided old face. How could he know anything about me, when I barely even knew myself? My longings were blurry and furtive, hidden even from me.

My anger, however, was murderously clear.

"Fuck you!" I shouted and shoved him away as Jimmy gasped in horror. Jimmy still idolized the Captain, thought he was some kind'a traveling magician who knew about foreign countries and dark scary stuff, but I knew different now. I saw him then for what he was, a fucked up old freak, and I hated him with something I'd never experienced before, a violent rage and the itch to inflict harm that can only be provoked by abject humiliation. Even now, when the mutilated finger was no longer touching my skin, that black tingle in my forehead reverberated. Liquid, like an oily filth, seemed to be filling my skull. I backed away from the Captain, then I started to run. I yelled out, "C'mon, Jimmy!" thinking he'd follow me like he always did, but I never looked back to check. By the time I stopped running, I was already half-way back home.

And Jimmy was nowhere in sight.

«« —»»

TONY'S FIREWORKS EMPORIUM turns out to be in a cinderblock roadhouse that must have been a low-rent drinking establishment at one time. Beer decals cover the grimy windows and a jukebox with an Out of Order sign taped to the front stands just inside the doors. The proprietor blows onion breath in my face and tries to sell me on attending a Demo Show tomorrow night. "Bring the kids, learn 'em how to use firecrackers without blowing off a hand or a finger!" He barely listens as I describe the Captain, but as I'm leaving, he cups his crotch like a lost friend and says, "Hold on there, I did see this t-shirt might interest you."

"A t-shirt?" I figure he's trying to sell me some crap, and when he plops a meaty paw on my shoulder, I have to fight the knee-jerk reaction to deck him. "Last year, 'bout this time," he goes on, oblivious to how close he just came to spitting out teeth, "my grandkids was visiting from Mobile. Brats the bunch of 'em, but I love 'em to death. Oldest boy come in here wearin' a shirt's got KablAM! on the front. Said he bought it at a tent a few exits up. Brolin Road, I think it was. Pissed me the hell off him spending his money when I'd'a gave him one 'a my awesome "It's Blow Shit Up Day" t-shirts for free!

"You wanna see one? I got 'em in all colors and sizes," he says, rummaging around under the counter as I bolt out the door.

Exits flash past on 55 South, a gaudy smear of fast food outlets, gas stations and mini-marts until finally, near a sprawling development of tract houses on the outskirts of Brookhaven, I spot the Brolin

Road exit. Beyond it, a circle of colorful pennants flap outside an orange and yellow tent and a trio of signs spaced a few hundred feet apart exclaim, in ascending order: GREAT DEALS—BUY ONE, GET ONE FREE!—FIREWORKS! Adrenalin sparks through my veins and my blood pressure soars into heart attack territory as I screech off the exit and park on the edge of a litter-strewn lot.

This time of night, there's only three other vehicles, one of which is a white van with Galaxy Pyrotechnics on the side that obviously belongs to the vender. Most fireworks sellers put in a 24/7 shift in their tent, grabbing a few hours sleep on a cot rather than having to pack up all the inventory every night and unpack it again the next morning. Besides, there's always a few customers who trickle in—insomniacs, night shift workers, people half-pickled who decide now's the time to stock up on Whistling Moons or Glittering White Willows.

Pretty names, right? Almost romantic, like a perfume some painted-up crone in a high-end boutique spritzes at women as they walk by. Not really what you'd expect to call objects whose sole purpose for existing is to explode.

I park in a dark corner of the lot, well away from the other cars. Before I get out of the Ram, I reach under the passenger seat and check the hidden compartment I installed there years ago. It slides out at the flick of a lever, revealing the shiny black Glock 17 .9mm. Take it with me? My first impulse is no—after all, I'm only checking things out, and besides, after all these years, no way would the Captain recognize me as Marcus Bujeau, that angry, insecure kid who freaked out when he talked about demons.

But as I continue to stare at the tent through the mosquito-speckled windshield, an undercurrent of nausea roils my gut, and I change my mind—in addition to the nightmares that plague me the week of the Fourth, sometimes I also get hunches. And I remember those KablAM! t-shirts well—Jimmy and I'd each bought one that last July; he had his on the night he went missing. I tuck the Glock under my belt, concealing the bulge under my loose-fitting work shirt. I can feel the metal gouge into the small of my back as I stroll toward the tent.

《《—》》

The night Jimmy vanished, I thrashed awake, convinced I could feel the nip of needle teeth and hear the whir of spidery wings nesting in the furrows of my brain. In my confusion, I remembered only that the mogui-demons feared fireworks and knew there was only one place close by where I could get some.

Back at the Captain's tent, I could hear the rumble of his deep, drunken snores; my mouth filled with a loathing that clung to my tongue like decay. I snuck into the tent, struck a match, and began lighting and throwing the fireworks. Within seconds, the roof of the tent was ablaze, the air thick and unbreathable with the reek of gunpowder and sulphur. I staggered outside, dodging fireballs and screaming aerial repeaters, and watched the silhouette of the Captain stumbling about inside the tent, blinded and burning in a scorching cascade of color.

I woke up the second time that night terrified that the dream had been real and that I'd actually blown up the fireworks tent with the Captain inside.

But the next day, when I returned to the spot by the lake where the tent had been pitched, only an oval of trampled grass and holes for the tent poles remained.

Later, I went over to Jimmy's house, where his mother, frowzy and tipsy at ten in the morning, assured me that "he's just off someplace, he'll turn up." When, two days later, he still hadn't shown up, I told my parents I thought he'd been grabbed by the man who ran the fireworks tent, but nobody listened. Jimmy had a reputation as a wild child who split when his parents were fighting, but always came back sooner or later. For a while, suspicion focused on Jimmy's father, a belligerent boozer who was mean with his fists, but that ended when the old guy woke up dead one morning after suffering a massive stroke.

Before long, Jimmy's absence was as taken for granted and as little mourned as his father's.

And Captain KablAM never again set up his tent outside Metairie, which in my mind was proof of his guilt. I vowed to myself that when I got older, I'd hunt him down. Make him tell me what happened to Jimmy. I liked to imagine that when I got through with the superstitious old fuck, I'd crack his skull open and laugh when the mogui went flying out along with his brains.

Now, of course, I suspect Jimmy wasn't the only boy who fell prey to the Captain.

During the week leading up to the Fourth, I watch for Amber Alerts, do a daily computer check on the NCMEC, the National Center for Abused and Exploited Children, keep track of the activities of organizations like EquuSearch. What I've found chills me, but confirms my belief that those demons the Captain talked about where truly a reflection of his own damaged soul. There's always at least one boy in the ten-to-thirteen range who goes missing, always in the Gulf States, sometimes in a location leading me to believe I've missed the Captain by only a few miles and the shittiest of luck. It's like a sadistic game of hide and seek that I invariably lose, that sometimes drives me to waste precious time suppressing my frustration and rage in a bottle.

There was the Knox boy, who vanished on July 3, five years ago, from a swimming hole in Magnolia Springs, Alabama. The year before that, it was twelve-year-old Roy Dobbs Smith, missing from Denham Springs, Louisiana. Prior to that, fourteen-year-old Dorian Panaga, whose body turned up in a landfill outside Judsonia, Arkansas. Last year, I almost exhaled, I thought nobody had died, until I picked up a paper at a truck stop outside Spanish Fort, Alabama, and saw a picture of dozens of volunteers on foot and half a dozen riders from EquuSearch who were combing the woods looking for eleven-year-old Curtis May, big for his age, who'd disappeared on a wooded trail between his mom's trailer and a bait store. Never found little Curtis, so far as I know.

Occasionally, after a boy goes missing, I'll get a lead—somebody remembers seeing Captain KablAM selling out of a tent on this road or that, or someone claims to have bought fireworks from him and can describe his KablAM t-shirt, but no one can ever pin down an exact location or time, and nobody knows his real name. The Internet hasn't helped. Whatever the Captain's been doing all this time, he hasn't been posting on facebook or Twitter; he's got no presence online. He's like a mogui himself, elusive and greedy, emerging from hell to play its terrible games before vanishing back into my nightmares.

《《——》》

I mull over these things as I make my way past a handful of cars grouped within the arc of the sodium lights. Inside the tent, it's stuffy and stinking of sulphur and sweat and greasy fried food. Cluttered tables display an eye-popping confusion of canisters, tubes, and boxed assortments of fireworks—everything from the relatively innocuous poppers and snappers and smoke bombs to major firepower like the Saturn Missiles.

I don't know what I'm expecting when I go up to the counter, but it's not this: a plump bottle blonde, wearing tight cut-offs and a red halter top with a pink visco fuse looped around her neck as adornment. She's in her early twenties and fat in a fleshy, sensual way that goes well with the heavily tattooed arms and glossy, fuscia-lipsticked mouth underneath a slender black nose ring. Settled back in a chair, bare feet up on a stool, she's reading a copy of US Magazine, a can of Red Bull at her elbow.

When I finally pull her attention from the starlet-of-the-week's latest pregnancy, she sighs and heaves herself onto her feet, looking annoyed when I inquire about the t-shirts with KablAM on the back. "Kaboom? Naw, we got nothin' like that. This is your basic one-stop shopping fireworks store. You go to Walmart for your clothing needs, know what I'm saying?"

Before she can go back to her magazine, I give her a description of the Captain. She looks monumentally bored, fussing with a display stand of mortar tubes, but when I tell her the Captain worked out of Metairie years back, something flickers across her face.

Then she says in a flat voice, "Nope, never been to Metairie and don't know no kabob dude either. People don't stay put in this business. Maybe this guy's moved on, y'know what I'm saying?" She glances over to where a tall, gangly guy is ripping the cellophane off a box of aerial repeaters and lunges forward like she going to vault over the counter to get at him. Her screech fills the tent. "Hey, you opened that, fella, you just bought it, y'hear!" Rolls her stoned-looking green eyes. "Man, this fireworks business sucks, you know what I'm saying?"

I can feel the Glock scrape the bones at the small of my back. "You sure that name's not familiar?"

She picks up the copy of US, shakes it at me like you'd threaten a dog with a rolled-up newspaper. "Look, mister, I'm just helping out here while my boyfriend grabs a few z's at home. He's the fire-works expert, been at it his whole life. Me, I'm not into this pyrotechnic shit the way he is. I'm actually a body piercing techni-cian."

"Your boyfriend, when's he gonna be back?"

"When he gets here. Who knows?"

But she smiles as she says it, displaying bad teeth and a small silver stud driven through the tip of her tongue.

《《——》》

Heading back to my truck, I feel frustrated, discouraged, the 'hunch' I thought I was having probably no more than gas from the chicken fried steak I scarfed down earlier in a diner outside McComb. What I really want to do now is head down the road, but maybe I ought to stick around, come back later and talk to Body Tech's boyfriend.

Before I can consider this further, a patchwork of shadows reconfigures itself ahead to my left, well beyond range of the lights. My hand slides toward the gun, until I see it's a kid, maybe ten or eleven years-old, with shaggy wheat-colored hair and the kind of vacant expression you'd expect to see on an adult who's done time. He's leaning up against the saggy chain-link fence dividing the lot from the road. When he catches me looking, his fingers close over something hidden in his hand.

I nod to him and continue on toward my truck, but the image is hard to dispel—the scruffy, lonely-looking boy, just the kind of child that predators look for. Is he Body Tech's kid? Did he come here with the cellophane shredder? What's he doing out here by himself?

I feel a hitch in my chest, thinking about what happened to Jimmy, wondering for the millionth time if things would've been different if I hadn't been scared off by the Captain's creepy bullshit.

A few paces farther, I glance back and can't believe what I see. The kid's holding a green Bic lighter and he's flicking it idly, a tiny flame sprouting up each time he flexes his thumb.

I turn back and start toward him with care, the way I'd approach one of the feral cats Charmaine feeds in the yard out back of our house.

"Hey, little man, what're you doing with that?" I'm trying to sound casual and avuncular, like I do with my students at school, but my voice comes out reedy and timid—kid probably thinks I'm a jerk. Still I persist. "You got a tent full of fireworks right over there. You want to blow us all up?"

He smirks like the idea has its appeal. Gives an insolent shrug. *Click, click.*

I bend down and he holds up the lighter, daring me to try and snatch it. I can make out the logo of a Mexican restaurant I've seen advertised on a billboard—grinning cartoon Mexican under a floppy sombrero, *Maria's Cantina and Take-Out* on the side.

"What's your name?"

Click.

"Where your folks at?"

A shrug.

"I'll bet your parents wouldn't like you playing with that."

Click, click, click. Click.

I look around, wishing someone would show up to claim him, so I could unload on them about what I think of their parenting skills, a kid alone after midnight in a goddamned parking lot, literally playing with fire outside a tent full of explosives.

"Listen, this isn't a good place to hang out. It's not safe. You need a ride, you want me to call somebody to come pick you up?"

He sneers and pulls out an iPhone that's higher tech than my own.

Click, and fuck you.

Then he gives me the finger, bolts over the fence, and runs like a brat-out-of-hell toward a row of tract houses that back up to the field.

Sheesh. So much for trying to be a good guy.

A few minutes later, I climb into the Ram, the rear wheels flinging up gravel as I roar off.

《《——》》

I decide to bed down for the night and come back the next morning, see if I can talk to the boyfriend.

In the meantime, as I cruise up the frontage road looking for a motel without a No Vacancy sign this late at night, my mind keeps coming back to the boy with the lighter, wishing I could've helped him somehow, wondering if I should go back and try to find him.

I do nothing, of course, but the rumination uncoils a frightening thirst. Craving usurps everything else. I remember seeing a bar a few exists down, so I peel back onto the highway and backtrack. A couple of motels flash by with Vacancy sighs, but I ignore them—I'm on a new mission now. Before long—*bingo*—there's my oasis, the grungy and aptly-named Wayward Inn. It's bleak and window-less, an institutional grey, the kind of place I can imagine cops per-forming advanced interrogation techniques on suspected child molesters, but the handful of men hunched over the bar look too downtrodden to be menacing, as pitted and weather-beaten as the building itself.

Closing-time's less than an hour away, so I order a double Jack straight up, gulp it like soda, and glance at my watch. Two days, twenty-two hours, and six minutes until the evening of the Fourth of July.

Prime time for the Captain to kidnap and kill.

That's the last thing I remember.

《《——》》

It's funny how often I misplace things: sunglasses and cell phones. Key fobs and wristwatches.

Days.

Waking up with a black hole where memory should be in some place I don't recognize, in the bed of a woman I've never seen before who offers to cook me breakfast, shivering on the shore of a lake in a downpour, bare-chested and tick-bitten on a park bench. Once I came to and found myself driving the Ram over a hundred miles an hour along a two-lane road bordered by fields and farmlands. I thought I was outside Baton Rouge. Later I found out I was in eastern Mississippi and I'd lost almost forty-eight hours.

This time, the last thing I remember is the bartender at the Wayward Inn asking me if I wanted a cab, me telling him I was fine. Then there's a gap and next thing I recall, I'm lurching out of a different bar, even seedier than the last, a man's voice yelling after me not to come back. Pushed from behind, I stumble out into bright sunlight, trying to figure out where I'm supposed to be headed and where I can get my next drink.

Along with snatches of memory linger remnants of dreams, images that veer between horrific and luminous, beguiling and mad. Nearby, a child's sobbing and I want to respond, but that part of me, the Marcus Bujeau who longs to soothe and console, to nurture and love, is trapped in a dark, airless pit, where insects like tiny black semaphores hiss past in the dark, opening bloody cuts where they strike. When I struggle to pull myself out, the earth avalanches, dumping more dirt on top of me, as the screams of the boy in the distance merge with my own.

I wake up with my face mashed into the carpet of a derelict motel room, hurting in a dozen different places. A broken water glass lies a few feet away; whether I broke it by accident or hurled it into the wall, I don't know, but slivers of glass have imbedded themselves in my forearms and neck, leaving stipples of blood in the rug fibers. I have no memory of how I got here, don't know how long I've been blacked out, but an empty fifth of Jack sits on the coffee table, and a bottle of Smirnoff with only an inch or two left keeps my boots company by the bed. When I drag myself up and pull back the shades at the window, I see it's still dark, but whether it's closer to evening or dawn, I don't have a clue.

It comes back to me then, that before I got sidetracked by more pressing needs, I'd planned to go back to talk to the guy who runs PyroGalaxy.

Dizzy and nauseated, I flick on the channel selector on the TV and recoil with self-loathing when I see the date. I've been 'lost' for two days. It's now early evening on the Fourth of July.

At the front desk, I ask the way back to the freeway, the Asian clerk looking at me like I'm addled, since it's all of a quarter mile away. I'm too embarrassed to ask if I'm still in Mississippi, but then I spot the motel's address on the bill that he hands me, and it confirms that I'm still in Brookham.

Which means the PyroGalaxy tent is only a few miles away.

I'm going so fast I almost miss the exit, the Ram's tires digging for traction on the sharp curve, at the apex of which, just for an instant, I catch the red flash of the opening salvo of some distant display.

It's obvious that the vender is pulling up stakes—the only vehicle in the lot is the PyroGalaxy van, its doors open, boxes stacked up inside. A rangy dude in a ball cap, camo pants and a t-shirt that reads "Party Like It's 1776!" turns around as I enter.

"Closing up here," he says, lifting an armload of boxes down off a shelf.

"I'm not here to buy anything. Just want to ask a couple of questions."

His face twists like I've said something dirty. "If you're a reporter, I got nothing to say."

"I'm not a reporter." I don't really know what we're talking about, but I press on. "Look—Larry," I say, reading the tag on his shirt pocket, "guy up the road told me you sell t-shirts with KablAM on the front."

"Guy up the road ought'a mind his own business." He strides outside again, heaving the boxes into the back of the van and turns, furrows rippling his forehead. He's got crew-cut hair the same white-blond as Body Tech's and a narrow, tanned face that just misses being good-looking by a stingy mouth and a slightly off-center nose. A rat-tat of explosions erupts in the distance and we both turn toward the sound, where the horizon is lit up with brilliant peonies and strobes dripping silver and gold. Larry gestures with a thumb. "You gonna be late for the show at the Fairgrounds."

"That's not what I'm interested in."

"Why you askin' about those t-shirts anyway?"

"You have some?"

"Nooo," he says, drawing the word out like I'm simple. "I might'a had one or two last year that I came across going through inventory, but I sold 'em and never restocked. And you didn't answer my question. Why you want one?"

"I used to know a guy called himself Captain KablAM. Never knew his real name. I've been trying to look him up. Old time's sake, y'know."

"Hmmm." The guy scratches his head like he's probing for lice, revealing a tattoo of a rattlesnake with criss-crossing diamond-shaped scales on its coils. "Yeah, I can tell you…"

In the distance, there's a rapid-fire series of reports as splashy multi-colored fountains illuminate the night sky. As one, Larry and I both turn toward it, and although my mouth opens to ask the next question, I find myself strangely mute. I cannot *not* look. "Where he is?" I finally say.

He gives me a slow smile. "What'd he do, scam you out of some money?"

"We were friends back in Metairie's all. He'd want to see me."

"Yeah, he prob'ly would," Larry says, loping back toward the tent.

As I trot after him, I can feel the Glock digging into my spine and sweat streams down the side of my neck. When I try to flick it away, my fingers come away crimson—a cut from the glass in the motel room carpet has started bleeding again. I grope for a crumpled fast-food napkin in my pocket, and my hand brushes something that has no business being there, that stops me cold.

But before I can consider the implications of this, a ring tone starts up—Johnny Cash's gritty bass walking the line. "Dammit," says Larry, looking around for the phone, "I need to get that!"

He runs toward the same counter where Body Tech shook her magazine at me two nights ago, but just as he grabs for it, Cash falls mute. "Shit!"

He starts pushing buttons on the phone, but he's flustered now and whatever he's trying to make happen doesn't look like it's working too well. "Fuckin' phones," he says, then looks at me, vaguely apologetic. "Sorry, my nerves are shot to hell. I thought that might be the cops."

Which causes the nightmare to come slamming back with sickening clarity, the slime and stench of the hole I was trapped in, the icepick-keen screams of the unseen boy.

My stomach clenches and I wonder what the Captain's done now.

"Look, I really need to find him."

Larry scowls. "Try Roselawn Cemetery in Baton Rouge. That's been his address for the last seven years."

I literally sway on my feet, like a man in a cartoon who's been bashed with a plank.

"Surprised he didn't go sooner, tell you the truth, the way he sucked down them cancer sticks."

He mistakes the floored look on my face for grief and adds, "Hey, sorry to drop it on you like that, man. I miss him, too."

"You knew him pretty well?"

"Hell, yeah, he basically raised me."

My eyes flick back to his face, and this time I look beyond the surliness and the stress lines, past the frown of a hard-working young guy pissed off because he missed a phone call. I take in the cornflower blue eyes, the gaze too old for its years, my mouth opening and closing soundlessly.

And I wonder why it took me so long and how I could have failed to realize how much people change and how little.

He takes my silence for interest and explains, "I had some troubles as a kid—a drunk mom, a father who liked to use me for a punching bag. One Fourth of July, I begged the Captain to take me with him when he left town. I knew my parents wouldn't look for me too hard, and I was right. The Captain took me in, taught me the fireworks trade, which was all I ever really wanted to do anyway." He gives a small, lopsided smile. "My girlfriend says I'll never get anywhere in life, but what the hell? Where's there to get to but here?"

I open my mouth again and this time words come, "Jimmy? Jimmy Limbo?"

He stiffens and for a second, a frown line deep enough to lose a fish hook in twitches over one eye. Then he just shakes his head and laughs to himself and it's Jimmy's laugh from all those years ago, soft and fuck-you indifferent. "Naw, you got the wrong guy, man." Taps his name tag. "I'm Larry."

Cash's voice starts its gritty rumble and he grabs the phone, face going grave as he reassures the person on the other end that he's on the way home.

When he ends the call, I catch him by the arm— "Wait, Jimmy—" but he shakes me off, angry now, "Like I said, you got me confused with somebody else, Mister. And this ain't a night I feel inclined to make small talk. You understand?"

Without even bothering to close up the tent, he strides back outside with me on his heels, drenched in sweat like I've just run a marathon.

"Why the hurry? What's going on?"

"You don't watch the news?" He shakes his head, staring off toward the fairgrounds where the sky fractures with glittery brocades and whistling stars. "A boy walking up the road got attacked last night. A guy who'd been hiding in the field grabbed him. Broke his arm, banged him up bad. Kid said he was about to pass out, when somebody started setting off fireworks. Lit the whole sky up for a few seconds, and the scumbag took off. My girlfriend's tore up. She knows the boy, used to babysit for him. Cops'll find the fucker, though." He drives a fist into his palm. "But hope to Christ I find him first."

《《—》》

It's funny how I misplace things, all right. Car keys and cell phones and sunglasses.

Not so funny when I find something I didn't know I had to begin with, something that shouldn't be there at all.

I walk through the tent, flicking the lighter from *Juanita's Cantina and Take-Out* in one hand, a High and Mighty I've just lit the fuse to clutched in the other.

At the last moment, I throw it at the ceiling where it explodes and ignites a chain reaction like the end of the world.

Flames gobble the roof of the tent and zip down the sides, setting off furious detonations, supernovas of color and great clouds of scorching blue smoke.

Seconds after I stumble outside, the tent's blown to smithereens, and the night sky jigsaws into an electric pandemonium fit to dwarf any fireworks finale on earth, enough to scare all the demons between here and China straight back to hell.

Except for the ones that are living in me, and there's only one cure for that.

When the last of the explosions sputter and die, I put the gun in my mouth.

LUCY TAYLOR is the author of seven novels, including *Dancing with Demons, Spree, Nailed, Saving Souls, Eternal Hearts,* and the Stoker-award winning *The Safety of Unknown Cities.* Her stories have appeared in over a hundred magazines and anthologies, including *The Mammoth Book of Historical Erotica, The Best of Cemetery Dance, Twentieth Century Gothic, The Year's Best Fantasy and Horror,* and the *Century's Best Horror Fiction.*

Most recently her work has appeared in *The Mammoth Book of Horror presents The Best of Lucy Taylor, Danse Macabre, Exotic Gothic 5,* and the *Best Horror of the Year #5.*

Taylor lives in New Mexico, where she volunteers with cat rescue organization, attends Buddhist retreats, and plots daring escapes to exotic and fantastical places.

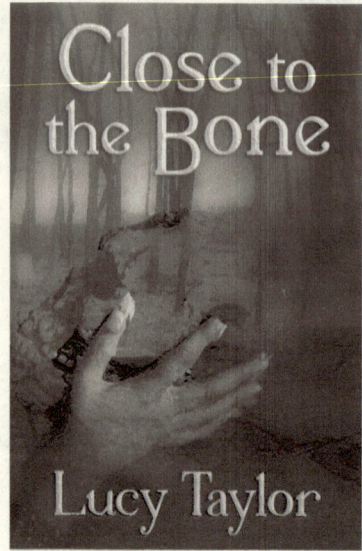

Close to the Bone

BY Lucy Taylor

Trade Paperback	ISBN 978-1623300241
E-Book	ISBN 9781623300296

Lucy Taylor writes the kind of stories for which the word visceral was intended; this collection is graphic both in sexual content and violence...gritty, disturbing tales of real people in the grip of madness. – Silver Salamander Press

Lucy Taylor, a writer known for her intense erotic horror fiction. – Wayne Edwards

OVERVIEW: These are intense stories of erotic horror, everything from a pair of sexually obsessed wrestling groupies to a family whose house mysteriously fills up with water. There's a touch of Southern Gothic, too– when it comes to Lucy Taylor's inspiration for these tales, she says "I think growing up in Richmond, Virginia, didn't hurt."

This erotic horror short story collection was Nominated for Best Collection from the Horror Writer's Association. Available in this completely new edition which features original wrap-around cover art and completely re-typeset.

STORIES FEATURED:
· Close to the Bone
· Animal Souls
· The Best in the Business
· Virgin, Cages
· Knockouts
· Fear of Phobias
· Slips
· The English Teacher
· The Family Underwater

OVERLOOK CONNECTION PRESS
PO Box 1934 • HIRAM, GA • 30141
PHONE: 678-567-9777
EMAIL: overlookcn@aol.com
www.overlookconnection.com

THE SILENCE BETWEEN THE SCREAMS

BY LUCY TAYLOR

The Silence Between the Screams **features cover art by Rick Sardinha.**

First Edition Hard Cover ISBN 1892950642 $39.95
Trade Paperback ISBN 1892950650 $10.95

A Silence Between The Screams is a collection of original short fiction that also features the previously released novella "Spree" ˉwhich hasn't been available for years. Now "Spree" and this collection of original short fiction has been published together for the first time. *The Silence Between The Screams*, the title story, takes us on a ride with a family that soon discovers that the fabric that makes up our world is not as sound as once thought. That revenge comes in all shapes and sizes in "A Hairy Chest, A Big Dick, and a Harley." Between survival and sacrifice the decisions are decided in "Hymns to Old Gods," and, well, you'll just have to read what this Bram Stoker Award-Winning author, Lucy Taylor, has in store for you.

Also published as a signed limited under the title *A Hairy Chest, A Big Dick, and A Harley* also featuring original cover art by Rick Sardinha. The text is the same, however the limited has many extra features, and interior art.

OVERLOOK CONNECTION PRESS
PO BOX 1934 • HIRAM, GA • 30141
PHONE: 678-567-9777 • FAX: 770-222-6192
EMAIL: overlookcn@aol.com
www.overlookconnection.com

THE SAFETY OF UNKNOWN CITIES
BY LUCY TAYLOR

- **Trade Paperback**   ISBN: 1-892950-12-X $14.95
- **Hard Cover-Signed**   ISBN: 1-892950-14-6 $39.95

THE SAFETY OF UNKNOWN CITIES
Winner of Best First Novel from the
Horror Writer's Association!
- Winner of the International Horror Critics Guild Award for Best First Novel
- Winner of the Deathrealm Award for Best Novel

• • OCP EDITION FEATURES • •

- Exclusive Introduction for The Overlook Connection Press edition by Lucy Taylor
- Original Cover illustration by renowned artist Neal McPheeters

Despite the often graphic sex in *Cities*, the book is also about the desperate human need for connection. Val, of course tries to achieve it by "changing partners with the same frequency that she changed countries." In a less forthright way, Breen suffers from a similar pattern. As a young boy burglarizing houses, he realized that he could, in a sense, become intimate with those he stole from by going through their personal items, their letters, diaries, whatever. Then later, he made the jump to a darker form of intimacy—the perusal of the contents of their bodies.

—From the OCP Introduction to *Safety of Unknown Cities* by Lucy Taylor

NOW AVAILABLE IN AN
AFFORDABLE EDITION
FROM THE OVERLOOK
CONNECTION PRESS

"Lucy Taylor's *The Safety of Unknown Cities* is one of the most impressive debut novels... centered around relationship-driven fiction catalyzed by horrific events mostly realistic, sometimes supernatural. *The Safety of Unknown Cities* is very much a supernatural horror novel. Indeed it's sexual, it's graphically written, but it's also...an affecting and powerful novel about heartbreak and the untimely destruction of childhood. If reading the book strikes familiar chords, the resonance's might be with either Clive Barker for an unflinching approach to highly charged subject matter, or with Poppy Z. Brite for sheer candor...an adventurous novel of a quality that absolutely demands an audience."

—Edward Bryant, *Locus*

OVERLOOK CONNECTION PRESS
PO Box 1934 • Hiram, GA • 30141
PHONE: 678-567-9777 • FAX: 770-222-6192
EMAIL: overlookcn@aol.com
www.overlookconnection.com